TO NANCY

Acknowledgements

My sincerest thanks to Nancy, Julie Jepsen-Grant, Bill Grant, Judith M. Moretz, and Larry Sydes for their invaluable assistance in the development of *Assault on the Crown*.

Assault on the Crown

Happy Birthday Jim! Best wishes during this coming decade!
Danard 3/24/90

DANARD EMANUELSON

Danard Emanuelson
358/1200

Epsilon Books • Walnut Creek, Ca.

This Epsilon book is a COLLECTORS LIMITED FIRST EDITION quality soft cover. First printing November, 1989.

ASSAULT ON THE CROWN

This book is a work of fiction. Names, characters, places, and incidents are the product of the author's imagination or are used fictitiously, and any resemblance to actual persons, living or dead, is entirely coincidental.

Copyright ©1989 by Danard Emanuelson

All rights reserved under International and Pan-American Copyright conventions. This book may not be reproduced or transmitted in whole or in part, by mimeograph or any other means, without permission. For information write: Epsilon Books, 1026 Sheppard Road, Walnut Creek, CA. 94598

ISBN 0-9624917-0-5

Library of Congress Catalog Card Number: 89-81787

PRINTED IN THE UNITED STATES OF AMERICA

"To love God with all thy heart and thy neighbor as thyself is the sum of religion."

——Thomas Jefferson

"I say the mission of government, henceforth, in civilized lands, is not repression alone and not authority alone, not even of law, nor by that favorite standard of the eminent writer, the rule of the best men, the born heroes and captains of the race . . . but higher than the highest arbitrary rule, to train communities through all their grades, beginning with individuals and ending there again, to rule themselves."

——Walt Whitman
Democratic Vistas, 1871

1

The Visitor

The two men inside the farmhouse watched the visitor get out of his car. He reached across the seat for his overcoat, put it on, and buttoned up the collar to protect against the cold October breeze. He reached into the car again and pulled out a small valise. The visitor shut the car door and stood for a moment, surveying the Irish landscape. Behind him a few trees and bushes hid the car from the country road. He began to walk slowly up the rutted dirt driveway towards the farmhouse.

"Right on time. 'Tis a good sign, lad," said the older man watching the visitor.

The younger man picked up the binoculars, focused them, and scanned the length of the country road as far as he could see in both directions. "Seems clear enough," he said, and turned his attention to the visitor. "Why, he's an old man. He walks slow with a slight limp, kind of shabby looking."

"Perhaps he's old and perhaps not. It's his

reputation, you know, that brought him to us. He has a way with the make believe. Some people call him the Magician; he's here one minute and disappears into thin air the next. Don't be too hasty." The older man looked out the window of the farmhouse, squinting his myopic eyes, but couldn't make out any of the visitor's features.

"Suppose he doesn't accept the project?" asked the younger man.

"Well, I've been over that with the Board. We'll just have to chance it. He's scrupulously honest, they say, a man of high principles and integrity, no less. Hard to find these days in his line of work."

When the visitor began his slow, orchestrated walk up the slight hill to the farmhouse, he thought they had chosen the location well. It was familiar to him. The green valleys and fields below surrounded the farmhouse on three sides. A rocky, impassable hillside guarded the back. The hill appeared to have been ripped and torn in a frenzy by some giant claw, leaving craters and crevices, sharp cliffs, and loose rocks. The patchy clouds cast moving shadows over the rough and broken hillside, giving it a foreboding look; an imposing barrier to those who might want to pass. From the farmhouse one could see for miles in all three directions.

Yes, the location was a good one, in the South, the Republic of Ireland, as he had requested, across the border from Northern Ireland. During a quiet period of the "Troubles" the Republic had been born in 1937, created by DeValera, back in power, in a flash of brilliance, without a drop of blood shed, and the South began enjoying the liberties of a free nation. Not so in the North, which split off and remained British. When the thought of the North, Ulster to some, crossed the visitor's mind, the old pain in his ribs returned, his nose hurt, his face stung, and his palms became sweaty. The reaction was always the same, lasting until he forced it to disappear into some hidden, inaccessible sanctuary of his brain. *Damn! Would it forever be this way?*

The cool breeze brought to him the occasional odor of cow dung, sheep dip and fresh country grasses. The gleaming white farmhouse, with traditional thatched roof, small barn and open garage in back, neat landscaping, and countless animals dotting the landscape, suggested a well-run and modestly profitable operation.

It has been a long time and the visitor had forgotten which Gaelic King defended this farmland when it was invaded by the Vikings. He wondered now which of the small forests dotting the valleys below were used by the landowners and peasants, often for months at a time, to hide from the plunderers and rapists from Norway. Ironic, he thought, that the island was united only once in its history — when Gaelic King Brian Boru, the first High King elected by all the Kings, led the Irish dynasties to victory over the Vikings and drove them from the island forever. After Boru was killed in the final battle, the dynasties never truly united again. The traitor Dermot MacMurchada brought the Norman invaders over to help him regain his kingdom, and so began eight hundred years of the "Troubles." Strange, he thought, don't they know unity of the North with the South is only a twisted myth created by DeValera?

He was almost to the farmhouse when he decided to stop and take in the smells and the many shades of green and yellow and purple of the countryside. The scene reminded him of a time almost twenty-five years ago when he had travelled from Belfast along this same country road with his mother, father, and two brothers to picnic in the country. The family was happier then, but not long after, his life had been turned upside-down.

He was about to begin again when he sensed movement at an outcropping of rocks not too far away. He remained motionless for a moment, but nothing changed. Imagination, he guessed.

He walked up to the door and reached out to knock, when the door opened suddenly. Standing before him was a tall, heavy-set man about fifty-five years old with dark brown hair greying at the temples, bright piercing blue eyes, a square, smiling face, and a few soft wrinkle lines around the eyes. His firmly set mouth and ruddy complexion accented his features. Maybe it was the way he stood — the visitor could not be sure — but the man possessed a quiet confidence, subtle but unmistakable.

"Good morning," the man said, and politely waited for the visitor to say the proper words.

"It's been a long journey from Dublin. I'm told this is a good stopping point," replied the visitor.

"Ah, 'tis you then, please come — "

The whine of the bullet, the crack of splintering wood, and the solid thud of the bullet burying itself in the door frame above and to the right of the visitor's head shocked him. His instincts drove him flat to the floor, half in the doorway and half out of it. He felt two strong hands grab his shoulders and drag him through the doorway; and as he rolled over he saw the tall man kick the door shut.

"Bastard," muttered the man, and he yelled, "Kevin, do you have him?"

"Yes, sir," came a reply from somewhere in the house, "one of our 'unfriendlies'."

A second bullet hit the frame and a third bullet buried itself in the door, and after that, silence.

"That's a helluva a way to be introduced," said the visitor as he got up and dusted himself off, a rush of adrenalin heating him up.

"I'm sorry about this. I don't know how they found us. They're playing games. We'd both be dead if they had wanted it that way."

"Comforting thought," replied the visitor, wondering if he had made the right decision in coming here. He noticed that the tall man seemed unperturbed.

"Come this way." And the man with quiet confidence led him through an entryway into a small sitting room complete with comfortable sofa, two easy chairs, two small side tables, and a larger than necessary fireplace, all tastefully done in a rustic, Irish style of long ago. Someone had tried to preserve a sense of history, except that it was betrayed by the inevitable TV set in one corner of the room. A number of small prints and family photographs hung in appropriate places. The bright, clean linoleum floor was carpeted, with a few throw rugs strategically placed. Three windows provided a broad view of the surrounding country.

The fireplace warmed the room considerably. The visitor caught the odor of freshly brewed coffee as he handed the man his overcoat, sat down on the sofa, and placed the battered valise beside him. A tall, slender young man stood by a window peering through a pair of binoculars. Without turning he said, "It was Ian Sommers, Father, he's behind a small bunch of rocks below."

"One of these days soon we'll have to do something about those fellows. Let me introduce myself. I'm Professor William Banks, and this is my son Kevin. I'll bring us some coffee and if you like, a spot of whiskey."

"The whisky will help, thank you," said the visitor, still trying to slow his adrenalin down.

"I'm sorry for the inconvenience. You wanted to meet across the border and I thought we would be alone here. I was mistaken. It's a long drive from Dublin and I trust you had a good flight from wherever you came?"

"Yes, it was fine. In your letter to my office in Switzerland you said something about a Northern Ireland project of international importance. I admit I'm curious. I normally avoid anything connected with Ireland, North or South. Judging from that little greeting, perhaps I should have stayed home."

The professor brought in a carafe of whisky and a pot of hot coffee on a tray with cups brimming, and a separate small glass of whiskey for each of them. The visitor smelled the familiar aroma of Bushmills, picked up his glass, raised his arm in a silent toast, and took a healthy swallow.

The visitor noticed that young Kevin seemed tense as he moved his search from window to window. He guessed him to be in his early thirties. He wondered how well Kevin could defend himself; perhaps he was stronger than he appeared.

"You're a hard man to track down," said the professor as he settled into a chair opposite the visitor. "We spent the better part of a year conducting a secret search for you. We finally made two contacts; one in Austria, a young duchess. Seems you recovered some jewels for her. The other, a private detective in Paris whom you helped locate a missing person. We understand you're a freelance agent; a kind of soldier of fortune; a salvager of sorts. You stay within the law, but sometimes skirt it slightly, or so the stories go. It was the French detective who finally relented and gave us your address in Bern. The duchess refused. The detective gave us bits and pieces of some of your projects. It was he who called you the Magician. We considered other men, but after hearing some facts and a few rumors, you're our first choice. You have just the qualifications we need."

The professor studied the old man with his white hair, beard, and mustache subtly camouflaging alert blue eyes behind large horned rimmed glasses.

"It's obvious you're not old, your hands give you away."

"I'm not trying to hide the fact that I'm young," said the visitor, "the disguise is good cover. However, you'll never learn my true identity. That's the way I work. I got into this business ten years ago quite by accident. As a matter of fact, the duchess was my first project. We were, ah, very good friends. I helped her in many ways. She's very loyal."

The visitor took a sip of coffee. "I do one or two cases a year. The rest of the time I have other business interests that keep me busy, usually for about six months a year. If I retrieve something I get half its value as fee. I enjoy the free-lance work; I'm good at it and it breaks up the monotony of my normal business. At times a project has been dangerous, but I've developed a variety of methods to prevent bloodshed. Once in a while I have to, ah, incapacitate someone, but it rarely results in aches or pains. I've had a few close calls, but the outcome has away been good.

"I have a close associate, an assistant, who lives with me and sometimes works with me. As a matter of fact, he's waiting for me at Dublin airport in case I need some help." The visitor took another sip of coffee.

"Do you have time to take on a project that might take six months or more to complete?" asked the professor.

"Well, that's a long time, but I must admit I'm curious. I can't make any promises, but I assure you nothing said here will be repeated, except to my associate, and he's completely reliable."

The visitor looked over at Kevin Banks peering out a window with the binoculars and finished his coffee. His adrenalin was almost back to normal. "Incidentally, did you know there's a car, a light blue Volvo sedan, parked beside the road about a mile from here with a man in it?"

"That's Ian's partner. Wonder who it is this time?" asked Kevin, not expecting a reply.

The elder Banks poured them each another cup of coffee and filled the whiskey glasses again. "'Tis good you came. We appreciate it. I don't want to bore you with a lot of details, but it's safe to say that if you've not been to Ulster in the last few years, you'll need a little background to give you an idea of what we are about.

"I've been a lecturer and professor of economics at Queens University in Belfast for the past twenty-five years. I've a number of books and papers published, including recent work on the union of the European Economic Community. A plan is in the making to remove all the trade barriers between the twelve nations by 1992 and create a single, borderless internal market."

The visitor's side began to hurt and he strained to signal his brain to forget it. He remembered, now, seeing the young lecturer Banks when he himself attended Queens, but he had taken no classes from him. His side stopped hurting.

"Northern Ireland's economic decline is worsening," the professor went on. "She'll not see a piece of the action in 1992, perhaps never, unless something is done about it. It's a land at war; the tribalism is splitting the community farther and farther apart. The war will go on; people will continue to be needlessly killed; and Northern Ireland will be in ruins unless something is done about it."

The visitor noticed the man was slightly more animated, his deep, resonant voice rising subtly to demand attention. Kevin apparently noticed it too, but didn't seem concerned.

"Knowing your reputation for thoroughness," continued the professor, "you must have checked and know that I've been leading the Independence Party for the past ten years, gradually working towards independence for the North."

"Do you really believe it's possible?" asked the visitor without admitting that he had carefully researched the professor and current conditions.

"Aye," said William Banks, and he stiffened in his chair, back ramrod straight, "with all my heart and soul, now more than ever. You know, if only the Normans had done a complete job instead of their half-assed conquest, Ireland would be united today. Instead, they bungled and we are split. And so we shall remain. We are essentially a forgotten people, except for the notoriety of the war. We live for today and look to a bleak future. We have gang against gang. We have continuing conflicts and ineffectual political see-sawing. Unity with the South is an idle dream, a myth. Now it must be independence for the North."

The professor's voice revealed an excitement

that captured the visitor's complete attention. "To end the 'Troubles,' violence, and misery in the North, three things must happen: one, the British must leave; two, the South must withdraw Articles 2 and 3 from their constitution, that lay claim to the lands of the North, the lands of Ulster; and three, we must win our independence from the British."

He paused, poured a little whiskey into his coffee, and took a sip. "You know," continued the elder Banks, "we believe the 'British Guarantee,' giving the North freedom if it so votes, applies only for unity with the South, not independence. And the South cannot finance the four billion pounds a year it takes to support the North."

"How'll you prevent a civil war?" asked the visitor.

"We'll have no betrayal," replied the professor firmly, "the future plans will be printed for all to see. Our Transition Plan and economic program are being developed and our people are working hard to enlist others to help. We plan to get the attention of the people of Ulster and England, and the whole world, for that matter, and force the United Kingdom to free Northern Ireland.

"We want to do it without bloodshed or violence. We will not wait seventeen, twenty-seven, or two hundred and seventy years. We plan to win our independence quickly, with your help. There won't be time for civil war and the United Nations will be here to preserve the peace."

As Banks warmed to his subject, the visitor felt the power of the man emerge. He could tell that the professor wanted very much to convince him that his help was necessary. The professor pressed on: "We'll get the majority vote for independence, not unity with the South. We hope to make you a part of it."

"How can you believe independence will work?" asked the visitor. "I remember a few years ago the new Assembly of '82 was dissolved. You were a member of that assembly. You got nowhere; everyone was bickering. The British were hoping the new Assembly would work out some transfer of powers that would put Northern Ireland on a new course."

"True," replied the elder Banks, "it was a farce. Nobody could agree on much of anything; chaos caused by confusion, hatreds, old suspicions plus some unfortunate religious killings in Darkley in '83. It was the Anglo-Irish agreement of '85 between Britain and the South that mobilized the North's pro-British Unionists and led to an increase in violence. It gives the South a say in the North's affairs. Even the PIRA denounced the agreement as perpetuating British occupation. The Unionist majority of the Assembly voted to suspend Assembly business indefinitely. Later in the year the British dissolved the Assembly. The Assembly failed because it lacked a national purpose."

"How are you going to overcome tribalism and develop a sense of national purpose?" asked the skeptical visitor. And yet, his interest deepened as the professor kept talking.

"Our Independence Party is aimed at getting

people to come out from behind the walls of fear and begin thinking and acting like free and independent human beings. We've got one Catholic for every Protestant and they are learning to work together to solve problems. They're beginning to like working together.

"The idea is catching on, and we seem to be growing. Most people don't know it, but our membership has reached over twenty thousand. That, sir, is strictly confidential. We're at a point where we seem to be getting publicity. We've kept the movement relatively quiet up to now, but a strange thing is happening. People are becoming interested as word spreads, and we're growing so fast I cannot predict how big our membership will be in six months.

"The larger Unionist and loyalist groups are listening. They're not speaking out against us yet. They seem to be analyzing the situation; all strangely quiet," and the professor paused for a moment; "I've been talking too much. Let's see what my cousin left us for lunch. Perhaps you can tell us a bit more about yourself. By the way, our letter to you was addressed to Perry Wallace. May I use that name?"

"It's the name I use as a free-lance agent, yes," replied the visitor.

The professor and the visitor, now called Wallace, ate at a table in a small dining room next to the kitchen. The cousin had prepared a lunch of potato soup, cheeses, small sandwiches, and coffee. The professor stacked a small plate with an assortment of food and took it to Kevin at the window. Kevin looked at his father and said, "He sticks his head up once in a while just to let us know he's there." The professor went into the other room and sat down with Wallace.

"Perhaps now you can explain your 'unfriendly' with the gun. As for me, there's not much more I'm free to tell you," said Wallace. "I'm not married. My early years are obscure, long forgotten. I have a legitimate business in a country of my choosing. As I said earlier, about ten years ago I got into the business of helping people solve sticky problems or regain something of value or locate someone. I've worked for the Italians, the Swiss, the West Germans, and a number of very rich and prominent people. Perhaps I've been lucky, I haven't had to kill anyone in the process. Whatever your project is, no one gets hurt. If you want it any other way, we can stop right now and I can go on my way," and the visitor fixed his intense blue eyes on the professor, leaving no doubt as to the meaning of his words.

"Aye, 'tis one of the reasons we wanted to find you. This job must be done carefully and without hurting anyone. Our organization is founded on the principle of nonviolence. In the end, the South won their independence without bloodshed. We want to do the same."

"It's violence that is plaguing us today," continued the professor. "The British presence fosters violence that is causing a slow paralysis that chokes off political dialogue. For such a small community, it's political chaos. The different Unionist groups fight for control of the Protestant vote. The various Catholic groups fight for control of the Catholic community. And within each group the members argue over the right course to follow.

"The paramilitary groups, those private little armies of various Unionist groups, some legal and some not, are fighting for leadership in their private war with the PIRA and the South. One in particular, the right Reverend Sean McIver's Men of Iron, is particularly vicious. That's Ian Sommers out there with the rifle and one of his men down below in the Volvo. They belong to Sean McIver."

At the mention of his brother's name, the visitor — Jason Stark, alias Perry Wallace, alias the Magician, born Robert Brian McIver of Belfast — froze. His ribs began to ache, his nose hurt, his face stung, and his palms turned sweaty. He fought his emotions and tried to force the feelings away. He had not heard his brother's name spoken in over twenty years and had pushed the old memories into the deepest recesses of his brain. He had abandoned the name Robert Brian McIver when he left Belfast and Northern Ireland vowing never to return. He adopted the name Jason Stark as a permanent name, now recognized as a prominent and exceedingly wealthy London stockbroker. In his free-lance work, he used Perry Wallace, James Donnally, the Magician, and one or two aliases. Robert Brian McIver was "dead."

"Where did McIver come from?" asked Jason Stark, avoiding the eyes of the professor, trying to hide his shock and the pain.

"A Belfast protestant. Has two brothers, one disappeared over twenty years ago, the other runs the family clothing store downtown. It used to be owned by the father, but he died about three years ago. McIver's a raving bigot, with his own illegal paramilitary force, and a very dangerous man."

Jason Stark felt a stab of remorse, but not a strong one. He hadn't known that his father had died. He had often wondered how long the hard old man would live. He thought of Patricia and then the hatred for his brother came flooding back as he fought off more of those illusory pains.

"How many parishioners does he have?" asked Jason, trying to maintain his composure.

"About six hundred, not enough to create a political force, but enough to cause a lot of trouble. Right now he's harassing us, trying to get us to stop our movement.

"You know, it's a strange thing about the North," the professor continued. "There's a hidden current running among the people and the politicians, except for a few hard-liners like Reverend McIver. Without exception I believe the largest political parties will embrace independence. And I'm certain a number of nonsectarian political and social groups will support it. I don't believe freedom will cause wholesale panic among the Catholics in the North. If the right approach is made, the big Republican and Socialist groups will support us because they will view it as a step towards a united Ireland. The PIRA would have no other choice but to fade away and wait to see what happens."

"I like your idea of independence," said Jason, "but how do you expect to get the British to agree? It seems to me that it's going to take some very long and enduring political effort to bring it about."

The professor smiled, a twinkle in his eye. "Aye, it would seem that way, but we have a plan to polarize the people here and the people of England to the single idea of independence. We plan to electrify the world and focus international opinion in our favor."

"Just how and when do you expect to do that?" asked Jason.

"Just as soon as you can tell us whether you'll take on the project," said the professor, "and just as soon as you finish it."

"I'm not totally convinced that you can negotiate independence," said Jason. "Obviously the British want Northern Ireland for strategic defence. After the South's anti-World War II and anti-Falklands attitude, they can't be trusted to help Britain in any way with defence. Professor Banks, independence gives the North a chance to end their war. But it's hard for me to believe the Protestant majority would vote for it."

"We'll get the majority vote sooner than most people realize. We plan heavy one-on-one recruiting during the next six months. With a hard core of membership and a well publicized program, we'll get that vote! Perhaps a bit more information will help," and the professor picked up a small briefcase, opened it, and withdrew several sheets of paper. "Kevin and my ten-man Board of Directors are the only people besides myself aware of the project. Since the time we first organized we've slowly been building up reserves in a Swiss bank account. When we started we didn't know what we'd do with the money. Now we know. If you accept the project it'll be part of your job to tell us how much it'll cost."

He handed Jason a single sheet of paper. "This is the list of demands that we'll present to Britain's Prime Minister." He separated several more sheets and handed them to Jason. "This series of blue sheets is an outline of the Transition Plan to be placed in effect for an independent government of Northern Ireland. Why don't you take a moment to look them over. Then we'll talk about the project." The professor got up to join Kevin, and left Jason alone.

The list of demands was brief, clear, and reasonable. The final item began, "Amnesty for all those involved———" and someone had blacked out the last portion. The Transition Plan outline was lengthy but clearly well developed. Some of the items were marked "In Process," but a brief sentence or two outlined the intent.

When Jason finished reading he got up to stretch his legs. He went to the small, lone window in the room, spread the curtains, and looked out at the green and purple valleys below. When Juliana had forwarded the request to him from Bern, it had been the first time he thought of Ireland in a very long time. The old aches and pains had magically appeared, and he had forced them away. He had been tempted not to reply, to just forget the whole thing, but he couldn't. The memories kept flooding back, and the pains with it. It became a constant struggle inside his brain. He was curious, yet reluctant. He was inexplicably drawn to the meeting. He had requested it be held in the South thinking it would ease the pain, but it hadn't.

He was here. More curious than ever. Professor Banks was certain and confident. His program was well constructed. He made independence sound exciting. But how long would it take to erase the hatreds, the misery, and the heartaches? Well, he couldn't leave without knowing. After all, he didn't have to accept. They would find someone else.

Jason went into the next room and joined Kevin and the professor. "How is it?" he asked.

"Ian left. He just got up, waved at us, and walked back to the road," replied Kevin. "No telling whether they left the area or not."

Jason handed the professor back his papers. "Very interesting, well organized, a great program. I would be willing to consider what you have in mind."

"Good!" replied the professor.

"But what's going to make the Prime Minister of England accept your demands?"

"Our project," replied the professor. And he handed Jason a single sheet of green paper. "Perhaps you'd better have a drink of whiskey before you read it."

Jason took the paper, read the first sentence, and sat down. "Yes, I believe I'll have a drink, thanks." He read on and then looked carefully, directly into the eyes of the professor, searching. "You can't be serious?"

"Very serious. We don't know if it's possible. It's the one thing that will electrify our people; spark that hidden current; give us an edge in our negotiations; and change our world. We want to get the attention of the British people and the rest of the world. We are very anxious now. We need to know if it can be done, when it can be done, and how much it will cost. Will you do it?"

2

Now You See Him: Now You Don't!

It was still light when Jason Stark left the farmhouse for Dublin. The sky was overcast, but visibility was good. It would be dark by the time he reached the airport.

The boldness of the professor's project had stunned him. After a more thorough discussion, he had agreed to check it out and report back in a week. They agreed to call the operation simply "The Project."

The professor had urged Jason to take Kevin along to Dublin with him, but Jason would have none of it. "It's better I handle any problems my own way. Kevin's liable to prompt something unexpected," he had explained, and in the end the professor relented.

Before he left the farmhouse Jason gave the professor a code and an address in Calais where Jason and Kevin could meet. He reached into his battered old valise and pulled out an instrument about the size of a small Walkman radio. "Here," he said, as he handed it to the professor, "is a little device my friend and I worked out. Put it on your phone line while you're talking, and switch on number one. The little red light will blink if your line is tapped. Put it in the center of a room, switch on number two, and the little red light will tell you if that room is bugged. Kevin can return it when we meet in Calais."

He was barely over the first ridge, out of sight of the farmhouse, when the blue Volvo was suddenly there in front of him, parked sideways across the road. The road was wider than the length of the small car; two men, one pointing a rifle at his windshield, and the other, an unarmed young man in a grey suit, filled the gap between the car and the edge of the road next to a wide ditch.

Jason slowed, then reacted. He pointed his car towards the narrow gap where the men stood, ducked down, and gunned the engine. A slight miscalculation and he would wind up in the ditch. He steadied his hands on the wheel and hoped he had made the right move. The car plunged forward; the two men scattered, and he sped by the Volvo with barely an inch to spare. His tires rimmed the ditch, but somehow held their traction and he was quickly back in the center of the road at full throttle. Jason looked back in time to see both men jumping into their car.

Ian Sommers thought he was ready when the car slowed, and he relaxed, thinking the car would stop. But when the car suddenly sped up and came roaring at him, he had no time to shoot, all he could do was react. "Jump, John, jump!" he yelled, and they both dove for cover. "Son of a bitch," he said as the car roared past, its tires spitting dust and rock at the two of them.

It was a scary ride along the narrow country road at top speed, but Jason knew his car would reach the motorway long before the Volvo. Once he pulled on to the broad, smooth pavement and merged within the safety of traffic going south, he relaxed. As he drove leisurely back to Dublin, gauging his speed to arrive just twenty minutes before flight time, his thoughts wandered to his early years, and again he fought back those unwanted pains. He wanted no one to know about Belfast. He was so meticulous about hiding his true identity that he had worked for five years to eliminate any trace of his Irish brogue and learn how to speak without any trace of British accent. But as hard as he tried, he couldn't rid himself of those mysterious, unwanted pains that leaped at him from the dark recesses of his brain every time he thought about the North.

It was just an odd coincidence that the professor chose him, a twist of fate he thought. He had hesitated about coming back to Ireland. When he left Belfast, at age eighteen, he had vowed never to return to the North; he was through forever with the land of hate. Well, he had come back due to irresistible curiosity and now, having been drawn into a dangerous game of political intrigue, he wondered if he could walk away from it.

He didn't need the work; after all, he was a millionaire. He had fled to England with next to nothing, worked hard, and earned his entrance to Oxford, graduating in finance. After an apprenticeship with one of the oldest brokerages in London, and with a little luck, he had bought his place on the exchange. It was then an exclusive club of just a hundred or so members. Astutely applying his intuitive genius for trading, his reputation soon grew as he became one of the richest brokers on the exchange.

Since the "Big Bang" of '87, when the exchange membership was greatly expanded, his brokerage business had tripled in size. He prepared carefully for the new look of the London Exchange and expanded his company shrewdly with new foreign business. He avoided insider trading like the plague. When he was away on one of his projects, he maintained daily contact with his two chief assistants and kept firm control of the business.

As Jason's car moved easily along in light traffic, he saw, reflected in the mirror, the blue Volvo following him. He was nearing Dublin and traffic was a little heavier; the sky was almost dark now, so he decided to try a few subtle maneuvers just to make sure it was Sean's men.

He sped up and moved from lane to lane, but the Volvo trailed at about the same distance. He slowed down and the Volvo backed off. *It's Sean's people all right.* The thought of his brother's name brought back the pain in his ribs, the pain in his nose, the stinging face, and the sweaty palms. He tried to shake it off. *I wonder how far my dear brother will go to preserve his warped ideas?*

Probably to the death.

As Jason swung onto the approach to Dublin airport, he was unaware of the black Austin, driven by Fred Press, the chief MI5 agent in Northern Ireland, following the Volvo. Jason pulled into the rental car area, wrote down the mileage, left the keys, picked up his small valise, and headed for the Godfrey Davis rental check-in counter. He remembered to walk slowly, with a slight limp and easy manner; an old man on his way home. He noticed the Volvo parked in a passenger loading zone, driver Ian Sommers watching. His partner, no doubt, was already waiting inside.

At the check-in counter, while paying his bill, Jason casually surveyed the area. Everyone moved in a blur of action except for a couple of security guards, a few auto rental customers, and two men, one near the toilet, the other standing next to a magazine rack. The man near the toilet wore a grey suit with no tie — Sean's man. He was young, about twenty-five, with a pleasant Irish face. The other man was dressed in a brown suede jacket, a Christmas present from Jason, with tan slacks and a small-brimmed wool cap. Beautiful, he thought, Craig is right on schedule. He'll know what to do. He caught Craig's eye and nodded almost imperceptibly towards the young man in the grey suit.

He paid cash, thanked the clerk, and slowly limped to the men's toilet carrying his battered blue cloth valise. Sean's man chose not to follow him. Jason selected a stall, checked his watch, stepped inside, and closed the door. The place smelled of urine. Moving swiftly, he opened the valise, removed a pair of black shoes, a pair of gold rimmed glasses, and a blue tweed, short-billed cap. He put them on the floor and turned the valise inside out, turning it into a smooth, rather expensive looking brown leather carry-bag. He quickly removed his hat, grey wig, goatee, and high-topped brown elevator shoes, placing each inside the bag as he went. Quickly he removed his pants, turned them inside out, changing the color from brown to blue, and put them back on. Next he reached down and unzipped the lower third of his overcoat, folded it up, and placed it inside the valise. He zipped up the valise, picked up the cap and glasses, and put them on, then slipped into the black loafer type shoes. From his coat pocket he pulled a small package containing a black mustache, removed it, and placed it above his upper lip. Again he reached into his coat pocket, this time extracting a package of soft plastic packing. He stuffed a piece inside each of his cheeks and molded them with his hands. Finally, he removed his top coat, now much shorter, turned it inside out, revealing a light blue and grey plaid design, and put it back on.

He flushed the toilet, opened the door, stepped out, and checked his watch. Just under two minutes. *Wonder if I will ever get it down to a minute and a half?*

Jason stepped out into the corridor, gave the young man in the grey suit a sidelong glance, and walked away with rapid, bouncy steps. The young man returned a casual gaze, looked back at the toilet exit, and then at his watch.

Craig watched the scene in fascination. He marvelled at Jason's quick changes. Old Merlin has done it again, he thought.

As soon as Jason turned left around a corner, out of sight of grey suit, he doubled his pace to the ticket counter where, fortunately with no wait, he got his boarding pass sooner than expected. He checked his watch again: Two more minutes gone. The man in the grey suit would be going into the toilet about now. Jason was sweating lightly as he slowed his pace and headed for his departure gate.

At that moment the young man in the grey suit casually entered the men's toilet. Craig Alexander moved into position. Fifteen seconds later the toilet door burst open and the young man in the grey suit came running out, only to crash into Craig, who had set his sturdy frame in position for a solid body block. The young man went sprawling down the corridor, hitting his right elbow and his head in the process. Dazed, he looked up at Craig, who was reaching down to help him up, saying, "I'm very sorry, old man, didn't expect anyone to come out of there so fast. You all right?"

"Yes, O.K." he replied, a little woozy as he got up. He stood for a moment to get his bearings, looked in both directions, and then, holding his elbow, started off, without knowing why, in the direction Jason had taken.

Jason checked his watch. Another four minutes had passed. The boarding gate would close in four more minutes. He had timed everything perfectly.

If Craig has done a good job we won't be seeing the young man. He reached the gate, flashed his boarding pass, and entered the plane to London. He checked his watch. Two minutes to closing. He was still sweating lightly as he removed his topcoat and settled in his seat. He fastened his seat belt, looked up and noticed one last passenger enter the plane. A man of average height in a brown leather jacket, with hard cut features and a grim look, began making his way slowly down the aisle, glancing left and right. Jason saw the man's eyes flicker as the man caught sight of him, passed by, and sat down a few rows behind Jason.

Jason wondered if he would enjoy his one brandy during the short flight to London.

* * *

Sean McIver was a tall, boney man with a brooding look about him. His eyes were like black pools of oil, accented by deep lines at the edges, his heavy eyebrows forming a slight questioning scowl. His heavy lips curled downward, creating an impression of constant disapproval. He was a preacher, the head of the New Protestant Convention Church, a separate church he had started himself six years earlier; but often his ways suggested something dark and evil.

He had been an elder and a paramilitary in one of the largest Protestant churches in Ulster until his opinions on the use of violence could no longer be tolerated. He was militant to the point of fanaticism. To him, anything was fair in the defence of God and the principles of Protestantism — his kind of Protestantism.

They gathered in the cellar office of his church a dismal, dark, musty-smelling place with a small cluttered desk, a table, four battered and scarred straight-back wooden chairs, and several file cabinets against one wall. To the left of his desk a locked door guarded an empty storeroom. Sean McIver sat behind the desk scowling at the other two men. In the dim light, when he moved his head, the fleeting shadows made his face appear skeletal and grotesque. He looked disgustedly at Ian Sommers. "You mean you couldn't stop him in the middle of nowhere, no one around? Why didn't you shoot?"

"No time, it happened too fast. We could have been killed. Had to get out of the way. Besides, there was no reason to try and kill him. We just wanted to find out what he was doing with Banks."

The reverend looked over at young John Larkey, his eyes burning: "You lost him? An old man with a limp who stood out like a sore thumb? Incredible."

"He just vanished," said the uncomfortable young man in the grey suit. "Just vanished into thin air. He went into the toilet and never came out. Several men went in and came out while I was waiting, but not him."

McIver hunched his shoulders, scowled again. "Well, he did come out. He came out as someone else. Think, man, can't you remember anyone who came out that he might have looked like?"

"No, Reverend, I can't remember any one of them. They just don't register. Maybe it was because I was knocked down when I ran out and smacked into that fellow."

"You ignoramus! That had to be someone helping him. A plant to divert you, get you rattled." He turned again to Ian Sommers, his senior operative. "Can't you find people with more experience than this man? What's happened to your organization?"

Ian Sommers sat stiffly in the chair, trying to look firm with resolve. "You know we only have twenty volunteer operatives. None are trained particularly well. They learn on the job, as they go, so to speak. Where in hell would we send them to get training? And where would we get the money if we could send them somewhere? Actually, John here is our brightest candidate."

"All right, all right, enough, I don't need a lot of excuses," said McIver.

"The man from the farmhouse was a professional," Ian continued. "He was good, very good. Not only did we lose him, but I believe we were being followed. I can't be sure. There was another car, a black Austin, behind us for a time. Then I lost him. I was concentrating on the old man. Perhaps I'm becoming paranoid.

"When John came back and told me the news, we both went back through the terminal trying to find the man that knocked him down. He had disappeared too. Then we checked on all the outgoing flights over an hour's span starting about fifteen minutes after we arrived. I didn't realize how damned busy Dublin Airport can get; three flights to London, two to Paris, two to the United States, one to Rome, one to Israel, and four other flights to different parts of the world. The man could have gone anywhere. Besides, we weren't prepared to leave Ireland and follow him."

Sean McIver glowered at him. "I hope your bones don't rot in hell for the pain you're giving me. So we have no idea what that traitorous professor is up to? Tell me, is John here the same man you placed in the Independence Party?"

"Yes, he managed to get in about a month ago."

"What do you have to report, John?" asked McIver. "I hope it's better than what I've heard so far."

"Well," the young man started, "you know that the party is half Protestant and half Catholic. It took me three months to find a Catholic to recommend me. That's how it works. One for one. Now I've got to go out and find a Catholic who I can recommend for membership."

"Like hell you will!" screamed McIver. "I'll not have the likes of you recruiting Papist pigs for some traitorous organization."

"It's the only way I can stay in the group," and John looked pleadingly at Ian, who sat up straight looking at McIver, not volunteering to enter the conversation. "Most of the members that I've met take a moderate view. They're drawing up a Transition Plan for the day when independence comes."

"Never!" cried McIver. "Over my dead body," and his face became flushed and his eyes took on a wild look, then glazed over. John thought he was looking at the devil. After a moment McIver seemed to get control of himself, frowned at John, and said in a disgusted tone: "Go on."

"The professor's got a lot of committees. I've been appointed to a committee on politics. We're supposed to look at how each political party will work in an independent Northern Ireland and develop recommendations on how to influence their thinking for better unification of the new country. We're looking for soft spots in ideologies. Ways to convert them over."

"Ha!" Sean McIver's lips curled in a sadistic laugh. "Have you figured out a way to convert my thinking? By God, you never will! Has your committee made any recommendations?"

"Yes, several. They're sent to a central committee of about forty people who review them and send the best on to the Board of Directors. We haven't seen any final results yet. They just keep asking for more ideas and from time to time send us a suggestion or two. It seems to be a long, slow process."

"Can you tell me what you recommended so far?" asked McIver.

For the first time, John stumbled a bit. "I — er, I've only been a member a short time and they haven't shown me all the recommendations they've made to date," he lied, then decided to give McIver something to put him off. "We're working on Sinn Fein. Sinn Fein wants a united socialist democratic Ireland. Won't have it any other way. We're thinking that if civil liberties, social reform, and a fair and just judicial system for Catholics as well as Protestants are guaranteed in an independent nation, Sinn Fein would at least want to become part of the system. They would bide their time waiting for a weakness in the new, independent country before they resume campaigning for a united Ireland. Facts are facts, the South can't handle us economically and Sinn Fein knows it. The question is, will they be realistic? If they wait, and we're reasonably sure they will, then Sinn Fein may give up the unification idea if the new government is to their liking."

"You sit there and tell me you are going to coddle those Papist jackals, let them tell us what to do? Never! There's no room for them here! We have to get them to go south, out of here forever. If we have to kill them we will! Better they leave forever!" And the Right Reverend Sean McIver was out of his chair, face red again, eyes rolling in his head, a certain animal wildness permeating his body; breathing heavily, he grabbed the desk, trying to regain his composure. John waited, not daring to speak. Ian Sommers held his breath. The reverend sat down, consciously trying to slow his breathing and regain his composure. "Can you tell me what the other committees do?"

"Not really. We're somewhat restricted to our own business. Haven't met many people from other committees. I know of one on the constitution, one on security, one on the economy, on the legal system, civil rights, and I would imagine a committee for every phase of government."

"You don't know a helluva lot," and McIver turned to Ian Sommers. "Do we have any other men in place?" he asked.

"No, we don't. We've tried several times since John got in, but our men are being put off."

"Well, John, you and Jack Brinker and George Dermont did a good job on that PIRA man, but you'll have to do better here," said the reverend. "I want more information on what's going on. Find out how many members Banks has. How much money they are collecting and where they are getting it." The reverend frowned at John. "Do you understand me?"

"Yes, sir. I can only say that I will try. That information is hard to come by. They're keeping a lid on membership and money. The Transition Plan will be assimilated and edited by the senior committee, then released for final approval by all of the membership. They don't want it released in bits and pieces because it may cause some, er, ah, disturbances if only parts of it leaked out."

"Damn right it could cause disturbances! I'm one that vows to disturb them. We're loyalists. Independence will lead to union with the South. And how many times have I said it is not our destiny to be governed by Papist pigs. The South is our enemy! They want to take over and put us out of our own country! Look at them, at one time fifteen percent of the South was Protestant, now it's three percent. The creeping plague. We'll not fall to the South. Our liberties are too precious." He stood up, his body shaking. He was sputtering, face red again, and eyes black with rage. "I'll die first and take those who try to rape and pillage our sacred Ulster with me!"

John had listened to him many times waving his arms and ranting away, but it was a controlled, rehearsed act. Now he was agitated beyond control, an outrageous raving bigot. John could smell the sweat pouring off him.

McIver moved over to John and with his long arms and giant hands picked him up by the collar and looked him in the eyes, making no effort to control his rage. "Don't think for a moment you'll be the only one in Banks's party working for me. I mean to get what I want. If you can't get it, I'll find somebody who will."

"I said I would try."

"Damned right you will. I want a report in two weeks, understand?"

"Yes, sir!" John was holding his breath.

McIver let go of John's collar, looked down at Ian Sommers and said, "Now get out, both of you."

The two operatives lost no time in leaving. The noise of their feet on the stairs faded rapidly and then only the sound of McIver's heavy breathing broke the silence of the musty room. He reached into his desk and pulled out a bottle of whiskey and a glass, poured three full measures, put down the bottle, picked up the glass, and drank it down in one scorching swallow. The strong, rich aroma of the whisky permeated the room, temporarily masking the dank odor. Dear God, he asked, how many battles left to fight? You created the Orange in 1795 to lick the Catholics and keep our land, to fight the likes of Wolf Tone, Jackson, and the French. They lost. We won. What now? By Your Holiness, I'll not give it up! His breathing was quieter now, he had stopped sweating. He poured another drink. It was plain from his operatives description that they had been following a professional. *I wonder what the professor wants with a professional?*

* * *

E Branch of MI5, British Security Service, was charged with internal security matters of the United Kingdom and its possessions. The office of the Director was located on the top floor, fifth level, of a new age modern building on Curzon Street between Green Park and Hyde Park. Director Richard Yates sat behind a large mahogany desk in a comfortable leather chair in a room with sparsely decorated walls and expensive carpet. Two locked file cabinets stood behind him guarding their secrets. He was tidy. A few papers, two telephones, and a small intercom unit on top of his desk allowed its highly polished surface to dominate the office.

The inevitable picture of the Queen, a picture of Winston Churchill congratulating him for heroism during "The War," and a picture of Captain Vernon Kell, the founder of MI5, hung on the walls. On a small bookcase next to the file cabinets stood a picture of his wife and two sons. In one corner of the room a discreet cabinet was stocked with fine whiskey, ice, hot water for tea, and hot coffee. It was a comfortable office designed to accommodate an efficient executive.

Fred Press, while in London, had decided to pay a rare visit to the Director. He sat opposite Yates in one of the three guest chairs. He admired his boss, a rotund man with a pale complexion and ruddy cheeks, a red nose and a small white mustache, and who wore pince-nez glasses. His eyes were crisp and clear, his mind sharp and inquisitive. Despite his age — he was almost sixty — Fred knew him to be light on his feet and quick. Fred thought he had heard all the stories about Yates. How he lied about his age and joined the army at sixteen, serving with distinction. After World War II Yates entered Eton to study languages. He had started with Scotland Yard, then was drafted into the Security Service years ago.

"Well, Fred, its good to see you again," Yates began. "It's been a while. I'm glad I was able to fit you in on such short notice. I've been reading your reports. Things are heating up again in the North, and the Prime Minister is very disgusted with the PIRA. She's looking for new ways to handle their terrorism. Please give it some more thought and let me know if you come up with anything. What brings you to London?"

"I played a hunch and followed a man. Never saw him before. Got on the plane at Dublin and then lost him at Heathrow."

"Umm, that's not like you. What happened?"

"I don't know, he just vanished. After he went through the customs booth, I stepped in front of the person behind him, flashed my ID, and got his name. The officer couldn't remember the address, just somewhere in London. When I got through the gate he was about fifteen yards ahead of me. The crowd was heavy, seemed like ten planes emptied all at once. I had his cap and coat in sight for about three or four minutes, then he just vanished. I pushed through the crowd, but never found him again.

"I'm not sure he was the same man that gave young John Larkey and Ian Sommers the slip. They work for that Protestant fanatic Reverend Sean McIver and were following an old man. A man who met with Professor Banks at a farmhouse just across the border in the South. You remember, he's the leader of the Independence Party.

"I picked up on young John standing outside a toilet, waiting. He was nervous and agitated. He went into the toilet and a few seconds later came crashing out and was knocked down by some guy walking by. A few moments earlier I'd spotted this fellow in a tweed cap and blue and grey short coat double timing it to a ticket desk for London. I was lucky to make the right plane with just a minute to spare. At least I have a description of him and a name, James Donnally. He is very good at disappearing. I think he's a professional. I'll file a report on it."

"Umm, what do you suppose the professor wants with a professional, and what does he do?"

"Don't know. Professor Banks's Independent Party is nonviolent with no paramilitary, wouldn't even think of it. So it's difficult to know what he's up to; what kind of professional the man may be. We have a telephone tap on Professor Banks's house. About two weeks ago he received a call from a man he wanted for a special project of some kind. The man asked him to hold the meeting in the South and to mail him the details. That's all we have. We couldn't trace the call. I set up to follow him south, and instead wound up following Sommers and Larkey. Don't know how they found out the professor was going across the border.

"While I'm here, I wonder when you might consider my request for more personnel? I realize that E Branch has been cut back because of the loss of colonial work, but activity in all areas in the North is increasing."

"Fred, I'm working on it. It's been six months since Henley was killed at that barn in Derry. Outright murder. Surprising no one took the credit. They usually do. Now we'll never know if it was the PIRA, who may have found out he was our man, or some Protestant paramilitary group that made a mistake. Henley was buried with full PIRA military honors."

"We're still guessing of course," replied Fred, "that it was a reprisal killing for the bombing of the Army barracks at Inglis outside London."

"Yes, quite a lot of publicity. We're going to have his body secretly exhumed and brought here for his family. About your request, I've had several discussions with the Director-General and he's made a recommendation to the Prime Minister. We want to get back in the PIRA and we want to get inside the Independence Party. The Prime Minister is stalling. She's waiting to see how long this recent increase in PIRA violence is going to last. The Director-General is pressing for two more agents now and three more after she makes up her mind about the PIRA."

"I can't thank you enough, Richard. The sooner we get more men, the better. The Independence Party is doing better than most people realize. Better than its leaders want to let on. I don't know what the Prime Minister's long range plans are, but one day soon the North may ask for independence."

"Umm, well yes, so far as I know we've no long-range plan in the government for Northern Ireland. Funny, I don't believe there's ever been one since the Norman invasion. The government has just been putting out fire after fire. I don't think we know the next step." Yates's tone of voice suggested a measure of disgust.

"It's an impasse, you know," said Fred, "the South'll not give up their claim to the North. The damned '85 Anglo-Irish agreement has agitated everyone in the North. With no Parliament and no Assembly, it's just the people. So we remain in control, the Army trying to keep the peace. The 'Troubles' won't end soon, not for Britain anyway. No plan, no solution."

Yates reached over, picked up a pen, and jotted down a note to himself. Fred Press waited until he had finished writing before asking, "Don't you think the Independence Party is a threat to our control of Northern Ireland?"

"Umm, perhaps sometime in the future. I gather from your reports, we've no immediate problem. They seem to be taking their time building membership. They're not making any waves. Professor Banks held only two seats in the Assembly. Not much of a force. Lots of prejudice, distrust, and hate to overcome."

Fred Press was uneasy. He wanted to tell Yates his intuition told him something was going to happen with the Independence Party sooner than expected. He had been trying to fit the puzzle together, but nothing jelled. "In addition to the wire tap at the professor's home, we've tapped his headquarters, and bugged it two months ago. Except for the one call about that special project, everything has been strictly party business or personal. He holds three or four meetings a week at the headquarters and a couple at his home.

"The odd thing is, they never discuss membership or money. All of that is written and handed in by the individual board member. No member seems to know what the others report on those two items. We've checked their bank balance and deposits fall short of what we estimate they collect. On one occasion we trailed Kevin Banks, the professor's eldest son, to Bern, where we think he made a deposit in a bank. The Swiss bank officials were very uncooperative."

The Director thought for a moment, "Umm, yes, I see. O.K., I agree we must infiltrate the Independence Party, and soon. I'll keep trying with the

Director-General."

"Thank you, sir. We'll keep you informed. By the way, if it's all right with you, while I'm here I'd like to pay a visit to Henley's widow."

"By all means," replied the director.

After Agent Press left, Yates got up and, lighting his favorite pipe, moved to the window. He looked out on the greater part of Hyde Park surprised, as always, to find himself suddenly gazing out on a sea of trees and green. He would spot an occasional jogger, people walking their dogs, mothers dragging their children, bicyclists, and once in a while a football game. It always relaxed him, and his mind would wander more freely. He wondered why Fred had come. It wasn't necessary, he could have filed a report. He had asked for help often enough during the last six months. No, something else was happening. He went back to his desk, sat down, and looked at the note he had scribbled to himself; "Fred is worried," it read.

I guess it's time to get serious, he thought. We'd better improve our efforts. I'll see the DG in the morning.

3

Northern Memories

The taxi from Heathrow dropped Jason off at his small estate just outside North London near Welham Green, Hertfordshire. The unpretentious three-story Edwardian house, built with fine Cotswold stone, was serviced with a long circular driveway set off nicely with lawn, shrubs, and well-placed spruce trees. He had purchased the house and surrounding ten acres from a bankrupt Earl and invested more than one million pounds gutting and updating the interior while maintaining the integrity of the original design.

The cellar included a well equipped shop-laboratory and small gymnasium where he and Craig practiced karate, lifted weights, and worked hard to keep fit. The first floor contained the living room, a dining room seating thirty, library, kitchen, a large bath, and his prize gallery room. The gallery doors were sealed to allow for precise temperature and humidity control to protect his priceless collection of impressionist works that included two

Renoirs, a Pissaro, two van Goghs, a Monet, and a large Caillebotte, plus sculptures by Degas, Rodin, and the American, Remington. It was a rich collection, carefully selected over years of regular visits to Sotheby's auction house. He had bought his first piece by borrowing the money. After that, he was earning enough money to make the winning bid for any item he wanted. At Sotheby's he was well known for his expertise in art.

Jason's bedroom with bath, his study, and four guest bedrooms with bath were located on the second floor. The study was completely furnished with office equipment, including a computer equipped with a terminal line direct to his office, and a fax unit.

Craig's apartment on the third floor was served by its own elevator from the ground on the east side of the house. Craig could come and go as he pleased except during those periods when Jason's schedule required his services. He was Jason's indispensable man Friday. Each week Jason set up a schedule and they would sit down and go over it, ironing out any conflicts.

They often went out together. In the early years, when Jason started earning big money and they cracked the edges of London society, it was rumored they were lovers. It wasn't long before the women they dated spread the word, emphatically, that they were not gay. Now the two were considered among the most eligible bachelors of London's upwardly mobile set.

Jason pulled out his keys, opened the front door,

and picked up his mail left on a small table in the entryway by his housekeeper, Mrs. Samuels. He climbed the circular staircase to the second floor, entered his bedroom, walked directly to a wall panel, and pressed a button. A hidden door slid open revealing a special, oversized closet. Craig called it Jason's "Merlin's Nest."

He opened his valise and emptied the contents, placing each in its appropriate spot. Then he undressed and hung his clothes on a rack full of clothes he used for disguises. The make-up table was a make-up artist's dream complete with various shades of skin foundation and skin base, latex eye pouches, latex ear parts, spirit gum, derma wax, all shades of pencils, putty for nose or eyes, and caps to create teeth of different shape and size. The collection included eyeshadow, highlighter, rouge of all shades, real hair mustaches, eyebrows, beards, wigs of different shapes and colors, and material with a special mold for making rubber masks.

This was part of Jason's secret side. He delighted in creating new disguises, then testing them out. Once he posed as an eccentric millionaire from America and completely fooled his two closest assistants over two days of wining and dining. Afterwards they sheepishly reported to Jason their failure to win the eccentric's account. He was pleased with the results and he and Craig had a good laugh. It was not just a hobby, but a passion. He worked constantly on quick changes, designing clothes that could convert rapidly into other colors, other styles. The time he spent during his early years in amateur theater work studying make-up, costuming, and magic taught him the sophisticated techniques of illusion. He had frequently performed a magic act in disguise before a live audience.

Jason slipped into a pair of jogging sweats, then checked his mail and dropped it off in his office. He switched on his computer and punched a couple of code numbers to check for messages: None. He went down to the kitchen, selected some cheese and crackers, poured a glass of milk, and took the small tray of snacks into the library. The fireplace had been prepared by Mrs. Samuels, and he torched it; the growing heat slowly warmed the room.

As he sat slumped in a chair opposite the fire, staring vacantly into the flames, he realized he was uneasy and drained. It had been a long day. He had started out relaxed about the trip to Ireland, even though he knew those crazy pains might return at any time. Perhaps it was the bullets, or perhaps the confrontation with Sean's men, but in the end he enjoyed the challenge of losing a tail. It didn't seem like enough stress to tire him. He was certain he had concealed his identity, as he had with all his clients. Lovely Juliana was his buffer from the outside world. After his first successful case, when he retrieved the duchess's jewels, Juliana had served as a clearing house for all his clients. Perhaps it was fighting off the memories of his early years in Ireland, perhaps it was "The Project." He knew that once Craig returned and they talked things over his uneasiness would go away.

As the fire became brighter and the room warmer, Jason finished the last of the crackers and milk and put the glass on the small table beside him. He was a bit more relaxed now, but a tinge of apprehension still gnawed at him. What made me do it? he wondered. I said I would never go back, but he professor's inquiry had been so cryptic I couldn't resist. Now it's possible this "Project" will take me to the North. I wonder if I can cross that border again.

Suddenly, without warning, the memories of Ireland came flooding back again. The unwanted pains hammered at him and he pushed them back. The land was so familiar, the air "seemed to smell green," a saying he used to tell Patricia. He was eighteen, attending Queens University in Belfast, just finishing his first year when he packed up and left. That was over twenty years ago. He never contacted his father and two brothers again. He rarely thought of Ireland. His mother had died just before he left, or else he might still be there.

He thought he had buried his given name, Robert Brian McIver, of Belfast, forever. His father, a militant Protestant loyalist and member of the Orange Order, owned a men's clothing store just off Donegal Square in the center of Belfast. Brother Sean was a bully with a mean streak. He would beat Robert Brian at every opportunity for the smallest trumped up reason. He would always hit him on the body so the bruises wouldn't show. Robert Brian never complained to his parents, but his absolute hatred for his brother slowly grew. Sean was sadistic and Robert Brian made every effort to keep out of his way. George, the classic follower, would never in his life make a decision on his own. He always agreed with their father or Sean.

Each night at the dinner table his father would say a prayer and recite the first few paragraphs of the oath of the Orange Order. He raved on with: "The Catholic Papist scum who plot against us to take away Ulster lands and jobs and make paupers out of us." During dinner he would recount a legend of William of Orange or Oliver Cromwell or Edward Carson. He never mentioned the flight of the Earls. He never mentioned the Treaty of Limerick and the Catholic Penal Laws when all of Ireland, North and South, was brutally controlled by Protestants. He never mentioned the loss of liberties or discrimination. He *was* discrimination. Robert Brian would look at his mother and roll his eyes. She let her eyes smile at him and they would go on trying to eat their dinner.

Robert Brian loved his mother deeply. Her indomitable spirit and cheerful outlook never faltered as she formed a wordless barrier between him and his father and brothers. His mother and he were much alike and the bond between them grew stronger as his father and brothers continued to recite the same themes of bigotry and hate. He worked in his father's store alongside his two brothers, when they weren't in school. Despite his bigotry, short temper, and strict discipline, his father paid them all fairly and Robert Brian saved his money. At the age of fifteen he bought his first stock, and he kept on buying after that. When he was seventeen he entered Queens.

Robert Brian met Patricia O'Neill Farley in his first accounting class; an exciting girl, full of life, with a passion for social reform. She was Catholic. He didn't care. Her clear, bright blue eyes, coal black hair and eyebrows, her soft milky skin and rosy cheeks captivated him.

Patricia was wary of Robert Brian McIver; she had heard his father was a bigot. But she soon felt the strength of his resolve and determination to break away and carve new paths. His square cut features, blue eyes, pleasing smile, and total honesty charmed her completely. They fell hopelessly in love.

They began taking occasional trips to the country. They would board a bus to Derry and when the houses thinned to an occasional farm, they left the bus and walked the countryside, talking and planning their future. They both knew what they were looking for, but never spoke of it; a private place to be alone, not bothered by anyone.

One afternoon they discovered a grove of trees near an abandoned feed barn. It was a peaceful place on a small hill where they could see for several miles. The morning rain had cleared for awhile, but when they reached the trees it began to rain again. They ran to the barn for cover and stood looking out at the rain. "'Tis coming down heavy, Robert." She looked up at the roof. "Ooh, 'tis leaking good in some spots, but it's dry over there."

He came up behind her and gently turned her to

him, not saying anything. He was shaking a little. He had kissed and held her many times before, but only briefly; they felt conspicuous even though they were alone and isolated. Now he looked into those bright blue eyes and kissed her warmly. She felt him shaking, hugged him hard, looked up at him and said, "Tis all right, Robert. I want you to love me. I love you so."

"I'm not sure how... I've never done it before," and he kissed her again harder, hungrier: "I love you, God how I love you."

"I've not... before, either, we'll just have to learn together." She turned away, got out the blanket, and put it in a dry place. "Over here."

They took off their jackets and he began fumbling with her blouse. She reached up to steady his shaking hands, then reached down and unbuckled his belt. Suddenly they stood alone without clothes; no more pretense, no shyness, only passion, young, pure and animal. They stared at each other as if trying to imprint the memory forever. Then they lay down on the blanket and between the hungry kisses and urgent, gentle feels, she helped him and whimpered a little when he penetrated. "Wait," she said. And he waited. And then they made love, once in a lifetime, never to be forgotten, first love. It was tentative, passionate, uncertain; and finally the full forces of awakening youth put them in uncontrollable spasms.

After that it became an agony to them. They couldn't help themselves. They returned to their special place time and again, as often as they could.

It was hell being apart and torment being together, until those deep, rumbling, uncontrollable spasms passed. Afterwards they lay in each others arms quietly and made small talk until reality returned and it was time to leave.

One day, when he was with Patricia at the barn, his mother died, unexpectedly, of a stroke. His father sent George to the University to find him, but George did not find him. When Robert Brian finally came home, they told him; he broke down and cried uncontrollably. Robert Brian didn't care about his father or his brothers. His mother was his source of strength and growing confidence. He would miss her. She ran his interference and now he would have to find the strength and courage to put up with his family until it was time to leave. He cried at night and took long walks trying to sort things out. He didn't see Patricia, and she understood.

Two weeks after his mother's death he met Patricia and they went off to the country. He wasn't in the mood for lovemaking, but he started fumbling around. She sensed his confusion. "Wait! I have something to tell you." He stopped. She grabbed his face and turned it to her and looked him straight in the eyes: "I'm pregnant. Five weeks. I just found out about it yesterday."

He was stunned. The suddenness of the news strangled him. He blinked, got up slowly, turned and walked out the broken doorway.

She sat there and cried softly, hands wrapped around her knees, rocking back and forth, trying to force back the sobs that were wrenching her body. She told him later that at that moment she believed he would never touch her again, never love her again, never see her again, never talk to her again. She had thought about it. She would not have an abortion. Somehow she would survive and raise his baby. Her family would never forgive her; she would leave home.

She was holding her stomach, sitting cross-legged, heaving deep spasmodic sobs when he was suddenly there, standing over her. He had walked a long way, first crying and feeling sorry for himself, telling himself about all the things he would miss, finally coming to grips with the truth of it. The real world had caught up with him, and he resolved not to be intimidated. He would make marriage work and he would succeed, later than planned, but he would succeed. He bent down and lifted her chin, wiped away the tears, and stared into her beautiful blue eyes. "We didn't plan it this way, you and I. It happened because we love each other. I love you. I will forever."

"Oh Robert, I'm so sorry it happened now," she said, as the sobs came heavier. "I thought I counted the days, but I must have missed. I can't give up the baby."

"Who said anything about giving it up? It's our baby and I'm proud of you. We'll start looking for a place of our own. When we get married, my father will never speak to me again, which is all right with me. I'll have to get a job. Maybe we can go to England."

"Robert, you can't quit school, it's your whole future."

"We'll get married soon. Maybe I can finish out the year before you start to show. That's when we'll have to find a place. I can get back to school later."

When they made love a little later, he had been more tender than ever before, more sensitive. He spoke softly and tried to be careful. During the two weeks since his mother had died, capped by the shock of a pregnancy, he had suddenly matured. No longer a boy with misty dreams, he became a man meeting a challenge. Patricia told him she would go with him anywhere, do anything to help him; that she was forever, happily in love with him.

Not long after that Robert Brian McIver would not, could not ever see his beloved Patricia again.

The fire crackled and sputtered low. Jason Stark was sweating and his side ached and his nose hurt and his face stung and he realized where he was and what he had been thinking about. He got up and went to a small cabinet, extracted a bottle of brandy, poured a full measure, and drank it down. He tried to shake off the haunting memories. He was a Londoner now, a millionaire. He didn't need bad memories.

He poured another drink and began thinking about his early years in London. He had spent his first six weeks in a cheap apartment in the SOHO District using the name of his friend Donald McVay. Then he met Craig Alexander at a small restaurant in the SOHO. As soon as they began talking, the bruised and troubled immigrant Irish lad with no job and an uncertain future won immediate friendship. Craig offered to share his apartment in Southwark not far from where he worked as a chemical technician for a small drug company. The rest was history.

"There you are!" And Jason's thoughts were interrupted when Craig suddenly entered the room. "Saw the lights on and decided to check in. That was quite a show you put on. I liked your outfits. The young chap in the grey suit didn't have a chance, got him with a solid body block and sent him sprawling. He looked awfully confused."

"I knew I could count on you," replied Jason. "I made the plane O.K., but someone followed me, a man in a brown leather jacket. Never saw him before. Not sure why he was tailing me. He boarded at the last minute and picked me out in my seat. I lost him at Heathrow when I suddenly ducked down in the crowd, removed my cap, glasses and coat, stepped to one side, and doubled back behind him. He gave up and caught a taxi. Don't know who he was."

"Sounds like Professor Banks is creating quite a stir with his independence thing, Jason. Who was the young fellow in the grey suit?"

"Unbelievable! It's a damned small world, Craig. He's a paramilitary agent for my unspeakable brother who is now a minister of his own church! I was shocked about that; my brother is the most unchristian Christian I have ever known." Then he told Craig about the farmhouse and the chase.

"Apparently he's not going to let the professor get too far without some kind of violence. I know him too well."

Craig whistled softly. "Here you are trying to avoid all your past connections, and you land right in the middle of it. Want to stop now?"

"Not yet. Did you find anything new about the professor?"

"Not really, it's rumored that his new membership count is growing faster. He is strict on the one Protestant to one Catholic idea and the committees, for this study and that study, are getting more enthusiastic and more dedicated. The professor has charisma, no doubt about it. The silent majority is beginning to take notice. The other political parties are waking up and getting a little bit wary. What does he want you to do?"

Jason got up and poured himself another drink, reached for another glass and poured Craig one, then handed it to him. "My friend, here's a toast to 'The Project.' It's a little scary, but I agreed to find out whether or not it's possible. The damned fool wants to 'sequester' the Crown Jewels from the Tower of London!"

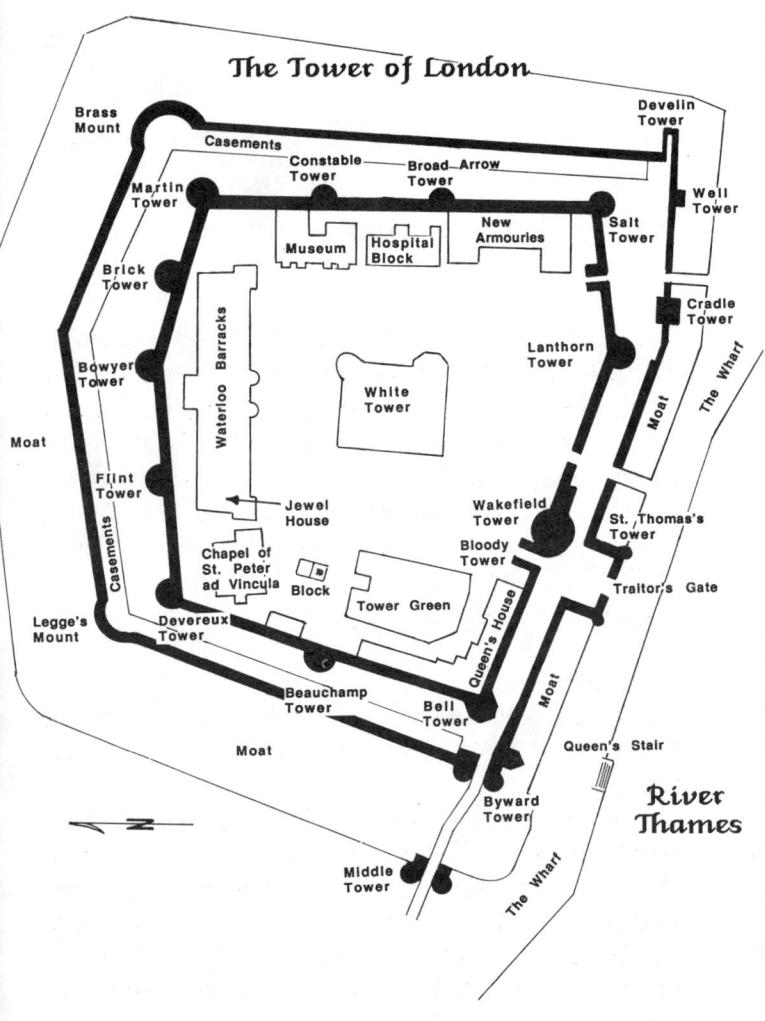

4

A Study of Stones

The Tower of London, its massive walls and central White Tower dominating the landscape, its hidden mysteries captivating the imagination, is revered as a symbol of Great Britain's strength, power, wealth, and glory. Each year its stature has grown. The government nurtures its history and proudly displays its treasures, inviting over two million visitors a year to soak up its charm.

Jason and Craig, arriving an hour before the 9:30 a.m. opening were nearly first in the queue. Jason wanted to check on early morning activities. It was misty, and the pavements were wet and full of shimmering reflections, but they didn't need an umbrella.

"You remember Claudette, don't you?" and Craig nodded yes. "That was eight years ago. Crazy about jewels," said Jason. "She wanted to come over from France to see the Crown Jewels. Very nearly had a fit when she saw them. I couldn't tear her away. Spent half a day down there in the vault. The guard finally chased us out."

"As I remember, quite a tantalizing woman," remarked Craig. "Too bad it didn't last longer."

"It was nice while it lasted, come to think of it. You know, m' friend, I'd forgotten just how magnificent this place is. That was my only visit. It's a helluva fortress."

"I gotta confess, Jason, this is my first trip after all the years I've been in London. When we were up on Tower Hill I must've counted ten or twelve turret towers on the inner wall; that wall's got to be forty feet high, maybe fifteen feet thick. True, the moat around the place has been filled in, but the outer wall is almost as high and the stone is massive. Can't get very near from the Thames or from the land side. Shoot you down before you took too many steps. It defies attack."

"Looks that way, doesn't it." Jason pulled out a small map that he had dredged up from his files and showed it to Craig. "I think we go through here at Byward Tower and can get out near St. James Tower. As I remember, the residents and employees use an entry east of Cradle Tower."

"Residents?" questioned Craig. "I didn't realize they had any."

"Mostly Yeoman Warders and their families, maybe 120 or 140, can't remember exactly. They live in the Casements inside the outer wall. The warders are all retired military; ex sergeant-majors. Quite an honor to get a spot here, you know. Long waiting list."

The ticket booth opened promptly at 9:30 and Jason and Craig walked to the Middle Tower entrance, where they were checked by a security guard with a hand held metal detector and cleared for entrance. They crossed the moat bridge and stopped beneath the Byward Tower, where they were met by a Yeoman Warder dressed in traditional Beefeater Tudor bonnet and black uniform trimmed with red. As soon as a small group formed, the Warder began his well rehearsed history of the Tower.

"Ladies and gentlemen," he began in his most proper English voice, tugging at one of the most beautiful beards Jason had ever seen, "it was William the Conqueror, wanting to create an unconquerable fortress, who started building the White Tower in 1066. It lay within the Roman walls and was meant to control and protect London. It took thirty-five years to complete. Later, during the reigns of Henry III, Edward I, and Edward II in the thirteenth and early fourteenth centuries, the Tower was expanded near to what it is today. Their enlargements carried the Tower boundaries east beyond the Roman walls."

The Warder led the small group slowly between the outer and inner walls, stopping briefly at each Tower while he summarized its history.

"Ladies and gentlemen," he continued, "the Tower has been a fortress, a palace, and a prison, and has housed the mint, the public records and the Royal Menagerie. It was used as a palace by all the kings and queens through James I in the early 1600s, although the last to live here was Henry III in the mid-thirteenth century. The Tower has never been captured in battle; but once, in 1215, some unhappy barons raised an army and held the Tower in pledge until King John agreed to sign the Magna Carta, the world's most famous document of freedom."

Walking between the massive walls, Craig heard the echo of the small group's footsteps break the silence of the morning, and when the Warder's voice struck the right place, he could hear it a second time. This is crazy, he thought, downright impossible. But, as Jason had instructed, he kept a mental note of everything he saw and heard.

"From earliest times," continued the Warder, "the Tower has been the guardian of the Crown Jewels. In 1671 Colonel Thomas Blood and two of his aides came to the Tower and stole the Crown Jewels, only to be caught in the act by the Keeper's son. Blood was pardoned by King Charles II, who was suspected of engineering the theft because he needed money. In 1841, the Great Armoury was gutted by fire and only the heroism of the Keeper of the Regalia and his wife saved the Crown Jewels. The Armoury was replaced with Waterloo Barracks, which now houses the Crown Jewels and Coronation Regalia." The Warder guided them past Traitors' Gate through the archway beneath Bloody Tower and onto the Tower grounds, finally stopping next to the White Tower.

"Ladies and gentlemen, before I take you up to the Chopping Block and turn you over to another Warder, let me say that I hope you enjoy your visit to the Tower. And by the way, we have a family of ravens who inhabit the Tower. Their wings are clipped so they can't leave, but they are brazen creatures and get into quite a bit of mischief. You ladies be careful, because they've been known to nip at a pretty leg. Legend has it the Tower will fall if the ravens ever leave."

Craig doubted a coup was possible. *But wouldn't it be a laugh if we snatched the ravens too!*

"Over there," whispered Jason, tugging at Craig's arm," is our target."

Craig looked over at the corner of the Waterloo Barracks and his doubts grew deeper. "This is getting ridiculous!" he told Jason.

"Perhaps, ladies and gentlemen," their new guide began, "what attracts visitors to the Tower as much as a peek at the Crown Jewels, is its macabre and bloody history. The Chapel Royal of St. Peter ad Vincula is suspected of guarding some 2000 bodies buried beneath its flagstone floor, all victims of beheadings or hangings. The Tower Green over there is an overflow burial site." And the Warder droned on with grim tales of executions, murders, and suicides. Then he dismissed the group to roam as they wished.

"You know, Jason," said Craig, as they slowly walked to queue up at the Jewel House, "these fellows don't talk much about the religious wars that raged here up until about 170 years ago. You know as well as I do that when the Catholics were in power, they killed Protestants, and when the Protestants took over they killed Catholics. They even purged the Jews once. Seems to me it started with William the Conqueror and ended with George

IV, see-saw back and forth between Catholic and Protestant, the struggle spilling over and mirrored in Ireland. Now Protestants here outnumber Catholics ten to one. Makes you wonder sometimes if our Protestant English government is afraid to let Northern Ireland become Catholic."

"Perhaps," responded Jason, "the deep down inbred Protestant-Catholic dichotomy, with its subtle discriminations, still persists among our leaders. They're supposed to be liberal in that regard, you know."

The two men stood silent for a few moments in the queue to the west entrance to Waterloo Barracks. Then Craig leaned over and whispered in Jason's ear, "You know, this place is awesome. The jewels have never been stolen. The professor must be out of his mind."

Jason smiled, "Anything's possible, keep your eyes open." They entered the well lit main floor, Upper Chamber, of the Jewel House, passing a security guard standing at the entry door. The low murmurs of the crowd and the sound of shuffling feet echoing off the walls created only a slight distraction for Jason and Craig. A few paces inside, a Yeoman Warder told them they could, if they wished, bypass the six large glass cases containing historic flagons, maces, military medals, and ceremonial robes, and go directly down to the vault of the jewels in the Lower Chamber. Jason motioned to Craig to follow him through the array of cases. "You know, Craig, each one of these items alone would bring a fortune."

"The swords are beautiful, tremendous workmanship," remarked Craig, "and those gold flagons and dishes bring out the larceny in my heart." When they finished inspecting the last case containing the Coronation robes, the Warder directed them to the stairway leading down to the vault.

Jason counted the forty-nine steps down and noticed that the large vault door, now against the wall in the open position, was similar to bank vault doors that he knew were equipped with an electronically controlled time lock. In the vault, two more Warders were on duty, one on the inside left of the vault on the upper level, directing people to keep moving along the lower level past the circular case containing the Crown Jewels. If one wished a longer look he could step out of line and move to the upper level. The second Warder stood on the inside right of the Vault, near the entrance, to answer questions and make sure visitors exited properly. Craig followed Jason to the upper level so they could examine the jewels at a more leisurely pace, and let the crowd slip by.

Craig stood there confused. The collection created so much glitter bouncing around from within the cases that he couldn't concentrate on any one piece. He turned his attention to the vault itself. The room appeared to be about thirty by sixty feet with a carpeted floor and textured concrete walls and ceiling. He wondered how thick they were. He noticed ventilation slots about one foot high at the top of the walls around the entire room. In each of the four upper corners was a television security camera. The sixty-three piece collection of treasures and Crown Jewels were located in a large central glass case with fourteen separate compartments. Damn! he thought, this job is impossible.

As they moved slowly around the cases, Jason was taking notes, and then he nodded to Craig and whispered, "That's what we want. Everything in, ah, let's see, case number eleven." We're in luck, he thought, the eleven principal pieces of the Coronation Regalia were still displayed all in one case. The Imperial State Crown, the Sovereign's Orb, the Sceptre with the Cross, the Sceptre with the Dove, the Coronation Ring, and the Jewelled State Sword were the exact six items targeted by Professor Banks.

Jason and Craig paused overlooking case number eleven as Jason continued his sketching of the placement of the pieces. Craig was thinking how hopeless this all seemed. *It's mind boggling to think anyone in his right mind would attempt such a thing. God! Look at that crown. It's so glittery and bright I can't look at it directly for too long. Must be a couple thousand diamonds all sending light spikes to your eyes. If I move my head, the glitter gets excited and seems brighter.* To think that he might touch it, carry it, or handle it in any way sent shivers down his spine, and raised up a crop of goosebumps. The collection of diamonds, rubies, sapphires, emeralds, and pearls framed in gold and silver, all in one place, the crown, seemed all at once to Craig just too much to think about. He began to sweat, though the temperature in the room was on the cool side.

Jason remembered from his earlier visit the way Claudette had drooled over the Second Star of Africa mounted on the front crown; the huge diamond of over 300 carats dazzled the eyes. The even larger First Star of Africa was mounted on top of the Sceptre with the Cross. It was over 500 carats, and Claudette went wild. She couldn't take her eyes off the shimmering bright diamond. She spent so much time looking in awe at the Coronation Regalia that she wheedled out of the Warder the exact function of each of the pieces used during the Coronation ceremony. When they finally threw her out, she told Jason she was determined to return the next two days. He was glad he didn't have to go.

Jason and Craig stood on the upper level in awe, captivated by the collection. "Fantastic," exclaimed Craig, "they are real, aren't they?"

"Yes indeed," replied Jason, "we British are too civilized and too proud of the jewels to deceive the public." The two men moved slowly around the case on the upper level, each making note of the case construction, room dimensions, and lighting.

"Let's go back to the beginning and drop down to the lower line for a closer look," said Jason.

Once in the lower line they were forced to keep moving. The collection was astonishing. Like all the tourists they slowed as they became hypnotized by the brilliance and dancing spikes of light from the Coronation Regalia in case number eleven. The incredible collection was too astonishing for the average man to totally absorb in one short visit.

Jason took a close look at the heavy door of the vault when they left. He counted the forty-nine steps up the West staircase. To the left of the top of the stairs Jason stopped at a small table and purchased, from an attractive middle-aged woman, a handsome colored booklet giving a detailed description of the Crown Jewels and a map of the location and identification of each piece in the vault case. Leaving the Jewel House through the southwest exit they passed a middle-aged security guard who bid them a polite good day. In all they counted three Yeoman Warders, two security guards, and one lady sales clerk, none with weapons.

When they were clear of the building and other visitors, Craig looked at Jason and said, "I think your Irish friend is mad! I don't believe we can find out enough in a week to be certain of any plan that might have the slightest possibility of working. Too much snooping might rouse some suspicion."

"You may be right. Most visitors only stop here once. Well, we'll have to do our best; we'll use a disguise or two. It'll be fun." They joined a tour of the Chapel of St. Peter ad Vincula and listened to a few sordid tales of some of those beheaded and buried beneath the stones. They wandered the Tower Green, a delightful park covered with trees, to get a closer look at the Queen's House located in the center of a row of L-shaped Tudor houses and the administrative offices along the inner West ward.

They walked to the Wakefield Tower adjacent to the Bloody Tower on the south inner ward, up the stairway from the ground floor guard room to the upper floor vaulted chamber and up to the turret. They took the walk east along the south inner ward passing through four of the towers, ending at Martin Tower on the northeast corner.

They passed the New Armouries, Hospital Block, and the Museum of the Royal Regiment of Fusiliers. The view from the wall and the Towers offered a spectacular overlook of the grounds and the Casements. They descended the dark stairway of the Martin Tower and exited opposite the Waterloo Barracks. Throughout their meanderings, Craig snapped random pictures of everything in sight.

Jason led the way to the White Tower, the central structure of the Tower, to get a few pictures from the two north turrets. When they reached the top floor they found the stairway entrance to the northwest turret chained. Jason distracted one of the security guards while Craig slipped under the chain and went up to the top, snapped a few pictures from the glassed-in windows, and returned while Jason was still deep in conversation with the guard.

"O.K., I think I have enough pictures, Jason, time to go," he said, and the two men left. They found the restaurant, ate a late lunch, bought more books and detailed maps of the Tower, and returned home.

For the next three days they visited the Tower, each time in a different disguise. Each evening they developed a new list of questions. They knew that the Coronation Regalia was removed from case number eleven and worn by the Queen at the opening of Parliament each November. During the month of February the Jewel house was closed for cleaning and renovation. The Coronation Regalia would be removed and worn by the Queen for an occasional state affair or an official photograph of the Queen. Each day the list of questions seemed to get longer.

Jason, in the guise of a tourist, arranged for a pass to watch the Ceremony of the Keys held each night at ten. It gave him an opportunity to check out night activity. Now he saw more sentries posted, at rest, each dressed in camouflage battle dress, each with a semi-automatic rifle loaded with a thirty-round clip. It unsettled him a little. He had noticed only one daytime sentry, a Fusilier equipped with a standard army rifle, on duty at the Waterloo Barracks.

He watched in fascination as the Chief Warder joined an escort consisting of a sergeant and three men who were detailed to help him close and lock the three gates. While he waited for the small group to return with the keys, Jason noticed the lighting was more artistic than security effective. Dark, almost pitch-black areas existed throughout the grounds, providing easy cover for a night operation. The Chief Warder returned and recited century-old words that ended the brief ceremony. He then carried the keys to the Queen's House, where they were secured for the night. Jason filed the information away for future reference.

On the fifth day the two men remained at home and outlined four possible plans. They spent several hours reviewing photographs, maps and their notes, adding comments to each of the plans.

"At first I really believed this whole idea was the work of a madman," said Craig. "The Crown Jewels are the most unprotected, yet protected jewels in the world. More than anything they're protected by the intimidation of the Tower itself. It's a massive, imposing fortress. Yet I see possibilities, dangerous perhaps, but possibilities."

Jason looked up from their largest map. "Let's not give up yet. The first two plans are weak and we might as well forget them." They concentrated on the next two and broke for a workout followed by lunch. Back at work, late in the afternoon, they finally agreed the boldest plan held the most chance for success. When they totaled up the estimated cost it was also the most expensive. "Damn," said Craig, "I think it has a good chance. It's unique and even a little brave. No one gets hurt, at least not on paper. You have my vote. Who's going to head it up?"

"I'm thinking about it. If I do it, will you help?"

"I didn't think you were a thief. You've always stayed within the law except in rare emergencies. Why change your stripes now? You certainly don't need the money or the work."

"I'm worried. In this line of work there are few saints. I can think of three or four men who would gladly do this job, but no one I could trust. They wouldn't hesitate to kill, and they might decide to keep the jewels. If I do it, I have control of the situation and control of the jewels. The professor won't know until the last moment that the jewels will never leave England." Jason laughed. "The British have a law against it. Not even the Queen can take them out of England. The professor claims it's 'sequestering,' not theft. He will just hold them hostage for a while. Well, maybe so. Even the Tower has been held hostage 'til old John signed the Magna Carta."

With a whimsical smile he went on: "I guess I can rationalize any situation. I worry that Northern Ireland will become an economic wasteland. The British do-nothing policy is making the situation worse every day. The South's support of the PIRA helps not at all, and their real fear of the economic consequences that unification would bring keeps them spilling out meaningless rhetoric. Independence is a clear course of action, and the professor's program for nationalism and economic progress is well thought out. Civil war might occur, but I doubt it. Too many of the factions at one time or another have said they would welcome independence. But the truth is they don't know how to go about it. At least Professor Banks has a plan. The question comes down to whether I tell him it can be done, and if I tell him, will he want me to do it, and if he wants me to do it, will I?"

"Do you suppose those crazies in the North will try to murder the professor once they find out what he is up to?" asked Craig. "And if they don't do it before he gets his independence, they will surely do it afterward."

"Once negotiations are underway, he'll have the

protection of the British and the United Nations. Before that, he's at risk. Later, unless I miss my guess, he'll become the first president or prime minister of the new independent country and will have plenty of his own protection. My own brother is the most dangerous threat; however, he can be neutralized."

"Jason, I've known you for over twenty years now and you've been like a brother to me. You've helped me earn more money than I ever dreamed possible, and you've been kind and considerate. I've done everything you have asked me to do, but this is insanity." Craig swallowed the last of his brandy, got up and stirred the fire, and turned to Jason: "But if you want me to help you, I will."

"You're a true friend, Craig. I wouldn't think of doing this project without you. Tell you what, let's sleep on it one more night."

* * *

Professor William Banks got up to add some wood to the fire, then, at an old family cabinet he poured a small glass of Bushmills and let the familiar aroma greet his nose, and linger, before he drank it. It was late, and he walked to the window and looked out at the lighted sky of Belfast. He wondered if a common bond, solid and binding, could ever occur between Protestant and Catholic. It seemed to him that in the many committee meetings he had attended the two tribes were getting on very well. He detected a genuine feeling of cooperation as they worked towards a system that could bring lasting peace and prosperity to the North. True, some members had been roughed up by the Catholic protection boys, and some had received veiled threats from the Protestant fringe, but the harassment had subsided for now. A few crazies like Reverend McIver worried him. The man would cause trouble, but he couldn't worry about where or when.

Lately more of the silent majority on both sides had become interested, and he wondered if the hardheads would ever come around. Over one thousand new members in the last week and a half. He was astounded that membership had climbed so fast. Contributions were climbing, too; £300,000 in the Bank of England and another £700,000 in a Swiss bank. A newspaper wag called it the silent movement of the silent majority. The idea was catching on, but he had serious doubts whether an independent North could be established without bloodshed. It was not in the Irish nature to accept big changes without some show of violence. Success would all be a matter of surprise and timing. Whenever he thought about "The Project" he got nervous. It had been eight days and still no word from Perry Wallace. His report was overdue, and this bothered him. Perhaps the mail was slow; in England that was not unusual. They had agreed on a code, and he had put the cipher in his wallet. Kevin was prepared to leave for Calais on a moments notice.

He had no idea whether "sequestering" was possible. It was a crazy idea. He had been to the Tower once in his life. The jewels were magnificent, but he couldn't for the life of him imagine how to get them out. *If the Magician says it can't be done we'll have to go for one more opinion.* And he was less certain of the next man on the list. Well, time would tell.

Surprise and quickness were his primary objectives. He would be happy to let the United Nations control the borders and police the public. A little time to get organized would prevent a wholesale exodus of Catholics to the South, which he didn't expect anyway, and prevent the PIRA from sealing off the three Catholic counties of Armagh, Fermanagh, and Tyrone. He did not want a civil war, and the party's contingency plans were designed to prevent it.

The new Provisionals possessed little respect for human life and when they took over the "Original" IRA he had quit in utter disgust. It rankled him that the new breed was now called IRA instead of PIRA as he stubbornly continued to call them. Their bungling violence had put the North at an even lower position on the British national agenda. Well, he hoped his planning would take the PIRA out of the picture for a long time, maybe forever.

NATO and the Americans would bring great pressure to bear to keep the North British for strategic defence. Well, he had one of his more silent committees working on a treaty, some land concessions, and what to do about the American bases.

He was thinking of the tremendous public relations effort it would take to bring world opinion and pressure to bear on the South, the final link in the triangle, to close down the PIRA and give up their claim to Ulster, when Kevin entered the room and interrupted his thoughts.

"Father, it's come, the message, at least I think it is. He said he would mail it from Calais. I didn't get back to the office until late and it was in the afternoon post."

The elder Banks took the envelope over to his desk, drew out a magnifying glass, and inspected it for signs of tampering; he could see none. The postal inspector who had received it back from MI5 had admired their professional work. He slit it open and read the cryptic message: "'Twelve-twenty, O.K.', that's wonderful, it means he can do it."

Kevin smiled: "Twelve-twenty, that's next week."

"Yes," and the professor pulled out the code Wallace had given him. "But remember it means he will meet you in Calais at 11:00 a.m. on the morning of the 17th. Well now, I wonder what he has in mind?"

* * *

Kevin felt uncomfortable and conspicuous as he walked the short distance from the hotel to the little restaurant with the outdoor tables on the sidewalk in Calais. He believed everyone was watching him. He had never dressed up in any disguise before, let alone that of a priest. They had scrambled around trying to locate a suit that would fit him. Finally one of the Board members, a Catholic, approached a priest he knew that was about Kevin's size and asked the priest to loan him a suit. The priest was curious, but didn't press for answers.

He was always happy to get away from the movement for a few days, or even one day; coordinating meetings and reports, and managing the office and accounts was becoming more difficult each day with the rapid growth of members. Sometimes it seemed to him he was walking in his father's shadow, though he knew it to be untrue. He loved his father and was proud of him. His father had taught him and his two brothers simple values: Truth, justice, freedom of expression, and respect for the other fellow no matter what his ideas and opinions may be. Each of them was taught independence, treated as an individual, and always allowed to express his own ideas and opinions. It sometimes led to fighting in their early years, but they grew out of it and learned to respect and love each other.

Kevin turned the corner and a cold wind sent a chill through his body. He spotted the restaurant a few meters ahead of him, stopped at a small gift shop, and peered in the window. He casually shifted his gaze first in one direction and then the other to check the people on the streets. No one seemed interested in him and none looked suspicious.

He walked through the door of the restaurant at precisely 11:00 am and saw Perry Wallace, dressed as an elderly priest, at a window table already sipping a cup of coffee. The restaurant was nearly empty; two men and a woman sat at separate tables in opposite corners reading and drinking coffee. The waiters were resetting the tables and preparing for the luncheon crowd. He tried to visualize Perry Wallace's true features behind the rich grey wig and matching mustache and beard, but couldn't. His nose seemed flatter and wider than the first time they met. Subtle changes made a big impact on his appearance.

"Good morning, Father, I trust you had a pleasant journey?" and Jason got up and extended his hand.

"Yes indeed, no sweat. Followed your instructions and here I am without a tail, at least I think so. Haven't tried this before."

"How did it go in London?"

"I went from Heathrow to Victoria Station, bought a ticket on the Circle Line, it was about 4:00 pm and the place was a madhouse. I waited until the last minute, then jammed my way onto a train. No room to breathe either and it was hot down there. I didn't see anyone following me. I got off at the next station, Sloane Square I believe, went up and over the tracks, returned to Victoria, caught the boat train to Dover, and here I am. I checked again on the boat but found no one. After customs I changed clothes in the toilet."

A waiter appeared for a moment and stood silent, looking bored, until Kevin said "I'll have coffee and a biscuit please." The waiter apparently understood English and left without saying a word, but was back in less than a minute with his order, and poured Jason more coffee.

As he glanced up to thank the waiter, Jason recognized a man entering the restaurant as definitely British, MI5 or equivalent, and definitely interested in them. He was the same man who had boarded Jason's flight in Dublin at the very last moment and trailed him at Heathrow. "It appears, Kevin, I'll have to give you a lesson or two on how to lose a tail. Our man just appeared."

Kevin quickly handed Jason the small detector Jason had loaned them before he left the farmhouse. "It works. Our phones are tapped and the office is bugged." Jason switched it to the number two position and set it next to his coffee cup.

The man selected a table a few feet away from them, sat down, fumbled inside his coat pocket for a moment, pulled out a pack of cigarettes, extracted one, laid the package on the table, and lit his cigarette.

The little red light on the instrument started blinking. Kevin glanced at the man, but he didn't look familiar, "What do we do now?"

"Nothing. Enjoy your coffee. We have plenty of time and I have something for you to read. Give it back when you're through. Refer to the items by number only." Jason reached over and placed a small piece of paper next to Kevin's coffee cup. Kevin read it quickly:

        1. It can be done.
        2. Need five months.

3. Need only you from Northern Ireland.
4. £1,300,000 - equipment and personnel.
5. I will head project. Will not disclose method now.
6. Will call you on the 25th for yes or no answer.

He read it again, then shoved it back to Jason, who folded it and put it back in his pocket. "You are certain?" asked Kevin.

"Yes."

"No. 4 is quite a bit. No. 5 will not fly, we need the method."

"No. 4 is honest," replied Jason. "As for the other, you will know in due time. Let's leave now."

Jason paid the check and they left the restaurant.

"I'll walk you back to your hotel." And Jason quickly turned to see if the man had emerged from the restaurant. "He's still in there, so he can't hear us now. We selected the only safe way to do 'The Project,' but unfortunately it's the most expensive. You come over for training two weeks in advance. I'll explain the method only then, not before. You can take it or leave it. I doubt you can trust anyone else."

"You want us to accept this blindly? That's asking an awful lot."

Jason smiled at Kevin. "My friend, you are asking an awful lot! I guarantee it's a safe plan. If you don't approve of it when you hear it, you can cancel and you will eventually recover about half the money." Jason turned to see the man leave the restaurant and start in their direction. They stopped talking.

Kevin walked into the hotel and Jason hailed a taxi. The man from London got into a taxi and followed Jason. The taxi wandered around the city for an hour as the driver pointed out various places of interest to the kindly old priest. He told Jason once that he thought they were being followed, but Jason told him it was all right. Jason asked him to stop at the train depot. "I will pay you to this point, but I want you to go to the south entrance and wait for me. I'll only be a moment." He left the taxi and went to a luggage locker, picked up a small suitcase, made a few moves to shake his tail, and got back in the taxi at the south entrance. The driver took him back to the restaurant, where he enjoyed a leisurely lunch. The man from the plane to London, the same man from the restaurant, was still with him. He is good, Jason thought, I should have lost him at the depot but he hung on. Jason paid his check and walked slowly to the hotel where Kevin was staying, went through the entrance, and disappeared.

* * *

Director Richard Yates, a little curious at this second surprise visit, stared intently at Fred Press seated across the desk from him. "It's been less than two weeks since your last visit; what brings you this time?"

"We intercepted a coded message in the mail to Professor Banks. We increased surveillance and learned that young Kevin bought a ticket to London. I followed him and so did Sean McIver's man. I'm sure he suspected he was being followed, because he lost McIver's man in London. I stuck with him to the boat for Calais. When he arrived at Calais, he switched into a priest outfit and went to a hotel. Next day, dressed in the same disguise, he met an older priest. I managed to tape their conversation while they were in the restaurant." He placed a small recorder on the desk, switched it on, and played the tape.

The Director reached for his pipe, lit it, and looked at his senior agent in charge in Northern Ireland. "Can't make much out of that. What did the boys in cryptography have to say?"

"Only that number four probably had to do with money, nothing else. We made voice prints. Young Banks was reading from a piece of paper the old priest handed him. The old priest put it back in his pocket before they left." Then he explained how the old priest disappeared. "I checked with the people on duty at the hotel but none remembered seeing him."

"Umm. You know, Fred, you're not getting that far along in age. That's twice inside two weeks that you lost your man. That's not like you. He must be very good."

"I've been thinking the same thing. He must be the same man I followed from Dublin to London. First as a plumpish man in a blue and grey short coat and now as an old priest looking every bit the genuine article, no hint of makeup. He's very good.

No self respecting priest would suspect he is being followed and deliberately try to lose a tail. They are up to something."

"Umm. I've been rereading your reports. Banks's group seems to be picking up in membership. Surprising they can find any Protestants and Catholics who want to sit down together. Nevertheless, it means more money coming in, more committees, and more work on independence. After your last visit I talked with the Director-General and he in turn talked to the Prime Minister. You'll soon be getting the men you requested. Two now, and we expect to get two more for you within two months. It would appear that Professor Banks is up to something, and we should do what we can to find out."

"Thanks very much, Richard. I'll file my report and keep you posted."

When Fred Press left, Yates picked up the phone and called the office of files and information. "Please see if you can develop a list of people whose M.O. includes an excellent aptitude in the use of disguise."

5

Casting the Die

Maria Donna Costell lay on her back, on his bed, breathing hard. She moved and he slapped her hard: "Be still, bitch," he said. Half drunk, Don Roberto Milano was on top of her, all 200 pounds of him, in the process of raping her. He liked to rough up his women. It was his way of getting back at a mother who hated him. Maria dared not cry out because his bodyguards were in the next room.

He had surprised her, caught her off guard, in the process of putting the little black book away when he came into his bedroom. Fortunately he did not notice her putting it back; he had only one thing in mind and he was drunk. As she turned from the dresser with the mirror, he suddenly slapped her, dragged her to the bed, put a knife to her throat, and forced her arms beneath her. He was strong and moved her 118 pound body around quickly.

Now he was straddling her, leaning on his left fist holding the knife, his right hand ripping at her blouse. Suddenly it was open and he took the knife and carefully cut her brassiere. She could feel the sharp blade touching the soft skin between her breasts, and she shuddered. She wriggled again briefly, but did not panic. She sensed his next move and was ready. He leaned on his left fist, with the knife still in it, and again raised up to reach her skirt with his right hand. The skirt was tight, stubborn, and didn't move much. She looked up at his sweaty face and bloodshot eyes and waited. He tried the second time and the skirt began to move. He kept fumbling at the skirt as his beefy hand moved up her thigh.

Now! she thought. Move! He's not going to rape me or anyone else. She rolled to her right and as he slapped her again she made certain her left arm was free. He was back up, breathing heavy. "Don't move, you little bitch, or I'll kill you." He started at her skirt again, his large hand coming up her thigh until it was almost to her crotch. It was his final move. She lashed out with an expert left-handed blow to his throat that nearly crushed his larynx. He would never again talk above a whisper. He dropped the knife and rolled over on his back gasping for air, both hands holding his throat. He squinted his eyes closed to shut out the awful pain and made whimpering, gurgling sounds. Now she was on all fours straddling him and he couldn't make a sound above a whisper. His erection was gone.

"You helpless bastard, you're through." She gave him a quick, effective chop across the bridge of the nose that broke it. and it started to bleed. She moved back, lifted her right leg slightly, and with all her strength kneed him in his groin, crushing his left testicle against his pubis bone and severely injuring the right testicle. He let out a little gasp and passed out from the pain.

Maria went to her purse, removed a small syringe, rolled him over on his stomach, and expertly injected him with a small dose of Seconal. Well, Don Roberto, she thought, you won't be dealing in sex or cocaine for a long time to come. Bon voyage! She went into the bath and took a shower to cleanse the slimy feel of his hands from her body. She used a little makeup to hide the red welts on the side of her face, fixed a small drink, and sat down to think. She now had the hard evidence to break one of the largest drug rings in Italy and its leader, Don Roberto, was now a helpless eunuch. The rest would be easy.

She decided to take the little black book filled with the names of all the members of the ring and their contacts and not bother to develop the film she had taken of it. She got up, unbolted the bedroom door and opened it a crack. Both men were still in the next room, but appeared to be dozing off. They knew of their boss's long brutalizing sessions with women and had settled down for the night. She softly closed the door, locked it, removed a roll of strong thin plastic wire from her purse, and looped it around the bed post making it into a double stranded rope. She opened the window and let herself down the two floors to the ground, retrieved the wire, and left.

Three blocks from Don Roberto's house, she found a phone and called Inspector Biraldi, chief of Rome's police drug unit. He had hired Maria three months earlier to infiltrate the suspected drug ring and look for hard evidence. She had dyed her hair blonde, wore brown contact lenses, reshaped her eyebrows, painted her lipstick in a much wider and thicker mouth, dressed in loud, flowery, cheap clothes, and called herself Anna Bionti. It took her two months to work her way up to Don Roberto, then a month of leading him on, knowing his insatiable appetite for women. Tonight she had finished her job.

She didn't have to wait long for the Inspector. His unit had been ready to move in on Don Roberto if she called.

"We will be eternally grateful, Maria, thank you for your help. I will send your pay, and half of any money we find among Don Roberto's things, before you leave tomorrow morning. You will not be mentioned in any of the reports. I have an ambulance on the way for Don Roberto. Sergeant Vitorio will take you home. Good work, thanks, and good luck."

The next morning it was the Inspector himself who brought her a huge sum of cash. "I couldn't trust anyone to bring it to you. We found a great deal of money at Don Roberto's, and this is your half plus what we owe you, as promised."

She paid another month's rent on the apartment, in case someone came looking for her. She put her hair in a bun beneath a large scarf, removed all makeup except what she needed to cover her disappearing welts, put on heavy dark glasses, and caught a flight to Nice. The newspapers were full of details of the biggest drug bust in Italian history. Don Roberto Milano had been hospitalized and would spend the rest of his life in jail. The police were still in the process of rounding up over one hundred suspects.

At thirty-two, Maria Donna Costell's natural beauty hid her tremendous strength. Her stunning figure was accented by long, wavy, almost jet black hair, olive skin, beautiful large blue eyes, and an extremely sensuous mouth. A former police woman proficient in five languages, she was now a free-lance agent-investigator. She kept in shape with daily workouts and long runs, and much practice at a private school for self defence where she had earned her black belt in karate.

When she arrived in Nice the taxi dropped her at her exclusive penthouse atop one of Nice's most fashionable condominiums. While she was away she had called Anne, her housekeeper, on a number of occasions to check for messages. An excited Anne met her at the door.

"It is good to see you back again, Maria; ah, but you need some rest, you look tired, and what have you done to your hair?"

"It was for my job. I'll get it fixed tomorrow. Yes, I'm tired. Messages?"

"On the table in the library. I separated out only one."

"Thank you, Anne, I could use some milk and

small sandwiches in the bedroom." She gathered the mail and took it into her bedroom. She opened the note that Anne had kept separate, and read it. It was from Jason. *Oh, Jason you're coming here! Wonderful! It has been too long.* She was instantly excited about his visit.

She had not seen Jason in over a year. She often wondered if they would ever be together again; two years ago when they fell in love, it seemed she would always be with him.

One man had hired them both. He had wanted the best. Instead of working separately, they decided to team up. It made the job easier and faster. When it was over they split almost two million pounds.

Afterwards, they spent the summer together and fell deeply in love. She told him everything about her life, but he drew the line about his early years. She learned nothing of his family or where he was born. When she pressed him, he would get up and walk away saying, "That's all dead, I can think of nothing of any interest or value to discuss, just forget about it."

He drew cool and distant whenever she suggested getting together for a long time. She suspected another women and gently accused him of it. He denied it saying, except for an occasional affair, he had no one serious in his life. She never quite believed him. Once she saw a gold wedding band hooked onto his key ring. She could feel something important within him not letting go. She let it drop. When summer was over they went their separate ways.

Now, she thought, he will be here day after tomorrow and I look like hell! Anne brought the snacks, set the bath water flowing, and was helping her out of her clothes when she saw the bruises on Maria's shoulders and arms. "Oh! What have you done? You should take better care of yourself. I will get some ice packs."

"The job was a little unpleasant at the end, but it turned out all right." Anne brought ice packs and put them on her bruises for a few moments; then Maria took a long, warming bath.

"Now please don't forget to wake me at noon tomorrow. Call the hairdresser for two o'clock, and oh yes, call this number in London and tell Mr. Stark that I'll meet him at the airport. Ask him for his flight number. It's all right, he understands French."

She went to bed, slept for the next twenty hours, and awoke completely refreshed, but a little stiff and sore. Anne applied more ice and the bruises looked a little better. The hairdresser cut her hair short, dyed it back to its natural black color, and gave her a facial and manicure. She shopped for a new outfit, returned home, and slept some more.

Jason arrived at the airport just before noon. Overjoyed, she hugged him and smothered him with kisses, and took a slightly embarrassed English-looking gentleman immediately to her favorite restaurant, one kept very secret by the locals.

"A small corner table and a little wine to start with, Jason. You look great, I can't see one more wrinkle."

"I don't need to tell you that you look smashing. Everyone in the restaurant is looking at you."

"I've been sleeping for the past two days. I just came off assignment. It was a little scary in the end, but it worked out. It was a drug case; tell you a little about it later. They found over £600,000 in this man's house. I would be delighted to treat you to another summer. I feel good now, but didn't know how really good I felt until I saw you. Oh, Jason, I've missed you. What brings you to Nice? Will you be staying long? Will you stay with me? Please." She didn't want him to get away from her again, not until she understood him better.

Jason felt embarrassed for not having called her since he had gone away. He suddenly realized how truly beautiful she was, and how much he had missed her. "Wait a minute, let me catch my breath, I won't be staying too long and yes, I'll stay with you unless you're just being polite, and I'll explain why I'm here a little later."

"Jason Stark, you know how I feel about you, I've truly missed you . . . very much . . . there hasn't been anyone else."

"I am sorry about last year, Maria, about the way it ended. I've wanted to explain what I couldn't bring myself to tell you about. I wanted to call you . . . several times . . . but . . . well, just didn't. I've thought about you often." The waiter interrupted and took their order.

"I want to clear it up, a little later perhaps, after a good lunch. You look hungry."

"I'm starving, and it's not just for food!" And she

looked into his eyes with a seductive smile.

As they ate lunch Maria studied him. He is a handsome devil, she thought, six feet tall of slim and solid body, a face with bright blue eyes and square, resolute features, self assured, and confident. He's honest, intelligent, and I love him very much. Why did I ever hold back?

They left the restaurant and she drove out along the coast towards Cannes. The sky was overcast, but the winds from the Mediterranean were soft and warm. She pulled into an overlook and they got out to stretch their legs. The sea was desolate, the rocky bluffs were steep and sharp and the occasional beach empty. She moved close to him. He could smell the sweetness of her, and a sudden buried longing gripped him. She turned to him and he kissed her gently. She threw her arms around him and kissed him hard. "We shouldn't be here. We should be home in bed."

"I'm almost sorry I came," he said.

She was startled, pushed him back. "What do you mean?"

"I apologize. It's not like it sounds. I mean . . . I came here to ask you to help me on a project that's a little dangerous, and, well, I don't want you to get hurt. That's all." He reached up and softly touched her hair, then put both arms around her, and pulled her close to him.

"Jason, you know I can take care of myself. It can't be any more difficult than my last job and besides I am a professional every bit as good as you are, right?"

"Yes, yes, but when I saw you at the airport I suddenly realized how much you really mean to me and what a damned fool I've been to go this long without seeing you. Now I'm confused."

She looked into his eyes, perplexed. "Tell me what's happening, why did you come here?"

He told her about "The Project," what her part would be, that now he wasn't so sure he wanted her involved. He explained why he felt he was the only one to carry it off. Someone else might never return the jewels, and he couldn't bear the thought.

She listened very carefully and waited patiently for him to finish. "For God's sake, Jason, you're not a thief, it is not your style. Why do you care if the damned things never get back? Why would you even consider doing it?"

Then he told her what he couldn't tell her before, about his early days in Belfast and his mother, about his father and two brothers and the way they were, and finally about Patricia, young, strong, fierce Patricia who was happy and pregnant, but in the end let the life go out of her: And how he could never bring himself to go back to Belfast, but knew that something must change the rottenness there. Maybe the professor could pull it off.

She could see the pain in his face and knew that he had been hurt deeply, more deeply than he realized. She looked at him and reached up with both hands, putting his face between them, and kissed him. "Thank you for telling me, let's go home."

She drove faster on the way back, not saying a

word; no more questions, no more wondering what was behind this complex man she had come to love. Jason stared numbly out at the empty sea, feeling as if a great burden had been lifted from his shoulders..

She mixed him a drink, then fixed one for herself, and they sat opposite one another in her living room. They stared at each other not knowing where to start. Suddenly she got up and walked slowly towards the bedroom. There was no mistaking the invitation of her movements. He smiled, drank his drink in one swallow, and followed her into the bedroom. As he closed the door he heard the shower water and knew what to do. It was not new to them, something they had come to enjoy during their long summer. He took off his clothes and joined her under the lukewarm spray of water. She kissed him and they began touching, the soap and water providing a smooth, silky film that made fingers and hands glide easily, sensuously over familiar places.

"You are bruised," he said, and kissed each one gently.

"They feel better now," she replied, "tell you about it later," and she kissed him in a way that only she could do, in a way that only he knew, and suddenly the lukewarm water could not quench the fire. They left the shower, not stopping to towel off, and when she was there on top of him, beside him, under him, she whispered: "Be easy, it's been a long time." And he was and they were patient, and then the abrupt release was almost too much to bear and it kept on and on and suddenly, they were quiet. "I love, you Jason." But he was already asleep and soon so was she.

Anne served them a delightful breakfast on the broad veranda that provided a breathtaking view of Nice. Not only was Jason in love with Maria, but he had great admiration for her strength, character and determination to succeed. She was living in one of the most exclusive cities in France with all the material things she could ever want. He knew she worked hard and took some dangerous risks at times, but she was very successful, and her wealth had increased dramatically during the last few years. She taught herself from poor beginnings to become knowledgeable and sophisticated with a passion for art and a discerning taste in clothes and decorating. Their tastes in art were much alike; their work gave them a great deal in common.

Over coffee Jason looked at Maria with unashamed lust. "You know, Maria, I suppose you're right. I should reconsider the damned thing. It's crazy."

"Well, you've good enough reason to see it through."

"I know the professor's plan is very good. If he accepts my terms when I call him tomorrow, I can still cancel any time within the first month and not much money will have been wasted."

"Do you really think you would cancel once you started?"

"No, I guess not. I'm afraid someone else might do it and I don't like the possible consequences. Something drastic needs to happen in Northern Ireland in order to stop the constant killings and save it from eventual destruction. If the professor's programs are given a chance to work, within five years the North will be a far different place to live and work for both tribes. I want to see people like my brother neutralized and something like this might do it."

"Jason, I've been trying to work out my part and I want to help you. I have no clients for the next few months so my time is free. I'm not quite ready to classify this as anything other than thievery, but if you're gong to do it then I want to be the one to help. I don't want some other woman taking my part. You didn't have anyone else in mind did you? I know you'll protect me."

"You know, come to think of it, I had no one else in mind." He smiled at Maria. "I don't think there's another woman alive whom I could trust to help." Although now he was reluctant to put her in any sort of danger, he suddenly realized that he couldn't do it without her. She was the only woman professional he knew that could pull it off. "Without you I can't do the project; O.K., you're in."

"I'm sure it'll be all right," she said, "now let's go back to bed."

* * *

The Reverend Sean McIver looked up from his tiny basement desk and scowled at John Larkey and Ian Sommers. "Well, John, you've had another two weeks in the Independence Party, what have you to report?"

"The organization is getting more members every day," answered John, "and Professor Banks is spending more nights and weekends attending meetings and collecting money all over the six counties."

"How many members?"

"I don't know, and I don't think many people do know. They keep it quiet. I could make a guess."

"Strange they should do that, wouldn't they be proud of their members?"

"They seem to be playing a waiting game," replied John.

"For what? What in the hell are they waiting for?" the reverend's voice growing louder now.

"I don't know."

"Damnation, John, it's just like before, you don't know a helluva lot," he turned to Ian Sommers. "Can't we get someone else in besides John here?"

"We haven't made any more progress since the last time we talked about it," said Ian. "Someone in the group knows our congregation pretty well and they're keeping us out. However, I've found a new man for the congregation and he has agreed to infiltrate."

This was news, and John decided he would talk to Kevin about it at the first opportunity.

The reverend looked at John. "Well, what's your estimate?"

"About seven thousand members." John lied; in fact, he knew it was at least four times that amount.

"That's not much for as long as the professor has been working at it. It looks like it may be a long time before anyone takes him seriously. How much money does he have?"

"Another guess," replied John, "maybe £150,000."

The reverend scowled at John. "Is he buying any weapons?"

"I thought I told you he's nonviolent."

"Hah! He won't get anywhere in this country without weapons. If he tries for independence he'll need them to fight the civil war. Hah! He's too soft for independence. What was that committee you're working on?"

"Politics," and John sat up in his chair a little straighter, dreading the next question.

"Well, have you made any recommendations?"

"Only the one I told you about last time for Sinn Fein. Now we're working on the Ulster Defence Association. You know they sponsored an independence movement back about 1979, but it died out. The committee thinks they can strike a responsive chord, if the right information is given to the UDA, and get their support."

"Maybe they can and maybe not," said the reverend, "the UDA seems to have changed their tune since then. Anything else?"

"No sir."

The reverend frowned at John. "You're just a bundle of information, aren't you? Well, keep trying." He turned to Ian. "Well, what've you been up to lately?"

"We've been keeping close tabs on the professor's son Kevin and learned he was going to London on the sixteenth. The boy went to London and that's as far as we could check."

"What do you mean?" and Sean McIver's face began turning bright red.

"I followed him to London and he got in the middle of the rush hour at Victoria Station and it was sardine time. He waited for a train and at the last moment shoved his way on board. I couldn't reach him in time to get on. I didn't think he was that smart."

The Reverend McIver was seething now, about ready to explode, "Damnation! That's twice within two weeks you've lost your man. What the hell is wrong? Something fishy is going on and I think we better get to the bottom of it. Now keep on trying to get the information we need and report back next week. Get the hell out of here."

* * *

Director Richard Yates was reading Fred Press's latest report:

> We have confirmed that the membership of the Independence Party has reached more than 30,000. Rough calculations indicate the amount of money that should be in the Bank of England is well beyond the £300,000 on deposit now and should be close to £1,000,000. They no doubt have an unreported £700,000 in a bank in Switzerland. Membership is climb-

ing and at the present rate it's expected to reach a total of about 250,000 by next March, making it close to the largest political movement in Northern Ireland. It's a low-key movement and they're quietly turning people around. I believe Northern Ireland is headed for secession from the United Kingdom within the next two years.

Director Yates put down Fred's report, picked up the phone, called the Director-General, and requested a meeting with the Prime Minister.

* * *

Jason drove Maria to Monaco, checked into a hotel and placed a call to the professor. When Professor Banks answered he recognized Jason's voice and simply said "Yes" into the phone and hung up. Jason dialed a number in Paris and told Craig he could begin negotiations for some of the equipment they needed. They spent the next two days in Monaco relaxing before Jason returned to England to begin work. Maria would follow three weeks later.

* * *

It had been almost six months since he first met Jason as Perry Wallace at the farmhouse and now, in mid-March, Kevin was on his way to meet him again. He was sure he was followed from Belfast by Ian Sommers and had quite a time losing him in London. The man was getting smarter, Kevin thought, but he made a couple of underground rail car switches, doubled back to Victoria Station, then walked through the entryway to the Grosvenor Hotel, out through the main entrance of the Hotel, and caught a taxi. He switched taxis and finally lost Ian. Then he went to the Barbican apartment that Jason had told him he had leased two years before as a safe house in another case.

When Jason arrived at the apartment, he went over the details of the entire plan with Kevin as the two ate lunch. Jason told him about all the other options they had considered and finally discarded.

"I must say I had my doubts, and I still do," said Kevin. "It's a daring plan; depends on timing, surprise, and confusion. Everything must be perfect. One slip and it's all over." Kevin reflected on his own training at Sandhurst. Unlike his two brothers, who attended Queens, he was sent to England for a military education. It was tough on him. And when he finished he went directly into the Army. He distinguished himself in the Falklands War, but shortly after it was over he resigned his commission. The military was not his idea of a life's work. When he returned home, his father asked him to help him win independence. He looked at Jason with a quizzical smile. "For something not thought possible, I agree with you, it's the best approach. In fact, it's so unique I believe it'll work."

"Good," replied Jason, and he withdrew a map of the Tower from his pocket and spread it open on the table between them. He showed Kevin the route he would take, his objective, and area of responsibility. "Once inside the Tower you'll be entirely on your own. My associate will not be far away, but he'll have his own work to do."

Next, he gave Kevin a list of all the highly specialized equipment he would be carrying. Kevin was surprised. "Did you dream all this up? Where are you getting it and how're you going to sneak it all into the country?"

"My friend and I have been designing the equipment for a long time. A man in Amsterdam is building all the special gear. He ships them out as books in small lots as he completes them."

"What if a sentry starts shooting?" asked Kevin.

"Remember, the whole plan revolves around surprise and confusion. You are the surprise, and the equipment will add the confusion. It's split-second timing that will do them in." The two discussed the plan in every detail and Jason showed Kevin how to put on a false mustache and reshape his nose.

During the next week and a half Kevin visited the Tower every day. He varied the time of his visits and sometimes glued on the mustache, fixed his nose, and sometimes wore different dark glasses. He was there, first in line on two occasions to check the early morning routine. He browsed in the gift shop and purchased several books on the Jewels and Tower history. The clerk who waited on him was a dowdy middle-aged woman with greying hair tied in a bun, long mousy dress, horned rimmed glasses, and a bumpy, misshapen nose. He's handsome, thought the clerk, little does he know we'll soon meet.

Jason delivered Kevin's gear two days before the operation. Jason surprised Kevin when he pulled out a rubber mask. Kevin tried it on. "It fits perfectly," remarked Kevin. "How do you do it?" He looked in the mirror; "I look a little bit like a young Winston Churchill."

"It's the artist in me, I guess," replied Jason. "Each of us has a mask like it. When we're all together we'll look like brothers. I used an old picture of Churchill as a model, but I made some subtle changes on each mask. You know, most people are not very observant. The masks I design fit so well that you can talk with someone face to face for a long time before they begin to suspect you're wearing one."

They went over in careful detail each piece of gear and then went over the timetable. Jason handed him a wrist watch with a large dial and bright digital readout. "Wear this; consider it a gift; each of us has one set to the exact same second."

Kevin was impressed with the thoroughness and quickness of the operation and had little to add to improve it. "I hope your timetables are accurate. It means hardly any exposure."

"I wish the operation were quicker, but we've squeezed every second out of it," answered Jason.

"We've rehearsed every move, and that's the best we can do. We've the exact footage of the paths to be followed. I trust you've been practicing up at the playing field on Bunhill Row?"

"Yes sir!" answered Kevin. "I'll probably never forget the damned timing as long as I live."

"Good," laughed Jason, "everyone else feels the same way. I guess we're ready. We can't be off more then fifteen seconds for the whole exercise, unless it's the time allowed to cut the hole in the case. We don't know what kind of glass it is. If it's tempered glass it'll explode in seconds with a little heat; if it's heavy, single plate, it'll cut nicely; if it's laminated we can burn through but it'll take a little more time. We've practiced on everything and we're using worst case times. All in all, it's quick, but not quick enough."

Jason spent another hour going over the plan again, then told Kevin. "We'll pick you up day after tomorrow at 4:30 a.m. if the weather is good. If not, then on the following morning. Get plenty of sleep tomorrow night."

Kevin spent much of the next day going over the plan again and again. He checked his false identity papers and made certain that his own papers were in the hidden flat compartment built into his small valise. He tried to think of anything he had missed, but could think of nothing. Perry Wallace's plan was excellent and carefully prepared. But, still, the risk was tremendous, and he felt uneasy.

He wondered about the whole idea. It seemed almost too ridiculous. He remembered the wild arguments among the Board members when they suddenly realized the project was possible. Before that, they went along with the idea thinking it wasn't possible, just a good idea to dream about. Now they realized it could happen and it bothered them. They argued the difference between "thieving" and "sequestering." His father was very persuasive. He felt confident "The Project" would succeed. "Look," he told them, "the British stole half the world away from their rightful owners and it took centuries for those people to get their land back by one means or another, including war and revolution. We are just getting a hold of a priceless set of bargaining chips so we can chart a new course for Northern Ireland, a place the British never really owned."

It was his father's charisma that won out through the long hours of arguments. His father once told him that he had taken special voice training to lower his voice and speech training to get rid of his thick brogue. It had almost worked; there remained a very slight brogue that added excitement to his speech. Once he chided his father: "You should have been a TV anchorman, a preacher, maybe even a pied piper without a pipe. You talk, people listen. You lead, people follow. They just invented a new word for you, 'Charisma'." His father popped out of his chair, did a little jig, and in a singsong voice sang, "Ho,ho, ha,ha, I've got 'Ch-ar-is-ma'," and he grabbed his mother and danced her lightly around the room. His mother, father, and he enjoyed a hearty laugh. But then his father turned serious: "Tis a tough and dangerous road we've chosen to follow, perhaps a little 'Charisma' will help us along the way."

Kevin slept fitfully during that last night, the doubts and fears creeping into his consciousness. *It would be a tough and dangerous road tomorrow.* He was ready to go when Jason picked him up in a large van at 4:30 on the morning of March 28th.

6

March 28th
Assault!

8:30 am

The cold winds of late March had subsided and the heavy rains that caused wet hair and feet on children had stopped, leaving puddles, whipped up by passing cars, splashing pedestrians. The diminishing streams and creeks of water on the streets of London turned into raging torrents in the sewers. In fact on this morning the grayness that shrouded the city during the past two weeks turned to a silvery haze accented by a sun that occasionally pushed its way through the many clouds struggling to separate. Here and there on the skyline flashes of gold and silver bounced off buildings or bridges or church towers. It was a good morning for tourist photographers.

Mrs. Penelope Ashford, alias Maria Donna Costell, was standing inside the doorway of the small furnished apartment she.had rented four months ago just a few blocks from the Tower of London on Wentworth Street. She had vacuumed the place twice thoroughly this morning and carefully scrubbed all the places she might have touched during the last four months, even though she had meticulously worn rubber gloves almost every moment she had occupied the place.

"This is ridiculous," she muttered to herself, "I'm neat, but this is almost too much," for she had vacuumed carefully every day. The neighbors thought she had a fetish about being clean. She reached down and removed the small paper dust bag from the vacuum and replaced it with a fresh one, turned the vacuum on for a moment, and then turned it off, removed the second bag, and installed a third one. She placed the two bags in a small plastic bag that contained odds and ends she had cleaned up. Craig had picked up all her things last evening except what she was wearing and what she had packed in the oversized purse. This is the cleanest place in London, she thought; nothing is here, no fingerprints, no fibres, no hair, no makeup, no clothes, not a thing has been left behind. She retraced her steps and went over everything again. She had paid cash for the next month's rent to make sure nothing would be disturbed, although nothing remained to be disturbed.

Satisfied she had thought of everything and done everything that Jason had suggested, she opened the door a crack, removed one of her rubber gloves and put it the plastic bag, picked up the bag and put her purse over her shoulder, opened the door, stepped quietly out, and locked it gently behind her. She quickly removed the other glove, put it in the bag, and left the apartment house for the last time.

The air was a little chilly, and as she pulled her

coat collar around her neck she noticed there was no wind and the sun was trying to make it through clouds that seemed to have covered London forever. She had plenty of time, she thought, as she walked towards the Tower she had come to know so well. She waited until she reached the corner of Mansell and Portsoken before dumping the plastic bag in a street trash can. She passed one of the hundreds of telephone switch boxes mounted on the streets and corners of London. These relay-switch boxes were testimony to the antiquity of the government operated telephone system that not long ago had become private. She noticed the new small metal box mounted on one side and painted to match the old color exactly. The little box with its shaped charge of explosives looked like it was part of the original equipment. Well, she thought, they'll have to modernize this section after today.

Maria checked her watch and decided to stop at Tower Hill for a moment. It always sent a chill down her spine when she was reminded of the hundreds of burnings at the stake, beheadings and hangings that must have occurred at this place over the centuries. Beheading, burning, or hanging was not on her list of ways to die. How many, hundreds, thousands? She didn't know and couldn't guess. *Well they have stopped killings in England pretty well, but they're still going strong in Ireland.* During the past four months Jason had taught her a great deal about the "Troubles," a never-ending struggle, recounting the long and bloody Irish conflict with the English and today's political maneuverings of the various groups in the North and the South. She had begun to believe in what they were about to do.

From Tower Hill one has a good view of the Tower, the Thames, and a few historic sections of London's skyline. As she glanced down at the Tower, clouds blocked the sun for an instant and cast a dark and foreboding aura over the Tower grounds. She tried to sense anything unusual nudging her intuition, but found nothing and breathed a little easier. It will work if I do my job, she thought, and I know I can do it.

She remembered when she had arrived in London four months before with forged documents and visa. Everything was arranged when she appeared at the Assistant Personnel Director's office in the Department of the Environment. Mrs. Penelope Ashford, alias Maria, arrived with the proper forged British documents and a letter of commendation from the Prime Minister herself. That very morning one of the young girls working for the Department at the Tower of London had given short notice. It seemed that she had been saving her money for a French college and suddenly received £10,000 from a mysterious aunt, and decided to leave for France.

Mrs. Ashford, a widow, explained that a friend who knew of the sudden opening called her that very morning when she found out the girl was leaving. "I need to be close to my aunt who is ill and lives near the Tower. I've found a small apartment on Wentworth Street," she told the personnel man.

The Assistant Director explained that rules required notification on a circular so those with seniority could request the position. But he was aware of the shortage of help and knew no one would request the position because of the lower pay; he was putting up a good front. Mrs. Ashford was a rather dowdy middle-aged widow with a slightly bent and knobby nose, dark brown eyes — Maria was wearing brown contacts — behind horned rimmed glasses, and slightly greying reddish hair pulled back in a tight bun. She wore a long print dress with long sleeves and appeared every bit the average English matron.

What he remembered later when he was unmercifully interrogated was her soft enticing voice and the most sensuous mouth he had ever seen. In fact, he remembered during the interview that every time she spoke, his eyes automatically went to her mouth.

She reached over and touched his hand in a motherly way. "I know what the rules say, but you have the authority to make exceptions, and I've had more government service than most of the people in your department. I've only been away from my job in Whitehall for three weeks to get properly situated. If I can't work at the Tower for the government I'll have to find work nearby in the private sector. I can tell you have an understanding character, won't you please reconsider?"

He'd been watching the words form on her lips and her mouth open and close softly; her voice was soothing. He was not aware of his seduction at the time; he capitulated. "Could you start tomorrow?"

Later, when asked repeatedly why he hired her, he realized her mouth was young and erotic.

"Most certainly, thank you very much, dear sir; and you'll never regret it. I appreciate everything you've done for me."

He sent the necessary forms to payroll and inserted her papers into a manila folder and sent them to central files. He called Mrs. Thomas, the manager of the gift shops and restaurant operation, and told her Mrs. Ashford would report to work next day. He didn't bother to back-check with Whitehall for confirmation of her previous service. Exactly three months and twenty-seven days later her file, containing forged medical reports, false fingerprints, letters of commendation, work history, and photograph, disappeared from the department's central file room.

As Maria left his office she thought, Jason was right, he's a bureaucratic jerk and not very smart.

Maria's first day at the main gift shop was hectic; she wanted to learn fast and make a good impression. She prided herself on being efficient and good at whatever she did, and she worked extra hard that day. Back at her small apartment that evening, she snacked, then sagged into bed exhausted. Thank God I don't have to work like this for a living, she thought, and promptly fell asleep.

During those first few weeks she earned high marks from Mrs. Thomas for her efficiency and innovative ideas. She was credited with a small but noticeable increase in sales after she made several suggestions on displays that caught the eye of the bored tourist looking for something special to jump out at him. She quickly ingratiated herself with everyone on the staff with her matronly advice on personal matters that always seemed to be the right answer for a special problem.

She became particularly interested in Mrs. Appleton, the small, attractive widow in her late fifties who handled the sales table at the top of the stairs that lead the tourists from the Jewel House vault. After her husband died, Mrs. Appleton had moved to London to live with her sister. Meeting so many new people every day was her source of entertainment and the work provided a tidy pension supplement that allowed her to live comfortably.

Maria learned that Mrs. Appleton had a brother with an ailing wife living in Bishop's Stortford. A close-knit family, the two sisters would often visit them on the weekends. After a month, Maria was occasionally sent to help Mrs. Appleton at the Jewel House. She had tried very hard to sell more than anyone else and succeeded. Mrs. Appleton was taken with her quiet charm and energy and suggested to Mrs. Thomas that Penny Ashford be the one to take her place whenever she was on holiday. She told Mrs. Thomas that Penny was so quick that she could handle the job without any extra help.

Maria had spent her lunch hours prowling the Tower grounds and offices. She managed to get a list of all the residents, a list of the various shifts of Warders and Fusiliers, and the sentry points, and found the location of the emergency power generator and communications center. On her days off Maria would board the underground to Victoria Station and take a taxi to Jason's. She couldn't wait to get him into bed, and afterwards they would review all of the information she had collected during the week. If Jason had a question she usually knew the answer or would have it for him the following week.

She took every early morning opportunity to go down those forty-nine steps to the vault with a tin of cookies for the two Warders opening the vault. She told Jason they call her the "Cookie Lady."

"Each morning at exactly 9:20 a.m.," she told Jason, "the automatic time lock snaps open and one of the Warders immediately tumbles the new combination, spins the wheel handle, and the two men open the heavy door and push it back against the wall. Once inside, they check the lights, cameras, the jewel case, and the floors to make certain everything is ready for the first assault by visitors. The whole process takes no more than five minutes, usually only three.

"The lock combination is changed each afternoon. The Chief Warder gets a magnetic card from the Keeper who obtains random numbers from a special imprint machine. The Chief Warder goes to the vault after the 5:00 p.m. closing time and waits until the vault had been cleaned, then makes an inspection, closes the vault door, spins the wheel, and inserts the magnetic card, automatically setting up the combination for the next day. The next morning the Warder on duty picks up the combination from the Chief Warder, who gets it only after he inserts the card in the printing unit and only after 9:00 a.m.

"The morning shift in the Jewel House consists of three Warders, two security guards, and Mrs. Appleton at the sales table. They're very punctual you know; always arrive at 9:15 a.m. or before to make sure everything is in order," she told him.

"No matter who's on shift?"

"Yes," she said, "must be the military in them."

They went to the floor diagram they'd made and tried to place everyone's movements on the diagram between 9:15 and 9:30 a.m. Over the next several weeks, whenever in the Jewel House, Maria carefully recorded the habits of all the people. She discovered who was lazy and who meticulously checked every last detail before the opening. Gradually they worked out a plan and began the tedious task of rehearsing it at every opportunity.

On this cold March morning Maria walked on from Tower Hill past the main gift shop and restaurant, waving at one of the girls through the window, and arrived at the Cradle Tower employee entrance at precisely 9:05 a.m. She recognized the constable. "Good morning, Tom," and she put on her best smile for the familiar security guard.

"Good morning, Mrs. Ashford, how do you like the clearing weather?"

"Just fine," and she displayed her cookie tin and two thermos bottles, and opened her large purse. He gave her a quick pass with the metal detector and cancelled the beep when it passed over the cookie tin and the two thermoses.

"O.K., you have a good day, Mum."

She walked quickly along the roadway between the inner wall and the outer wall towards the Byward Tower, the main visitor entrance. As she passed the gate entrance near St. Thomas's Tower she slipped in behind the thick walls, pulled a small round object from her cookie tin, and placed it in the keyhole of the lock on the gate.

She continued on to the little gift shop, located inside the outer wall next to Byward Tower, stopped, looked quickly in both directions, opened the door with a key Craig had made from an imprint, and went inside. She wanted to be positive no one would see her go to the Byward Tower gate door. She took out another round object, opened the gift shop door, and looked up and down the long roadway. No one in sight, so she went quickly to the door. Even as she moved it would be difficult to spot her because of the many days spent locating a coat with a color to blend in with the ancient wood of the door. She slipped the round object into the keyhole of the huge wooden door, then turned and headed back towards the Bloody Tower entrance to the inner grounds. She saw three people enter from the Cradle Tower gate but they looked neither left nor right, each intent on thoughts of their own.

She passed by the magnificent White Tower and thought, I won't be seeing you again for quite a long time, I hope nothing happens to the ravens. She knocked on the southwest exit door of the Jewel House and Renner, a security guard, opened it.

"Ah, good morning, Mrs. Ashford, how are you this fine morning? I thought it would be Mrs. Appleton on duty today?"

"She was called away suddenly and I'm filling in for her. You won't mind, will you? I brought some of your favorite cookies."

"Well, come right in then."

She glanced at her watch — it was 9:13:05 a.m. — and walked to the small table where she took off her coat and put down her oversized purse, with the cookie tin and thermoses inside, and pulled out the cash box from a drawer. She looked around quickly and counted people. The two Warders assigned to the vault below were standing at the top of the stairs chatting with the Warder assigned to the upper chamber. Renner went over and resumed his conversation with security guard Baker, who was assigned to the entrance door.

Hurry up, boys, she thought, it's almost 9:16 a.m. *God! It's going slow,* and her hands began to sweat and her underarms felt moist. *Stop it! This won't do! Get hold of yourself!* But she knew down deep that once she made her first move everything would be all right. It was the damned wait that always got to her. She quickly put on a pair of thin rubber gloves without being seen and unpacked a couple of boxes, placing the booklets on the table. She checked her purse, opened the cookie tin, pressed a tiny button, and a small bottom drawer popped out, exposing its hidden contents. She pushed it back in and it snapped into place. She looked over just as the two Warders started down the stairs. Baker and

Renner kept on chatting, joined by the third Warder. She checked her watch again, this time closer, it was 9:19:30 a.m.

* * *

Jason had waited patiently, constantly checking long-range and short-range weather forecasts, finally selecting today as the time to move. He was glad he didn't have to cancel. The weather was perfect; it was hazy and absolutely no wind at the moment, ideal for what he had in mind. At 8:30 a.m. Jason was sitting on the deck of the barge, beneath the lightweight tarpaulin covering the equipment, reviewing details of the plan for the last time with Craig and Kevin as the barge moved slowly up the Thames.

When Kevin had entered the van at 4:30 a.m., he had shaken hands with the first two team members. They were dressed, as he was, in British Army battle fatigues, and in the dim light their rubber masks made them look like brothers. They didn't talk. Jason drove the van to Redbridge and picked up two more men; then on to Havering where they picked up the final two team members. They all shook hands and wished each other good luck, but kept talk to a minimum. Jason drove to M 25 and cut South to A 13 towards Canvey Island. When they arrived at the end of the small dirt road on Canvey Island, Craig untied a small skiff and motored the first team, with their allotment of gear, out to their assigned barge. The two-man team disappeared under the huge oddly shaped tent-like tarpaulin. Craig picked up team number two and repeated the performance. Jason introduced Kevin to Ivan Someroff and to Craig, posing as James Donnally, and then Craig took the two men out to the third barge.

Craig motored the skiff back to shore. While Jason waited with the skiff Craig drove the van back to the edge of the small village, parked it on a side street, and jogged the half mile back. They motored out to the third barge, and offloaded the rest of the gear as Kevin and Ivan stored it away. Jason set the rudder on the small skiff and sent it going upstream. It would eventually be found beached opposite Northwick. Soon after, the three barges made their way up the Thames.

9:23:15 am

A small tube of Thermit ignited and welded the lock mechanism of the Byward Tower gate; a few seconds later a similar tube melted the lock mechanism of the gate at St. Thomas's Tower, and now both locks were welded tight in the locked position and the gates sealed. No one could get in or out until repairs could be made.

9:24:10 am

Captain Theodore Block, Teddy to his friends, sat at the wheel of the tugboat *Maggie II* as it chugged its way up the Thames. He had picked up the three barges with their strange looking cargo in a cove off Canvey Island just East of Thames Haven. He couldn't make out what was under the tarps but it didn't matter because they had paid him an extra £300 to keep to a strict timetable. The man who gave him the money had said something about a film and told him cameras would be ready at exactly 9:25 a.m. at Tower Bridge and London Bridge. The man made Captain Block reset his watch exactly to the second. He would be on time, precisely, if only to maintain his reputation as the best tug captain on the Thames.

The Thames was calm and the *Maggie II* moved along nicely. Captain Block was watching the time closely and kept making minor adjustments to the speed so that he would be certain to pass under the Tower Bridge on time. He looked back at the three barges; nothing had changed. They passed the Navy patrol boat anchored at its base near Greenwich, where the Lieutenant on duty, suffering a hangover, paid scant attention. When the *Maggie II* passed under the bridge it was exactly 9:25 a.m., a tribute to Block's skill as a pilot. He cut the speed to two knots, as instructed, and looked up for the movie cameras on London Bridge. Ninety seconds later he felt the tug jump ahead a little and turned around to see the first of three helicopters take off from the barges. With the cabin door closed and the heavy sound of his own engines holding his attention, he hadn't heard the sound of the helicopters warming up. The covers had been removed from all three and were dragging in the water. Suddenly the second and third lifted off and were in the air, moving off towards the Tower of

London.

With much less load the tug surged forward a little. Some movie, Block thought, and increased his speed to ten knots as instructed. He had done what his client had asked, but after a few moments he realized they had filed a destination and cargo plan with Customs and the Navy. He was supposed to anchor the barges off Lois Road Power Station fully loaded. He decided to check in with the dispatcher, slowed down again, picked up his radiophone, and called the office.

"Hello, Jack, the load is gone. What do you want me to do?"

"What do you mean gone? Gone overboard?"

"In a manner of speaking, yes, they flew off. We were hauling three helicopters that just now flew off towards the Tower of London; they were painted in British Army camouflage and colors."

"What did they do with the tarps?"

"They are dragging in the water."

"Well, slow down and have the crew get them on deck; then turn around and bring the barges home."

"Will do. Over and out."

Jack looked at the manifest and found it was paid for by a Mr. James Donnally, not the British Army, at the Class A rate, and decided there would be plenty of time to check it out later. He was having a busy morning. It was a decision he would regret for a long time.

9:26:05 am

It was agony for Maria. The three men were still

chatting in the middle of the room, but she knew that any second now they would split up. She had been idly moving things around on the table, and now it was almost time. She looked up and as if on cue, the three men split up. Thank God for habit and punctuality, she thought, and quickly removed her gloves, picked up the cookie tin, and moved towards security guard Renner as he walked towards the exit door. "Mr. Renner I wonder if you could explain the interesting lock on the exit door if you have time."

"Be delighted, Ma'am."

Once in the entryway out of sight of the other two men, she turned and asked if he would like a cookie.

"Yes indeed, Mrs. Ashford," and as he reached for a cookie she caught him square in the nostrils with a small spray bottle. He took one breath and slowly sank to the floor. From her pocket she removed a titanium wire loop, put it over the two door handles, and opened the door a crack. No one could enter unless they carried special wire cutters.

She quickly moved around to the entrance door where the other security guard and a Warder were preparing to open it. "Have a cookie gentlemen," she said. And as they turned to reach for the cookies, she squirted first one and then the other with two perfectly rehearsed moves. Both men went down. She took another thin wire loop and wrapped it around the door handles. Running to the steps to the vault she muttered, "These cursed forty nine steps," and took the first level two steps at a time, slowing quickly for the final level to the vault.

ASSAULT ON THE CROWN

She reached bottom with forty-five seconds to spare.

9:26:10 am

Two Warders arrived at the Byward Tower gate and tried inserting the key but it wouldn't go in the lock. One Warder struggled with the key and then gave up. The other was peering into the keyhole when they heard the blade beat of a helicopter.

9:26:30 am

Unit One left its barge with pilot Hans Sortheim at the controls and his assistant Brad Justin in the jump seat. It had been a tricky takeoff, but the special hold-down clamps mounted on the barge floor made it easier. One rope pull on the special release mechanism untethered all four hold-down clamps at once. All three helicopters were French Aerospatiale-Westland SA 341 Gazelle military utility type, a favorite of the British Army, the French Army, and the Kuwaiti Air Force. Its rotor diameter was 34 feet and cruising speed 148 mph. The three had been outfitted with a thin hollow aluminum casing that stretched between the two landing skids, and a special three-inch vertical tube extending from inside the cockpit through the fuselage and down through the casing. The add-on thin aluminum casing was a personnel carrier that doubled as a disguised pontoon. The cockpit had been stripped of all but the essential instruments and a large clock had been placed to one side of the panel. They had gone over the operational timing so often that Hans could recite check points to the exact second. The second pilot seat was removed and only the rear bench seat remained, where Brad Justin sat alertly prepared to do his job. In front of him were three boxes of small cannisters shaped like little bombs, complete with directional fins.

* * *

Frank Dilling lifted Unit Two off its barge just ten seconds after Unit one and flew in the direction of the Tower. His flight path over Wakefield Tower would take them to the Chapel of St. Peter ad Vincula, where he would turn around and begin the work of sealing off the West side of the inner Tower grounds. There was plenty of time, so he pulled up and waited a bit before moving forward to his target.

* * *

Jason sat in the cockpit of Unit Three with pilot Ivan Someroff, while Craig and Kevin were strapped to the thin aluminum pontoon below. They had taken off a few seconds late, but within the tolerances Jason had planned. He thought of Maria and what she would be doing at that moment in the Jewel House. She had to take out all five men in the space of three to four minutes. The entire operation rested on her. She knew who would be on shift today, and because people tend to become creatures of habit, she knew almost precisely what their morning movements would be. He realized how much he had come to love Maria, and vowed never to subject her to danger again. Now, if she failed in the Jewel House and instead was somehow subdued herself, he and Craig were prepared to get her out quickly and abandon the project.

He checked the big clock on the panel and looked out to see the other two units getting into position. By now, he thought, Maria should be in the vault or in custody. They were hovering low and well out of sight of anyone on the Tower grounds. They were ready, and it sent a chill down his spine.

9:27:01 am

Chief Warder George Halliday was pleased with himself this cool, calm March morning because it marked the tenth anniversary of the start of his tour of duty at the Tower. He was sitting in his office staring out at the clouds fighting back the sunshine and thinking about his early years in the Army and the wars he had fought for the glory of Britain. Twice decorated on the battlefields of Europe during World War II, he stayed in the Army, fought in Korea with the United Nations forces, and spent his later years in the Army as an instructor. He had wanted to continue his service in some way, so he applied for a post at the Tower just before he retired. His long and exemplary service won him the assignment, and he and his wife moved into an apartment in the North Casement section of the Tower. Three years ago he had been promoted to Chief Warder, a post he hoped to keep for as long as he could. He had just celebrated his sixty-fourth birthday.

He got up out of his chair with a little more effort than in his younger days, poured more coffee, returned to his desk, and went over the duty roster again. No one had reported sick this day, so he had no relief problems. He checked his watch and knew that in three minutes the Tower would become a bustling community of employees replaying the history of the Tower and England for the tourists. Well, he thought, a little sunshine could make it a very busy day.

9:27:45 am

Four simultaneous explosions occurred at four separate streetside telephone switching boxes located within a mile of the Tower. The special shaped charge of explosives placed on the side of each box blew the insides apart without so much as bulging a box. A few pedestrians heard the noise, but not seeing smoke, fire, or damage anywhere, shrugged it off. The internal destruction to the boxes cut off all telephone communications to and from the Tower and all telephone service within a five-square-mile area around it.

* * *

Just as the phones went dead, a tiny noise generator started up that created radio interference for the next forty-five minutes, preventing any radio transmissions from the Tower to any other military or civilian emergency unit. The little noise generator, stuck under a table in the communications office, would not be found for several days.

* * *

At the entrance to the vault Maria slowed her breathing. "Gentlemen, I almost forgot your cookies," she called, then waited a few seconds until they came out through the vault door. Warder Neal reached for a cookie, but Warder Anderson, whose wife would soon be trapped in their apartment, hesitated. Now, Maria could not get at both of them with the spray in the way she had rehearsed; Warder Anderson was turned slightly away from her. She caught Warder Neal and as he started down, she stepped in front of Warder Anderson. But Anderson, who reacted faster than even he could imagine, caught a glimpse of her move, grabbed her wrist and her other arm, and shoved her back against the vault door, where the inner wheel caught her in the back. She gasped from the pain and dropped the spray and the cookie tin. He was about 60 years old, 180 pounds, and still fairly strong. Her back was arched and her wrists pinned against the top of the door. He wasn't quite sure what to do next. It was odd, he smelled her perfume and looked at her lips; he hesitated. She took the opportunity, squirmed for leverage, and brought her knee up into his groin. His heavy uniform softened the blow, but he still doubled over with pain and released her. She turned and hit him expertly on the back of the neck, and he went down. "Sorry, old man, this wasn't supposed to happen," she said.

She was breathing hard and almost panicked when the lights went out. *Where in the hell are the tin and the spray?*

9:28:00 am

Hans floated Unit One up and over the Customs House and turned East directly in line with the Byward Tower. He passed over Byward precisely on schedule and stopped where he could see the two Warders trying to open the gate. "O.K., Brad, do your stuff!" he yelled.

Brad Justin reached into the first box with a gloved hand, pulled out a cannister, and dropped it through the tube. "Bombs away," he hollered. He followed with two more, one from each of the other boxes. The first one hit the ground and startled the Warders when it began spewing out a foul smelling acrid form of tear gas that Craig had developed. It smelled bad and made you cry, but it was not toxic. Your eyes would stay shut for several minutes. The next two cannisters merely lay there with their digital clocks ticking away. One was set to go off in five minutes and the other set for ten minutes, giving a total of fifteen minutes of constant streaming tear gas.

The Warders at Byward Tower gate looked up in amazement, took one whiff of the gas, and ran to escape inside the gift shop; they were trapped for the next twenty minutes. The second batch was

ASSAULT ON THE CROWN

dropped between the archway below Bloody Tower and Traitors Gate across the corridor. The third batch was dropped at the St. Thomas's Tower gate and the fourth at the Cradle Tower gate. The south corridor between the outer wall and inner wall was now completely filled with the gas, effectively sealing the Tower from the outside world. The police and Army had no units within fifteen minutes of the Tower with enough gas masks to help out.

* * *

Mrs. Anderson was late for her appointment. Her husband, Yeoman Warder Anderson, was already on duty at the Jewel House and she was due to get her hair done at 10:00 a.m. She checked her watch at 9:28 a.m. She left her neat apartment house in the Casements near the Broad Arrow Tower and headed for her car parked near the Salt Tower. Then, reminiscent of her years dodging bombs in the London Blitz, she heard the helicopter, looked up, then saw a small bomb drop near the Salt Tower and explode in a cloud of smoke. She saw two more that did not explode. As the smoke drifted toward her she watched the helicopter move closer and drop three more between her apartment and the Broad Arrow Tower not more than twenty feet from where she stood. She caught a whiff of the acrid, foul smelling smoke and wondered. "Oh Dear, could it be ... could it be tear gas?" Her eyes began to water; she ran back to her apartment, fumbling for her keys. Hands shaking, she finally opened the door and went back inside. The air inside was still clean. She rushed to an open front window, quickly shut it and grabbed the phone to call the Chief Warder's office, but the phone was dead. She went back to the window and could see nothing but thick white gas. Oh dear, so much smoke, and she realized she was trapped until the foul smelling, eye smarting stuff cleared.

* * *

Frank Dilling swooped over the Chapel of St. Peter, and Robert Millicum, behind him on the bench seat, dropped the first cannister at precisely 9:28:00 a.m. The two Warders standing near the Site of the Block waiting for the first visitors saw the helicopter and saw the cannister drop and spew smoke. They were astonished to see another helicopter touch down near the entrance to the White Tower They stood frozen in shock, trying to make up their minds what to do when Millicum dropped the next two cannisters and tossed two percussion grenades from the open side of the cockpit to land about fifteen feet from them. The special explosive devices designed by Craig would disappear in harmless smoke, but the concussion would knock a man down if he was within ten feet. Both Warders fell backwards but did not hit the ground. Instead, a little dazed, their eyes beginning to water, they turned and ran for the Chief Warder's office.

***

Jason's Unit Three touched the ground between the White Tower entrance and the entrance to the Waterloo Barracks. Precisely at the same instant two explosions hit the ground from Dilling's Unit Two. Craig and Kevin rolled off the thin aluminum pontoon, each equipped with a powerful AK 47 charged with harmless soft clay bullets, a back pack of percussion grenades, and gas mask ready for use. As the bewildered Fusilier guard at the Waterloo Barracks entrance looked at the British Army uniforms and equipment, he hesitated; Christ! What kind of exercise is this? Then he raised his gun. Kevin tossed a grenade and the man went down. All that practice at Bunhill row throwing a cricket ball paid off, he thought.

Craig tossed two near the Warder and Constable standing on the steps to the White Tower. They were blown backwards, but managed to keep on their feet and scramble to safety inside the White Tower, shutting the door behind them. Craig ran up the steps and inserted a Thermit tube in the keyhole, where it went off immediately, melting the lock and imprisoning everyone inside. He turned around just as Kevin finished trussing up the Fusilier and threw a grenade at the entrance to the Fusilier Museum. Kevin now established his base at the entrance to Waterloo Barrack, where he could see any movement from the Museum, White Tower, or Hospital Block. Craig established his base near the entrance to the Jewel House, where he could handle any movements coming from the West side. Their objective was to cause noise and confusion with a constant barrage of grenades and occasional bursts from the AK 47's. In a few more seconds they put on their gas masks.

* * *

Chief Warder Halliday heard the gentle beat of a helicopter somewhere overhead and turned to look out the window just as the first cannister exploded near the Chapel, spewing out tear gas. Then he heard the two explosions and saw Warders Pickney and Shaw turn and run towards his office. Another gas cannister exploded, then another and another, followed by a smoke bomb, and then several explosions all in the space of a few seconds.

He blinked in astonishment as the West side of the Tower, from the Chapel to the Queen's House, suddenly became a wall of white gas and smoke accented by several exploding grenades. The smoke looked eerie settling in and around the trees of the Tower Green.

He caught a glimpse of an Army helicopter. *Damn! The Army is attacking for some stupid reason. Could it be an exercise? Why weren't we informed?* Then a sudden horrifying thought struck him and he picked up the phone to dial the Jewel House, but the phone was dead. He rushed to the communications office. The TV pictures of the vault were clear. No one was there; where were the two Warders?

9:28:45 am

Hans pointed Unit One north and, hovering, looked west along the South corridor. "Very good work, Mr. Justin, keep it up." Brad dropped another batch at Salt Tower, Broad Arrow Tower, and Martin Tower, effectively sealing up the East corridor, then they continued on around with more cannisters for the North and West corridors until they were back at Byward Tower. Hans checked the panel clock and it read 9:29:30 a.m. He pulled up immediately to his assigned altitude of 500 feet and hovered to watch the action below.

"Perfect," he said to Brad, "I didn't think it would be so easy."

"Right on, Captain."

"You are one helluva bombardier."

"I didn't think this old fashioned World War I scheme would work, but we didn't miss a target." Brad looked out the cockpit window. "Good! They are all working; not a dud in the bunch. The whole place looks like it's on fire."

* * *

Ivan Someroff lifted Unit Three off quickly after the two men rolled off and Jason began dropping cannisters along the east side of the inner grounds, first at the Museum, then the Hospital Block, in front of the New Armouries, and finally at the Lanthorn Tower entrance from the outer Ward. Ivan moved Unit Three west and then north over the White Tower and dropped Jason off in front of the

Jewel House exit door at precisely 9:29:45 a.m. Then he pulled up to 400 feet, where he waited, alone now, and watched in fascination the chaotic scene below.

* * *

Frank Dilling maneuvered Unit Two on a straight line from the Chapel to the Queen's House while Millicum dropped three cannisters at intervals of fifty feet. On the first return trip to the Chapel Millicum began tossing out smoke bombs and percussion grenades at short intervals. Now the west side of the Tower grounds, including the Tower Green and the area between the Block and the Chapel, resembled a battlefield filled with smoke and exploding grenades.

Dilling moved up to 300 feet to allow the gas and smoke to settle on the grounds forming a foul smelling, eye watering, opaque wall of white to anyone who might want to try and get through without a gas mask.

9:29:45 am

Jason, carrying a large back pack, two lightweight aluminum tubes next to it, and a small spray can in one hand, in case Maria was in trouble, made a dash for the door, cut the wire loop Maria had installed, and went inside. The cutter clamp retained the wire and he reached back and put the clamp with the wire in the bag he was carrying.

Inside, he looked around and saw the first of

Maria's victims on the floor. Jason was at the top of the stairs to the vault when the lights went out and he knew it was exactly 9:30 a.m. At that instant, at a small electric utility transformer station located not far from the Tower off Mincing Lane, transformer number A 4396 blew up, cutting off power service to the Tower and surrounding area. Also at that same instant a small explosion blew the main fuse box to the Tower's emergency diesel-driven generator unit, killing the emergency power supply. The Tower was now completely blacked out. He turned on his light and ran down the steps.

Maria was trying to visualize where the tin and spray had fallen, but her eyes hadn't adjusted yet. Jason reached the bottom of the stairs carrying a large light. "Good girl!" he said.

"Running late, Jason, hold the light a second and help me find my tin and spray." She found one near Warder Neal and the other almost beneath Warder Anderson. She pressed the button on the cookie tin, pulled out two hypodermic needles, and expertly injected both men in their wrists.

"Thanks. Am I glad to see you, Luv!" and she turned and ran up the stairs to inject the other three men, put on her army jump suit and fatigue hat, clean up, pack everything, and get ready to leave.

* * *

Halliday was still staring at the TV screens when suddenly the power was cut off and all four screens went black. He asked the radio operator to get him

Army headquarters on the battery operated emergency radio but all channels were jammed by static. *Christ! We're isolated!*

He ran back to his office, where Warder Pickney and Warder Shaw were drying their eyes. "Christ almighty, men, what in the hell is going on out there?"

"It's the Army, damn them, dropping tear gas, smoke and grenades," replied Pickney. "We saw helicopters, one overhead and one that touched down in front of the White Tower. Two British soldiers rolled off from underneath the chopper and it took off. Then two grenades hit awful close, we got a whiff of the gas and came in here. That's the most foul smelling stuff I ever smelled and it gets to your eyes in a hurry, hardly see a damned thing."

The Chief Warder ran back out the office door, turned down the hall, and rushed outside. He got about ten feet before his eyes began to water, and he suddenly realized he would be blind within a few seconds. He closed them tightly, turned, and stumbled back towards the building just as a grenade landed about ten feet from him. The concussion knocked him down. He lay there dazed, feeling for shrapnel. He found none, realized he wasn't hurt, got up, and stumbled back to his office, trying to dry his eyes. "Pickney, get me some water."

9:30:30 am

Jason entered the vault, adjusted the light, and began work. He attached a "glass cup," a six-inch diameter rubber suction cup with handle and pump rod, to the outside of case number eleven, pumped it three times so that it was securely attached, then began making his nine-inch by twelve-inch cutout. He began to sweat. They had practiced dozens of cuts on all types of glass. If it was laminated glass he would have to burn through. If it was tempered, it wouldn't cut at all. So he had brought along a small twin unit of oxy-acetylene they had tested over one hundred times. Maria carried backup units hidden in the two thermoses she brought with her. They couldn't be too careful. If the glass was tempered, all he had to do was heat it in one spot for just a few seconds with the torch and the glass would explode into thousands of small pieces and the entire case would be open. It would mean a delay until Craig arrived to hold a canvas over the case to keep the tiny pieces of exploding glass inside.

The glass was cutting! But he couldn't yet be certain it was laminated. When he finished the cut Jason grabbed the handle on the cup and pulled with all his strength. The cutout was stubborn; could it be laminated? He tried again. The cutout popped out and he staggered backwards breathing a sigh of relief. He removed the cup, put it back in his pack, and put on a pair of white gloves. He picked up the thirty-inch long aluminum tube and unscrewed the top, revealing a velvet lined interior, with soft packing. He dumped the packing and reached through the opening to case number eleven. His hand trembled a bit as he removed the Imperial

State Crown and carefully placed it in the bottom of the can, then added packing on top.

* * *

Dilling saw Unit Three touch down again and a man jump out and run to the Southwest exit door of the Jewel House. "Now we have the entire Tower grounds to cover, so look sharp for anything that moves except for our two guys on the ground." He looked back at Millicum. "The Fusilier is down on the ground in front of the Waterloo Barracks."

He turned and crossed over Unit Three and Millicum tossed two percussion grenades at the entrance to the Museum. They could see no movement except for their two men on the ground. He moved south along the east corridor while Millicum kept tossing out grenades amidst the layers of smoke made by the tear gas cannisters. He checked his clock and it read 9:30:30 am. "Time for another round at the Tower Green. You know, we've only been here for two and a half minutes and the place looks like a flaming disaster."

"It sure is a mess," replied Millicum. "God, it looks like it's burning up! Only two men down there to cover the grounds with those soft pellet guns and do-nothing grenades! I hope they know what they're doing! Did you see the man go into the Jewel House?"

Frank Dilling made three more circular passes around the perimeter of the Tower Grounds and Millicum dropped occasional grenades to create noise and confusion. When the first smoke bombs stopped spewing out their white smoke he dropped a few more and noticed that the second batch of cannisters were firing off on time. He passed Unit One a few times on his route around the grounds, but noticed he was now hovering at 500 feet, while Unit Three was on the north side hovering at 400 feet.

9:33:30 am

Maria was still wiping things down with a wet cloth when Craig came bursting in through the Jewel House door carrying a small light. She waved to him and said, "You are very punctual."

"So are you," and Craig took the stairs to the vault two at time.

The moment Craig entered the vault, Jason breathed another sigh of relief: "Good, you made it, now get to work." Jason reached in and pulled out the Orb, and handed it to Craig, who proceeded to pack it on top of the Crown, and followed it with more packing on top. Next came the Coronation Ring. Craig placed it on top and screwed the lid back on the tube. Jason reached into the case and pulled out the Sceptre with Dove while Craig was opening the fifty-inch long aluminum tube. Craig placed the Sceptre with Dove inside as Jason followed with the Sceptre with Cross and Jeweled State Sword. Craig gingerly slid the sword into the center section of the tube, then screwed on the lid.

"Done," said Jason. "Let's get out of here." He reached for the small oxy-acetylene pack and put it back in his pack, checked and found nothing left behind, picked up his pack and light, and the two of them rushed up the stairs with Craig lugging both cannisters.

"All together these things weigh quite a bit," complained Craig.

"Come on now, no more than a light golf bag," replied Jason. "You didn't eat enough this morning." He checked his watch as they reached the top of the stairs, where Maria was ready and waiting. It was 9:37:30 a.m. We did it, he thought, only seven minutes and forty-five seconds!.

* * *

Hans saw that Unit Two was busy circling the inner grounds, dropping percussion grenades. He stayed in position until 9:36:00 am to make sure all of the second-round cannisters went off. One didn't at Broad Arrow on the east side, so he dropped down, moved over to the spot, and Brad dropped another one. "Good, it fired," said Hans, and he moved back up in position. At 9:37 a.m. the last of the second batch fired.

"Let's get the hell out of here!" Hans said to Brad.

"Tally ho, old boy," replied Brad.

"We'll touch down in fourteen minutes." Hans banked Unit One to the south towards Croydon and cranked her up to 120 mph.

9:37 am

"How much more time?" asked Millicum in Unit

Two.

"Stop worrying. It's 9:37, we have exactly one minute left and look there, Unit One is on his way home." He turned to watch Unit Three begin his descent to touch down and said to Millicum, "Drop two grenades at the Block and two more at the White Tower, two at Waterloo, and two at the Museum, the more confusion the better. Millicum followed his instructions as Frank maneuvered the helicopter. They saw no one moving among the white clouds of tear gas and smoke and occasional exploding grenades. He turned and saw one man on the ground run for the helicopter just as three figures emerged from the exit of the Jewel House. Hmm, he thought, only two went in; none of my business, though. "Time to go home, Mr. Millicum, we've done our job." He checked his panel clock; it read exactly 9:37:45 a.m.

Dilling turned Unit Two south towards Bromley at a cruising speed of 120 mph.

"I wonder what kind of mess they left behind? I wonder what the booty is, wonder what it's for?" asked Millicum.

"None of our business, Mr. Millicum, we got paid well for our eleven minutes' work. Just make sure you get out of the country before all hell breaks loose."

"Yeah, £50,000 is not bad. Maybe there could be more? Whatever they got must be worth a good reward."

"Think, man. Did you ever see their natural faces? We don't even know the other two pilots or the other five involved. Who you gonna turn in? The last guy I worked with that tried to get a reward got a good one, a final resting place. So forget it. Go home and enjoy your money. Your reputation will be intact and who knows, one of those people may want to hire you again."

"Just an idle thought," replied Millicum. "Forget I ever said it." He knew the pilot was right. They had trained in separated teams and their client always had some phony disguise. They never saw the faces of the others, and when they got in the van, everyone had been wearing those crazy rubber masks. Although the mask had been comfortable up to now, it was beginning to itch, and Millicum would be happy when he could remove it. The whole plan was well thought out and nothing had been left to chance; even a double cross was covered.

"All right my friend, get ready to dump, we will be on water in about twelve minutes."

* * *

Pickney brought Halliday some water and he dabbed his eyes with it trying to wash out the irritation. It took several minutes before he could see clearly. By then it was almost 9:37 a.m., the explosions were still going on, and the white wall of smoke and gas seemed thicker now. He wondered if anyone in the Tower had been killed.

"Christ, why didn't we stock in a supply of gas masks and weapons here? This is ridiculous, sitting here helpless, not knowing what in the hell's going on out there," he told Pickney, wishing he were somewhere else, knowing that something extraordinary was happening beyond his control. Now he realized that British complacency and planning had never considered the possibility of such a daring and unique assault. "It's not the Army, it's someone else, after the jewels. We've got five unarmed men and a woman in there, I hope to God no one is dead." His office began filling up with all sorts of people wanting to know what to do. He finally told them to sit tight because at the moment no one could do anything. They were trapped!

9:38:03 am

All three went to the door, waited until Unit Three touched down, then charged it. Maria got into the cockpit with her pack and Craig handed her the two cannisters. Craig, Kevin, and Jason scrambled onto the aluminum pontoon-support and held onto the straps just as the helicopter took off at 9:38:03 a.m. The entire operation had taken just ten minutes, a little over eleven minutes from barge lift off; the gas cannisters would burn for another five minutes. Jason looked down at the smokey scene below and saw very little movement on the ground. Craig yelled above the noise of the beating blades, "Masterful—timing was perfect—well done, Jason!"

It was the first time Kevin had heard the name mentioned, and he filed it away for future reference. Craig caught himself, but it was too late.

Jason didn't seem to care.

Ivan flew south at 120 mph and 800 feet, towards Croydon, fifteen seconds behind pilot Dilling in Unit Two. They would touch down in approximately 15 minutes, but Ivan was certain he would never see Unit One or Unit Two again. Jason told Craig and Kevin to review touch down and escape. He followed the check points with his watch. South to Croydon, southwest to Oxted, then to avoid the traffic patterns of Gatwick Airport, they turned southeast, flying low along the railroad tracks to Ashurst, then cut west towards Ashurstwood.

From the cockpit Maria marveled at the beauty of the surrounding countryside with its green fields, rolling hills, and thick groves of trees. When they pulled up and over the last hill Maria got her first look at the mile-and-a-half long reservoir at Saint Hills. It was a beautiful, shimmering body of water, secluded, with not a person in sight. Thirty seconds later they touched down at the north end. Just before the helicopter touched water Jason inflated a rubber raft and the three men got into it. As the helicopter settled down on the water they pushed free and waited for the rotor to stop. Maria handed them the cannisters and climbed down and got into the raft. Pilot Ivan followed. Jason maneuvered the raft in close to the aluminum pontoon and unscrewed two large plugs. As the water began seeping into the pontoon, they pushed off and paddled to shore. Ivan looked back as the helicopter slowly sank below the surface.

"What a waste, it's such a good little flyer," he

said.

They went ashore at the Northeast corner of the reservoir, deflated the raft, and began the one-mile hike to a small back road that was not far from highway A 22. Dense woods surrounded the water reservoir. Jason, in the lead, picked his way through a trail that he and Craig had carefully selected after a number of scouting trips. Craig and Kevin brought up the rear, doing their best to cover up their tracks. No one did much talking, intent on walking the trail and carefully erasing any signs of their passage. After a half mile they crossed a small river, stopped, and buried the bulky rubber raft among a clump of trees.

When they reached the country road that led to highway A 22, the large rented van was still parked among some bushes and trees, hidden from the casual passerby, where Jason and Craig had left it the night before. Each now quickly stripped off their battle fatigues and put them in a large ruck sack that Jason had left in the van. Maria was now dressed in a trim-fitting grey jumpsuit and the men had changed into everyday casual clothes.

* * *

Back at the Tower the noise had stopped; no more helicopters and no more grenades popping off. Chief Warder Halliday checked his watch; it read a little after 9:38 a.m. He went to the door again and stuck his head outside. The smoke was still thick and spewing out from a few cannisters. It was chilling not to hear one small sound except for the gentle hiss of gas: almost complete silence. At 9:43 a.m. the smoke began to subside. The last cannister on the Tower grounds quit emitting gas at 9:50:17 a.m. and the air began to clear of smoke and that awful stench.

10:15:47 am

Craig took the driver's seat while the rest climbed into the back. The van was equipped with two benches on either side, and Maria and Jason sat opposite Kevin and Ivan. The two cannisters and their back packs lay on the floor between them. Craig switched on the ignition and headed north a mile to Forest Row, then turned north onto A 22. He drove the speed limit through East Grinstead over A264 to M 23 and up to Gatwick Airport, a distance of twelve miles.

When they were settled in the van, Kevin looked at Maria and wondered where he had seen the middle-aged woman before. He guessed it was the Tower, but he couldn't remember. He knew that Perry Wallace, also named Jason, was keen on disguises, and suspected she was younger and prettier than she looked. He noticed her mouth, and it gave him a sudden lusting urge, but he didn't seem to know why at the time. The pilot Ivan, Craig, and Perry Wallace wore a rubber mask like his, but each had slightly different features.

Kevin was upset with his father for allowing Wallace/Jason to keep the jewels in England. Kevin had insisted on some item that would prove that his father actually had access to the jewels.

"Did you get the ring?" he asked Jason.

"Yes," and Jason reached into his pocket and handed Kevin the Coronation Ring. Kevin looked at it. The large sapphire with its cross of rubies and surrounded by diamonds glimmered brightly in the dim light of the van. "Beautiful, even better looking than when it was sitting in the case."

"It is beautiful, may I see it?" asked Ivan, and Kevin handed him the ring.

"It is a brave thing you did today, I hope it's worth the price you might have to pay." He handed the ring back to Kevin and looked at the two cannisters on the floor between them, wondering what secrets they held. He said nothing for the rest of the trip. Kevin put the ring in a small pouch inside his pants, thinking he would hide it later.

They dropped Kevin off at Logan Air terminal at Gatwick where a chartered jet was waiting to take him to Prestwick airport forty minutes away. He shook hands with everyone and boarded the plane with his luggage. It was 10:40 am when he took off from Gatwick, a little over an hour since they left the Tower. Craig drove the van north up Motorway 23 to M 25, then doubled back to Reigate where Ivan could board a train to Folkstone and connect with the 2:00 pm boat to Boulogne. Ivan removed his mask before he left the van. "Thanks for the easy morning, it was fun," he said. "I hope you can stay out of reach of the authorities. I don't believe I'll have any problems."

"Thanks for a job well done," said Jason. "You

were superb; and if I ever need you again, I know where to look. Take care of yourself and have a safe trip home." Ivan picked up his bag and left. After Ivan left, Maria removed her makeup and Jason and Craig removed their rubber masks. They left Reigate and drove to Croydon, where they transferred all their gear and the jewels to Jason's Jaguar. He followed Craig to Heathrow, where Craig checked in the rented van. And then they drove back to Canvey Island to recover the other rented van before returning home in time for lunch, a little celebration, and rest.

* * *

Hans Sortheim piloted Unit One straight to its resting place at the bottom of a small, secluded reservoir between Hollingrove and Mountfield. The trip took a little more than fourteen minutes. High over the reservoir Brad Justin deactivated all the surplus cannisters and dumped them into the water below. They touched down, inflated the raft, collected their gear, pulled the plug on the pontoon, and paddled to shore as the helicopter sank slowly into the murky depths. Once on shore they walked into the woods surrounding the reservoir and buried the raft. They took off their battle fatigues and masks and buried them. Their rented van was parked a short distance from the reservoir, and they drove quickly along the country road to A 21, then turned south to Hastings, on the coast, where they checked in the van. They caught the earliest train to Ashford, where they could transfer to a train to Dover and catch the first boat to Calais.

* * *

Frank Dilling and Robert Millicum flew directly over Bromley and followed Route A 21 southeast all the way to the Bewl Bridge Reservoir near Ticehurst. It's the largest reservoir in the southeastern section of England, almost four miles long. Like the other two groups they scuttled their craft, paddled to shore, and made their way to a hidden rented automobile. Along the trail they removed their fatigues and masks and buried them. They drove to Ashford, turned in the car, and took a train to Folkstone, where they expected to catch the 2:00 p.m. boat to Boulogne. Once on board the train, Millicum couldn't resist discussing their morning. "It was quite a show. I wonder what is happening back at the Tower?"

"Best you forget about it, Mr. Millicum, you are now probably on the list of the world's most sought-after fugitives."

7

March 28th
The Awful Truth

Chief Warder Halliday went outside as soon as the smoke thinned, as some of the Warders, Fusiliers, and employees began filtering out into the smelly aftermath. The awful stench made his stomach want to turn over. He saw the Fusilier on the ground by the entrance to Waterloo Barracks struggling to get free. With Warder Pickney and Warder Shaw close behind, he ran to the exit door of the Jewel House, looked in, and saw Renner on the floor inside the door.

"Pickney, you help that Fusilier, and Shaw, you stand guard out here and let no one in." Halliday went in, closed the door behind him, checked Renner, and was relieved to find a heartbeat. And as he started down the stairs to the vault, something caught his eye. It was security guard Jackson and Warder Stone, lying on the floor near the entrance door. He ran down the stairs and in the dim light of the vault saw the two remaining Warders lying on the floor. Jesus, they look dead, he thought. He bent over and checked each man for a pulse, lifted their eyelids, and found them O.K. Thank God, he thought, and breathed a sigh of relief.

He had forgotten a flashlight; he lit a match, went into the vault and walked slowly around the jewel cases until he was stopped by the half-empty case.— number eleven. *Christ!* He lit another match. *Half the jewels are gone!* He rushed out and scrambled up the stairs, and checked the other two men. They were breathing normally; he was puffing hard.

Halliday went out the door. "Go get the nurse," he said to Shaw.

Pickney was back and the Fusilier was free. "Pickney, here are my car keys. Get over to the police station on Bishopgate Street and ask the sergeant in charge to call or radio Scotland Yard and get Kingsly, Head of the Criminal Investigation Division, over here right away. Tell him it's a matter of great urgency and national security. On your way out, tell the security guard on duty to close the gates and let no one in or out without my written permission. Hurry, we've no time to lose. Borrow a portable radio with an operator and bring them back with you." He looked at the Fusilier, a young man in his early twenties, "Are you O.K.?"

"Yes, sir. I can't see very well. My eyes still sting. Dirty bastards."

The nurse appeared with Warder Shaw. "Shaw, get me a torch from my office and bring it back on the double. Take this man with you and get someone to wash out his eyes." Shaw and the Fusilier left and he turned to the nurse. "There are five people in there, all unconscious. Tell me how they are as soon as you can."

The Fusilier Sergeant Major on duty at the Museum reported for instructions and Halliday told him to stand guard with Shaw. He hoped he was making the right moves. *When the news gets out all hell'll break loose.* Shaw returned with the flashlight and he took it and went back into the Jewel House. He took the forty-nine steps two at a time, passed the nurse checking the two Warders outside the vault door, went inside the vault, and took a careful walk around the jewel case. He found everything in place except at the case with the Coronation Regalia. He tried to remember exactly what had been in the case. The ampula and spoon, the spurs, the armills and the chalice and paten were still there, but my God! The Crown, the Orb, and the Sceptres, and yes, the Sword and Coronation Ring, were gone. He looked at the cut out opening, looked again inside the case, and the enormity of it hit him. He stood dumbfounded in shock. As the awful truth struck home, his knees weakened and his legs began to shake uncontrollably. He waited several minutes until he stopped shaking.

Halliday regained his composure and carefully checked the floor, walls, and ceiling of the vault and the remaining cases again. He walked out of the vault. The two Warders on the floor looked peaceful enough, asleep perhaps, and he wished it were all just a bad dream. His stomach felt sick.

At the top of the stairs the nurse was waiting for him. "They're all right; drugged and sleeping like babies. Each one has an injection mark on his wrist. Their respiration is slow, heartbeats all normal. They should come around soon."

"Thank God," he said, "and thank you very much. I would appreciate it if you say nothing to anyone."

"We should get them onto cots so I can monitor them for the next hour or so. Can you have cots brought here, and I'll stay until they come around? Is something missing from the vault?"

"Yes, I'm afraid so. I'll get some cots for these fellows. Move them to the east side of the upper chamber. Don't touch anything except the patients."

He went back outside, found the grounds filled with milling people and started issuing orders for cots, more tables and chairs, temporary portable lighting, and two men to help the nurse. Then he told Warder Shaw to assemble everyone on the Tower Green and have three or four clerks begin taking statements of each person's movements before, during, and after the raid. Warder Pickney returned at 10:25 a.m. with a portable radio and police operator. "Chief Inspector Kingsly is on his way." He asked the radio operator to place an emergency call to all police stations in England to report on sightings of British Army helicopters flying out of London within the last hour.

Kingsly, the prominent, well-regarded Head of Criminal Investigation for Scotland Yard, arrived with two assistants at 11:00 a.m. "What's happened here?" he asked Halliday.

"We've had a major crime," responded Halliday,

"and I doubt that England will ever be the same. The Crown Jewels are gone and I have no idea where to begin looking for them."

"Incredible," replied Kingsly. "I never thought it possible."

"Neither you nor a thousand other people in the government, but it's happened. I'm afraid we've lost valuable time and the thieves, whoever they are, have skipped the country." Halliday explained what had happened and took Kingsly on a very quick tour of the Jewel House.

Kingsly went back to his car and, with a radiophone relay, called the Prime Minister. When he returned he told Halliday: "The Prime Minister wants no news leaks to the public or the media until she receives a full report. I suggested that we shut down the entire island. She agreed to freeze all outgoing sea and air traffic and place the military on full combat defence alert. She's calling a meeting at 12:30 p.m. and expects me to be there with a full report."

* * *

When the Prime Minister put down the phone she was shaking and unsettled for the first time in her career. Now, she thought, how do I shut down the island? In all her experience the thought of closing the island for an emergency had never crossed her mind; and for that matter, no one in the government had ever suggested such a contingency plan. She started with the Secretary of State for Transport, then followed with the Secretary of State for Defence, the Secretary of State for Scotland, and finally the Secretary of State for the Home Department. It was already 11:20 a.m. when she finished the last call

She thought of the hundreds of fishing boats, transports, and cruise ships travelling the shores that would have to be stopped. The thousands of people caught in one of the worst "traveller jams" ever conceived. The orders to the airports and to the military were slow to develop. Shortly before noon Heathrow shut down, followed closely by Gatwick, and the many smaller airports in Britain and Scotland. All international flights coming in were diverted to airports on the continent. No one was told why; it remained a total mystery, except that it was some kind of national emergency. For the next twenty-four hours it would be total chaos.

* * *

At 11:20 a.m. Halliday decided he was still in charge at the Tower. He turned to Kingsly. "Perhaps we can gather enough clues to help you before you leave for the PM's meeting. Why don't you get your lab people over here and see if they can turn up something?" He went back inside the Jewel House again.

"I've got two of them coming around and on their feet," the nurse told him. "They're able to talk, but still a little faint. It looks like all five will be up and around in five or ten minutes."

Halliday went over to Renner, the security guard and the first to awake: "Can you tell me what happened?"

"It was Mrs. Ashford, sir, she was on duty . . . to sell books today for the gift shop . . . she offered me a cookie, like she usually does when she's here, and then all of a sudden she squirted me in the nose with something . . . that's the last thing I remember, 'til now."

"What time was that?"

"I don't know, let's see, it was right after the time lock went off and the two Warders went down to the vault to open it. Probably about 9:26 or so."

He went over to Warder Anderson. "How do you feel?" he asked

Anderson was groggy. "Like a fool. She got Neal with a squirt . . . from whatever it was she was carrying, but I got her wrists, and, well . . . she dropped everything. I had her with her back up against the vault door, but she kicked me in the balls." Anderson paused, trying to remember, trying to come to grips with it all. "I let go and I guess she hit me on the back of the neck and I went out. I'm pretty sore, but I guess I'll be O.K.. She was such a nice person. I can't believe she would do anything wrong . . . what happened, anyway?"

"You'll find out soon enough," and Halliday turned to the nurse. "Get these people over to your dispensary and get urine and blood samples for testing, and don't let them talk to anyone until I say so. You'll need a full spectrum of drug tests. Get the doctor here quickly to conduct a complete physical of all five men."

When Kingsly returned, Halliday led him into the upper chamber and they went slowly around the room, found the wire loop on the entrance door, left it there for the lab people, and finally stopped at the little table at the top of the stairs. "Here's where Mrs. Ashford worked. The gift shop always has someone here to sell souvenir books to visitors as they come up from the vault. Apparently she took all five men out. Seems to me she's only been working here for four or five months."

"We'll have the lab people give it a good going over," replied Kingsly. And the two of them went down the stairs to take another look at the vault.

"Is this the place the two Warders got it?" asked Kingsly.

"Yes," replied Halliday. "One lying with his head east and the other lying in the opposite direction." He showed Kingsly the cutout in case number eleven. "The important pieces of the Coronation Regalia are gone. Each item by itself is priceless. It's devastating, a real catastrophe, I just can't believe it. Except for the glass cutout itself, there's nothing on the floor or in the case left behind by the thieves. The place is clean. It was a well planned and organized raid, I doubt if you'll find anything."

Kingsly took out a small notebook and Halliday carefully described each item that was stolen. They went up the stairs and Halliday selected a booklet from a box behind the small sales table that described in detail the stolen items and handed it to Kingsly. Once outside, Halliday told Warder Shaw.

"When the Scotland Yard lab people get here, let them in and no one else."

The two men walked towards Halliday's office through the crowds of people gathered on the Tower Green, waiting to give their statements, and decided to interview a few individuals to pick up what they could.

It was the same story. Everyone had been trapped by the foul smelling, eye smarting gas and smoke. No one could agree whether three or four helicopters participated, but all agreed they were painted in British Army colors. The men were dressed in British Army battle fatigues.

Halliday found out that the Byward Tower gate and the St. Thomas Tower gate had been frozen shut. Apparently the raid started precisely at 9:28 am and was over in ten minutes. Incredible, he thought, it was mayhem for ten minutes while someone entered the vault and lifted the jewels.

Halliday and Kingsly tied up the loose ends before it was time for the PM's meeting. "We'll have a census and statements from everyone in the Tower by late this afternoon," said Halliday. "Our power and communications are down. No one has reported sick or hurt except for Warder Anderson's groin and neck; still some people with smarting eyes. Miraculous! The lingering odor of rotting onions is, however, bothering some people."

"The lab people have arrived, and my assistants will see the investigation through," said Kingsly. "They'll pick up the samples of urine and blood, gather in all the debris and cannisters from the

ASSAULT ON THE CROWN

grounds, and check out the gates and Jewel House. I'll have someone collect all the written statements. After that you can get someone in here to fix your power system and communications. I'll make sure the telephone people get on the job. I don't know what's wrong with your radios, but I'll put someone on it."

Halliday had sealed off the Tower. It was after 6:00 p.m. before anyone was allowed to leave; and then only if they swore to complete silence about the day's events. The Tower was officially closed to the public indefinitely.

* * *

Shipping was the easiest to shut down. Beginning at 11:50 a.m., Navy patrols stopped and searched several ships, ferries, fishing boats, and pleasure craft that had departed the island after 9:30 a.m.. Some had already reached the continent and escaped a search. But it didn't matter. The afternoon boats to Calais and Boulogne meant to carry the three pilots and two copilots to the continent never took on any passengers. Jason's alternate plan was placed into effect and each man found his way to separate, secluded lodgings scattered throughout England.

* * *

It was a sombre group that assembled at Westminster and settled into the cushioned chairs at the long table in the Cabinet Room. Besides the four Secretaries of State she had called, the group included Kingsly, the Chairman of the Joint Intelligence Committee, the Director-General of MI5, the Chief of MI6, and the Chief of Military Intelligence Service.

The Prime Minister, sitting at the head of the table, opened the meeting by saying, "This morning's events are shocking. I've informed the Queen. She's sick at heart and wants the Coronation Regalia back at all costs. We don't know who has taken the jewels or why. It could be an international plot or some very professional thieves expecting to gain millions by selling the jewels or demanding ransom. Hopefully the thieves will not cut up Cullinan I and II or any of the other large jewels. Chief Inspector Kingsly of Scotland Yard has been on the scene and will be in charge of coordinating the investigation until further notice. I've scheduled a press conference to explain our 'National Emergency.' Please proceed, Mr. Kingsly."

Kingsly recounted the events of the morning based on the information they had gathered. "It was the same for everyone in the Tower, they were trapped by gases that smelled like rotting onions, and which made the eyes water profusely on contact, but were apparently nontoxic, unlike CS gas. CS tear gas can be very toxic; it's been known to kill if too much is inhaled. The raiders sealed off the inner and outer walls of the Tower and the east and west sides of the inner grounds with tear gas, smoke, and exploding grenades. No one could get through unless they wore masks. They created mass confusion for a short period of time, ten minutes, and their plan worked extremely well.

"An employee, a Mrs. Ashford, drugged all five of the men on duty in the Jewel House. She fought with one of them and got the better of him. We're getting her file now and interviewing those who knew her best."

"How did she do all that?" asked a curious Prime Minister. And Kingsly related the events as they occurred.

"You now believe only three British Army helicopters were involved?" asked the Prime Minister. "And you have no idea where they went off to?"

"From the reports gathered from people outside the Tower, who thought it was some kind of Army exercise, they all headed out in a southerly direction."

The Prime Minister turned to the Secretary for Defence. "You had no exercise planned around the Tower and you've no helicopters in the London area?"

"That's correct Madam, no question about it, they were not British Army."

"How would someone get three helicopters into England without some kind of permit and licensing?"

"We'll have to check that out. We don't even have a decent description of the units. If you're going to ask for public help at your press conference, perhaps you can ask if any tourist took photographs of the helicopters."

"And at the same time perhaps someone along the route of the three helicopters could tell us where they sighted them," added Kingsly.

"Both good suggestions," said the Prime Minister, "The press conference is at 2:00 p.m. No interviews are to be given by any Tower personnel or any of your departments. All news releases will be issued by me at a news conference each day. Now let's get to work."

No one can remember for certain where Winston Churchill first raised his hand with the V for victory sign, but he did it many times on the steps of 10 Downing Street. Britain's prime ministers always made special announcements from this historic site. Because of terrorists activities, 10 Downing is sealed off from the public except by special permit. On this day a shocked and pale Prime Minister electrified the select gathering of media people with news that would rock the world. She described in detail what priceless pieces of the Regalia had been stolen and how.

"No," she had no idea why they were taken.

"Yes, three helicopters were used in the assault on the Tower."

"No, we don't know how many people were involved, or whom they represent."

"Yes, the Tower is closed indefinitely until power and communications can be restored."

"Yes, we need help from the public. Send any photographs or information to Chief Inspector Kingsly at Scotland Yard."

"No. Interviews of Tower personnel or investigators will not be allowed until we have pieced all the information together. All news releases will come from 10 Downing."

"Yes, outgoing traffic from our island will be shut down indefinitely until we can get our searching procedures organized."

She left the clamoring crowd of newspaper and television reporters and retreated inside, relieved the ordeal was over. She suspected that more than a thousand media people from all over the world would descend on London. But for the most part, airlines throughout the world had cancelled all flights to London for the immediate future.

8

March 28th
Killer Time?

Kevin Banks arrived at Prestwick Airport on the West coast of Scotland at 11:20 a.m. feeling physically and mentally drained from the raid on the Tower, but still too excited to sleep. The plan called for a drive from Prestwick to Stranraer on the Southwest coast of Scotland in the Dumfries and Galloway Region. A chartered fishing boat was due at Stranraer at 12:30 p.m. to take him back to Northern Ireland. He could sleep on board during the two-hour trip home.

A nice, young, attractive woman picked him up at the jet and drove him to the Godfrey Davis rental office. Still wearing the young Churchill mask designed by Jason, he carried the ID of one James Donnally, and toted a small valise. He picked up the prepaid rental car and took highway 77 South to Stranraer. The drive along the coast of the North Channel above the Irish Sea was beautiful as it wandered among the soft green rolling hills of sparsely populated Southern Scotland. The sun broke through clouds, changing large colored patches of sea from deep grey to bright blue and changing the colors of the hills from deep forest green, almost black in places, to bright yellow green. It's a peaceful scene, he thought, not like this morning. He yearned to stay somewhere close by for awhile and put everything behind him, but, so much to do and so little time.

Kevin felt the small pouch below his belt and again regretted his father's capitulation to Wallace/Jason in allowing the jewels to remain in England. He had wanted them under his complete control; no telling how events would turn out. From the moment Wallace/Jason had first described the plan he had been certain of its success. Wallace/Jason was smooth, a real pro, he thought. *I would feel much better if I knew his true identity.*

He turned onto a small side road just below the ruined Abbey at Crossragual and found a secluded cluster of trees, where he stopped the car and got out. It was time to get ready for the boat trip. He removed his mask, glad to do so — the damned thing was beginning to itch — and placed it in a pile with his false papers. Then he removed the ring from its pouch, packed it in cotton, dropped his pants, and placed the ring between the top rear of his right thigh muscle next to his his right testicle and taped it there with broad surgical tape. Only the most meticulous search would detect the extra lump. From his small valise he removed an old fishing jacket, a pair of pants, and an old pair of tennis shoes, and changed his clothes. He dug a small hole among the trees, put the mask, tape, and false ID in it, and filled it back up again. The hidden ring was only slightly uncomfortable when he got back in the car to continue the drive. He was only thirty miles from Stranraer; traffic was light, and he sped up to make certain he would meet the boat on time.

* * *

Kevin was alert and careful as he drove into Stranraer at 12:25 p.m. He found the petrol station that handled Godfrey Davis, checked in the car, and walked the short distance to the docks where, not far from the ferry slips, he found the fishing boat *Belfast Star* that would take him across the Northern Channel to Belfast.

He climbed aboard and the captain welcomed him in a surly way, as if the whole episode was an imposition. The captain's friends knew of his poor disposition, but Kevin didn't, and he took an immediate disliking to the man. He noticed four or five other people in the deck cabin, but couldn't make out their features. Good cover, he thought. Kevin went below with his small valise, found a bunk, climbed into it, and went to sleep as the boat began chugging its way out of the small harbor. Fifteen minutes later the Navy shut down the harbor.

An hour later the engines slowed and awakened him. He looked out the porthole and saw a Navy patrol boat swinging alongside. He decided to feign sleep. A few moments later a Navy lieutenant and two seamen were inside the cabin and woke him up. "May I see your identity papers please?" asked the lieutenant. Kevin showed him his drivers license. "Good. Catch anything?"

"Not much luck," replied Kevin, breathing a little hard. He didn't know what the captain or other people on board had told the lieutenant.

"Well, too bad. We have to make a quick search, so please open your bag." The lieutenant checked his bag while the two seamen thoroughly searched each compartment and lifted the bilge hatch cover. Satisfied, they left. "Sorry to have awakened you, old man, had to, you know. You can go back to sleep now."

Kevin watched the Navy patrol move off. As the captain cranked up the engines, the boat resumed its rhythmic pulsations. He wasn't sure what they had been looking for, but he guessed they had closed off the island and were looking for the jewels. A chill ran through him as the thought of being caught with the ring hit him. Kevin lay back down; it wasn't long before fatigue overtook adrenalin and he was asleep again.

On board the patrol boat the Navy lieutenant recorded the time and place he had stopped the fishing boat *Belfast Star* with its captain, one crew member and four fishermen from Belfast aboard. He didn't record their names.

An hour later, awakened by the rough motion of the boat, Kevin sat up quickly only to discover he was staring into the barrel of a .45 automatic, behind which was the familiar face of Ian Sommers, Reverend McIver's chief agent.

* * *

Shortly after 2:00 p.m., during her first of many press conferences on the subject, the Prime Minister shocked the world with the news of the missing Coronation Regalia, the centerpieces of the Crown Jewels. She pleaded for any information leading to their recovery.

In Belfast, Professor William Banks had been waiting anxiously all day for news, any news, of the attack. He had heard the bulletin about shutting down the island, but that was all. Now he was thrilled. *They did it! Unbelievable! Now we'll get their attention. Now we'll get our way. Now we'll get our independence!* The new constitution was almost finished, and he was extremely proud of it. He firmly believed a new North could become economically strong; several committees were generating excellent ideas.

His executive board was short on membership predictions for March. It was only 195,000 when they had expected 250,000. It was hard work getting people to yield to the idea of change as drastic as independence. But, surprisingly enough, within the last few weeks membership had risen at a more rapid rate than in previous months. The committee workers were more and more enthused about the results of grass roots deliberation over the various segments of a new government's operation and the outlook for a brighter economic future. The goal was to achieve economic independence from Britain within ten years.

The professor was anxious; tomorrow morning the State Sword and his letter of demands would be delivered to the Prime Minister. All hell would break loose. His letter included a planned call to the Prime Minister at 1:30 p.m. tomorrow, after she had had time to think about his demands. The following day he planned a recruitment day, when over 200,000 small pamphlets explaining the movement and the plan for independence would be released throughout Northern Ireland. He was elated and he was ready now for the final push. *Perhaps our recruiting effort will bring in another 50-75,000 members.* After his talk with the Prime Minister tomorrow he would hold a press conference.

It was 4:00 p.m. and Kevin was late. Well, he thought, the PM closed down the entire island. He had been hearing all day about the chaotic conditions at the airports and seaports. Perhaps Kevin's boat was held up at Stranraer. *It may be several hours before he gets home.* He poured himself a small glass of Bushmills, the familiar aroma causing a slight watering of his mouth, drank it down, and sat down to think. *I must go through with it, regardless whether or not Kevin makes it home today. We're too far along.* He looked out at the lights of Belfast, a long-standing habit of his, and contemplated his moves for tomorrow.

* * *

When Jason reached Canvey Island, after dropping off Kevin and Ivan, Craig and Maria helped wipe the parked van clean of prints. Then Craig drove it to Havering, with Jason and Maria close behind in his Jaguar, and checked it in. Along the way they heard the emergency radio announcement that the Prime Minister had mysteriously ordered a shutdown of the entire island and no one could leave by air or by sea. Jason smiled at Maria. "What chaos we've caused! Our teammates will have to stay on the island for a few days."

"Let's hope they don't find them or us, Jason," she remarked, just a little disturbed at the enormity of the effort the government must be mounting.

It was almost 1:00 p.m. when the trio reached home. Jason and Craig fixed lunch while Maria poured a small bottle of champagne for a toast. Although they were tired, they went over the entire operation again. Jason hoped Kevin would be traced from Gatwick to Stranraer. If the authorities found the ring, it would add legitimacy to the professor's claim that he was in control of the jewels. They would have to believe Kevin took part in the raid. All good circumstantial evidence.

The other members of the team, the pilots and bombardiers, could not be traced except by long arduous work and a lot of luck. Tracing them through the money paid them would be impossible. The munitions and the helicopters were all traceable, but the the individuals who bought them, Craig and Jason in disguise, with forged documents, would be impossible to trace. Everything seemed covered except for Maria, who was the most visible of all. Craig had lifted her employment records from the central files and destroyed them. Her apartment was clean. Because of her careful disguise, Maria's true identity seemed safely guarded.

Then Maria told them. "While I was waiting for the time to slip by, I nervously counted the money in the cash box. I didn't have the gloves on at the time, and I must have left my prints on the bills."

"Jesus, Maria, that's not like you," exclaimed Jason.

Then she smiled slyly and looked at Craig with a twinkle in her eye, "I couldn't remember which bills I touched, so I brought the cash box with me."

Jason and Craig laughed. "How much money did we steal?" asked Jason.

"A little over forty-two pounds."

"Wow! Save it and we'll send it back with the Jewels and put a little interest with it," and Jason laughed again, with relief.

"Speaking of the Jewels I'm dying to see them, to touch them, although I feel it's almost sacrilegious." And she looked at Jason with the expression of a small child about to put her hand in a cookie jar.

"How about now?" responded Jason, too tired to tease her. "Craig can bring the two cans upstairs and we'll put away the booty." And they went upstairs to Jason's bedroom, where he opened the hidden door to Merlin's Nest and began unpacking the two aluminum cans holding their precious cargo. He unscrewed the lid on the shorter can and withdrew the Sovereign's Ring and handed it to Maria.

Her hand shook slightly as she took it from him. Merlin's Nest was well lit and the bright blue sapphire, with its cross of rubies, surrounded by diamonds, sparkled with brilliance. "It's beautiful, but I thought I saw you give it to Kevin in the van?"

"That was a perfect imitation, made by an underground jeweler in Amsterdam. It cost quite a bit, but I figured that the Professor could use it as a memento. It's marked inside with the tiniest of dates to distinguish it from the original."

Craig put on soft white gloves, reached in, and removed the top packing, pulled out the Orb, and placed it on the table. Then he removed more packing and lifted out, ever so slowly, the State Crown. His hands trembled a little as he put it down on the table next to the Orb. "It's an eery feeling handling these things," he said. "They represent so much history and, God, how priceless! I'm glad we have them instead of someone else. They are magnificent."

"God! They're gorgeous," exclaimed Maria. "Just look at the sparkle and glitter that over 2800 diamonds create!" The brilliance of Cullinan II was overwhelming. She resisted the temptation to reach out and touch it, and instead put on a pair of soft white gloves.

"It's heavy!" she said as she picked up the crown. "I wouldn't want to wear it for very long." She wanted to try it on but could not bring herself to do it. "Only a king or queen should wear it," she said, replacing it on the table. It had all been an exciting game until now. The impact of their deed struck her again and she wondered what might happen if they were caught. It was not her nature to be fearful. She looked at Jason standing next to her, confident and self assured, and the thought went away.

"It weighs almost three pounds," said Jason as he opened the second can. Craig withdrew the State Sword and placed it in a special light-weight wooden crate they had constructed for delivery to the Prime Minister. Jason gently withdrew the two Sceptres and placed them on the table in front of the Crown and the Orb: "Behold! The symbols of the British Empire, in all their breathtaking beauty." The three stood gazing at the great collection in complete silence and awe for several minutes. It was difficult for them to focus on any one point. The shooting lights seem to command the eyes to move about, creating flashes that numbed them. Diamonds, sapphires, emeralds, rubies, and pearls were everywhere, precisely placed for maximum beauty.

With a great deal of reluctance they put away all the items in a special velvet-lined steel cabinet Jason and Craig had built in their cellar shop. They closed up the wooden crate and nailed it shut. Craig took it to his room along with the professor's letter to the Prime Minister.

They listened to the Prime Minister's news conference at two o'clock. "Well, there you have it," Jason remarked, "we're on the most wanted list.

After an afternoon of rest, Jason drove Maria to a pay phone where she placed a call to Belfast promptly at 6:00 p.m. The professor had been waiting: "What's your number, wait there." Maria gave him the number and hung up; five minutes later the phone rang. It was the professor. "Sorry, the phone is bugged; I drove to a pay phone. Kevin's not returned yet. His boat was probably held up. Go ahead and deliver the letter and the sword to the Prime Minister in the morning. I still plan to call the Prime Minister tomorrow afternoon. I'll ask her to withhold any announcement to the press until the morning of April first. I want to be sure Kevin is safe and I have the ring. Unfortunately, it will give them more time to track you down."

"I believe we're safe professor, but let me get Mr. Wallace."

Maria stayed with the car and Jason took the phone.

"I still want you to deliver the package to the Prime Minister tomorrow at 11:00 a.m.," the professor told him. "I intend to stall the Prime Minister until I have the ring. Kevin is late."

"He's no doubt O.K.," said Jason, trying to reassure the professor. "I'll call you tomorrow this same time for any more instructions."

* * *

Kevin, still looking into the barrel of the gun Ian Sommers held, stretched his stiff body and asked: "What's this all about, Ian?"

"Well, well, at last sleeping beauty is awake. So

you know my name? I didn't know I was famous."

"You like shooting at people, don't you?" and Kevin gave him a dark stare.

"Just a little target practice down on the farm. No bother. You'll be obliged to stay with me for the next few hours. You're about to take a short detour in Belfast. Once we get where we're going you'll know a bit more. I have two more men up on the deck. Don't try anything foolish. Hand me your bags and stand up, remove your jacket, and put it on the bunk." Kevin obeyed.

"Now turn around and face the bulkhead, put your hands on it, spread your legs, and lean forward." Sommers gave him a body search with one hand, the other still holding the gun, starting from the neck and slowly working down the upper body front to back. He then moved down to his hips and his legs, working slowly and carefully with one hand. Kevin caught his breath and prayed he would miss the ring. Sommers put his hand on the inside of Kevin's legs and worked up to the groin area. He stopped short when he felt Kevin's testicles and just missed touching the extra lump. Kevin let out his breath silently. Sommers stepped back: "Well, you're clean, as they say, now let's take a look at your jacket and bag."

He carefully felt every square inch of the jacket, which was empty, and then dumped out the contents of the valise on a small side seat in the cabin. He found two shirts, a pair of pants, some socks, a pair of dress shoes, and a small toilet case, which he opened and inspected. He looked up at Kevin.

"Traveling kind of light for such a long stay away?" Kevin made no reply. He felt inside the bag and found the small bottom compartment where Kevin had carried his extra papers, but it was empty. "Again, very clean. "You may repack your valise now, thank you."

What did you expect to find?" asked Kevin.

"Just wanted to be sure you weren't carrying a weapon."

Kevin felt the boat slow down and the quick jolt of the boat bumping a pier. "We're here," said Sommers. "Please walk slowly. I'll lead, my two friends will follow behind you to the car. Get in the middle of the back seat."

The captain stuck his head in the door and said, "Wait here. I want to go down and talk to the Customs man, he's a friend of mine." He returned shortly. "It's O.K., seems they're looking for a big package. I told him all we have is fish and some small carry bags."

"Thanks," said Sommers. He waved to the captain as they left the boat and reminded Kevin that he was a dead man if he tried anything. Kevin looked for an opportunity to run away or cry out, but the wharf was dead-ended, the car blocked the only way out, and Sommers had a gun stuck in his ribs. He recognized the wharf at the fishing village of Kearney on the Ardo Peninsula as he got into the car and caught a glimpse of the coastline of the Isle of Man.

One of the men drove and the other sat on his left while Sommers was on his right. Sommers reached over and placed a light colored headband over his eyes, followed by a heavy pair of sunglasses and a floppy hat with the brim down. "Sorry about this, but it's best you don't know where you're going."

Kevin listened for familiar sounds and tried to count turns and guess the time it took to get to wherever they were going, but he soon lost track. He caught the strong smell of coffee at one point, but couldn't think of where that might be. The sounds of traffic didn't mean much. The car finally slowed, made one last left turn, then moved ahead over a cobblestone driveway and stopped.

"You can get out on your left now," said Sommers. And he led him away from the car over the cobblestones. "We're going down some stairs now, so put a hand on my shoulder while I lead the way." Sommers stopped at the bottom and Kevin heard him unlock a door. Then Sommers lead him through a short corridor into a warm room that smelled dank.

"Ah, I see you found him, now maybe we'll get to the bottom of things. You may remove your blindfold, Mr. Banks," said a man with a deep voice. Kevin pulled it off, blinking in the dim light, and found himself staring at Reverend Sean McIver sitting behind a worn old desk piled high with papers, magazines, and books. Kevin had seen his picture in a newspaper some time ago, but now, seeing him in the flesh, he recoiled at the sinister aura the man projected. He was scowling at Kevin with his lips curled downward. His deep-set eyes of black ebony seemed to shoot bullets of tiny lights.

His black hair was streaked with grey, and the lines etched on his face, deepened by constant brooding scowls, made him look much older than his forty-eight years.

Kevin caught the little ups and downs in the tone of his voice as he spoke, revealing a hidden excitement in him that seemed almost uncontrollable. The man's wild rantings and ravings against the South and the Catholics were well known.

The reverend turned to the two men standing behind Sommers and said: "Go and join the others upstairs and wait for Ian here to finish with this fellow." They shrugged and left the room. Ian Sommers sat down in a chair in the corner of the room, fully expecting the reverend to go into one of his rages.

"We've been wondering where you've been for the last two weeks. Would you mind telling us?" asked McIver with a slight foreboding tone to his voice.

"I was vacationing in Scotland after a brief visit with a friend in London."

"Now then, Mr. Banks, three months ago your father went to America to raise money, is that true?"

"Yes."

"I understand it was a great deal of money that he raised, like maybe close to a million U.S. dollars. Is that not true?" The reverend was guessing, neither of his planted spies knew how much money the Independence Party had accumulated.

"I don't know, he never told me."

"You're lying."

"I'm sure it was a lot of money, my father is a very persuasive man."

"What does he intend to do with all that money?"

"You obviously know what the Independence Party is all about. We need money to help the organization grow, and get our independence."

"You don't need that kind of money to make your movement grow. Damnation! Your organization seems to be growing now without hardly any effort. There's more to it than that. You're raising a secret army; buying guns and ammunition to fend off the British in a revolt. That kind of money buys arms and men."

Kevin was relieved to find that McIver, if he knew anything at all about the jewels, did not connect it with him or the Independence Party. "I'm sorry, that's not true. You know we're non-violent. We've no paramilitary group. We've no guns. We've no bombs. We just have ordinary citizens, half Catholic and half Protestant, joining up and getting excited about independence and yes, we are growing."

"Damn! You people have got to stop this! We're English and we're Protestant; we don't need independence; we'll not have independence, and I'll see to that!"

Kevin was still standing, looking down at the man, and it seemed to him he was beginning to froth at the mouth. "We're not English," said Kevin, raising his voice, "we're Irish, Northern Ireland Irish, Ulster Irish! The English spent eight-hundred years trying to drown Ireland in misery and fear.

They didn't succeed in the South. The South beat them. And here, it was the 'Plantation' that saved this piece of the Island for Britain; and now they don't want it and we're headed for economic ruin."

"That's a damned lie," cried the reverend.

"No, it's not a lie, seventy-three percent of the people of Great Britain want to get rid of us."

Although he knew it was true, the reverend jumped out of his chair. "That's a lie!" His eyes became clouded with hysteria, mouth twisted in a peculiar, evil way, and his hands shook as he spread them out on his desk. He leaned over and looked into Kevin's eyes as if trying to draw power from the atmosphere to strike him dead. Kevin recoiled and for the first time felt raw fear.

"Let me tell you," McIver growled through a tightened jaw, "no matter what people think, no matter what the government thinks, no matter what movement you have, we'll not have independence so the South can suck us up with their filthy Papist ways. You'll die first, and I'll die to see us saved along with other loyalists whom God has given the right to protect themselves. If it means killing, then by God, killing it is!"

Kevin braced himself. "You can't stop us. We've come too far. You'll have to kill too many people."

The right Reverend McIver was livid; his entire body shook and his eyes rolled wildly about as if searching for something deep inside himself. "Shut up! Ian, put him in the storeroom. Your father won't sacrifice you for independence, we'll see to that, he'll stop it or..." and he turned and left the room.

Ian Sommers got up and opened the heavy, squealing wooden door set inside the thick support walls of the church basement. Inside the small storage room Kevin stared at the empty shelving, a cot, a chair, a bucket in the corner, and dim light bulb hanging from the center of the cement-and-stone ceiling. The room was damp and smelled musty, but was otherwise clean.

When Sommers closed the door behind him, Kevin could not even hear the sound of his footsteps leaving the office. He felt totally alone. A cold deadly fear struck at him: *Jesus, the maniac may kill me!*

9

March 29
Thrust and Parry

The City of London Courier Service, known in London as COLCS, stores its vans at a garage just off Sutherland Street in the Pimlico section of London. Two blocks away at a repair garage, Craig walked in dressed in a COLCS uniform. He claimed a van that had been serviced and stood waiting for one of the mechanics to deliver it back to COLCS. The manager was happy to let him drive it out, and didn't bother to check Craig's ID. It was not uncommon for someone to come by and pick up a repaired vehicle; COLCS was always in a hurry.

Craig picked up Maria, waiting in their car parked a few blocks away. Dressed in a COLCS uniform, she transferred the wooden box carrying the Sovereign's Sword and the letter for the Prime Minister to the van. Maria's hair was tucked tightly beneath the grey-blue cap. She wore dark sunglasses and thin gloves. Under casual inspection she could pass for a young man.

They arrived at 10 Downing Street gate at precisely 11:00 a.m., the day after the assault on the Tower complete with forged delivery and sales slip stating the delivery was a large candelabra purchased from Harrod's.

"You will have to leave the box here for a security check before we can take it into 10 Downing," said the guard after he reviewed the papers.

Maria replied in her best young man's voice: "That's expected. But the party wishes the large envelope to stay with the box and this small note to be delivered to the Prime Minister right away. It's very important, can you do it?"

"I can call down and they'll send someone to pick it up."

Maria waited while the guard placed the call, and when he hung up he told her, "It's all right, someone will be down in a minute. You gonna wait?"

"No, we're running late, other deliveries to make, thanks anyway," and she left in the van with Craig.

When the Prime Minister's secretary opened the note ten minutes later he was shocked at its contents. The note simply said that the guard at the security gate had a box with the Sovereign's Sword in it and a letter of explanation. He interrupted the Prime Minister, who was trying to concentrate on a speech but kept thinking anxiously of the jewels and the chaos at the airports.

"Have security check it out, open the box, and bring it to me along with the letter as quickly as possible." The Prime Minister called the guard at the gate and asked who had delivered it, then called

Kingsly at Scotland Yard and ordered him to stop and check all COLCS vans for two suspects. They were too late. The missing van was located thirty minutes later parked two blocks away from the repair garage, perfectly clean.

When the guards brought the sword to the Prime Minister, the breathtaking beauty of the magnificently jeweled scabbard of solid gold encrusted with jewels made her catch her breath. She reached out to touch it then remembered that Scotland Yard would want to check it carefully. Perhaps they would find a lead. She was always uncomfortable with opulent jewelry; it made her nervous. She wondered how much it would bring at auction in today's unpredictable market? A horrifying thought.

She opened the large manila envelope carefully, trying not to destroy any fingerprints. She gently removed a one-page letter with the tips of her fingers, careful not to touch the remaining two sheets containing the Transition Plan, placed it on her desk, and read:

29 March
Madam Prime Minister:

Please accept the return of the sword as a symbol of our faith and sincere desire to work towards a peaceful and lasting solution to the "Troubles" in Northern Ireland. This peaceful solution will only come in the form of complete independence for Northern Ireland.

Great Britain has long been unjust to the people of the North. We have been denied our own government and certain civil liberties. Northern Ireland is dying by economic strangulation. Independence is now the only solution to save her from destruction.

The Independence Party of Northern Ireland has sequestered the Coronation Regalia and is prepared to trade them for independence for Northern Ireland. All you have to do is follow our plan and the Crown Jewels will be returned to England:

    1. One week from today on April 4th dissolve Parliament and hold an election on April 5th asking the people of Great Britain if Northern Ireland should be allowed its independence.

    2. On April 5th hold an election in Northern Ireland on the question of independence.

    3. If either election favors independence, then on the following day you will request the United Nations to provide troops no later than April 12th, and a civil police force to replace those now active in Northern Ireland.

    4. On April 12th all British troops are to be withdrawn from Northern Ireland and the Royal Ulster Constabulary and Ulster Defence Regiment placed on indefinite leave until a new independent government forms new civil and military forces. All paramilitary units will be outlawed.

    5. Great Britain must accept the Transition Plan attached. This document is the blueprint for providing the economic foundation for our independence.

6. Finally, amnesty is to be granted all members of the Independence Party, including those who sequestered the jewels.

We now have something of great value to Great Britain, perhaps of greater value than Northern Ireland, but not of more value than the freedom of its people. The Regalia is safe, but I have not allowed myself to know where the jewels are being kept.

Please withhold this information from the media until we have had a chance to talk. I will call you at 1:30 p.m. today.

Sincerely,
Professor William Banks, President, NIIP

As the Prime Minister read the letter she paled at its contents, then she became angry. *How dare they! It's thievery, not "sequestering"! It's blackmail, not negotiating, and for what? More "Troubles" and a civil war? And what about the bloody Republic, the South, what does he think they will do? The man is crazy!*

She buzzed her secretary: "Get me Inspector Kingsly now!"

He was on the line within seconds. "Tell the others to get to 10 Downing as soon as possible, we have new developments."

At 11:30 a.m. she convened the meeting of the four Secretaries of State, four top intelligence people, and Kingsly, and gave them each a copy of the letter and the Transition Plan. "So now we know who

ASSAULT ON THE CROWN

took the jewels," she began, "and yet the professor claims he doesn't know where they are! I would tend to believe him." She was up pacing the floor, trying to settle her nerves. She spoke rapidly. "I know a little about him from his economic and political work, but I need to know more. I'll need to know soon whether we have a chance of recovering the jewels before we're forced into an election one week from today. I can't arrest him, it would do no good." She wanted to shoot the bastard. She went on exitedly. "I want to stall him and give us more time to locate the jewels, but once the news is out to the world press, public opinion and pressures from other governments will be compelling. It'll take a great deal of diplomacy to put off those elections for very long. We can only hope the radicals in the South and the North won't create an incident."

Inspector Kingsly replied first. "How soon we find the jewels is a most difficult question to answer. It's only been twenty-four hours and we still don't have much to show for our efforts. Recovering the jewels within a week, especially now that we know they'll keep them hidden, may prove insurmountable. We're fortunate to have received a beautiful video tape of the entire operation recorded from Tower Hill by a German tourist. Excellent film and we were able to time the entire sequence at exactly ten minutes."

"My God, that was awfully quick," replied the Prime Minister. She sat down, still excited. "The tourist should receive a token of our appreciation. I'll have my secretary think of something."

"In every way it was a well-planned attack, Madam. The urine and blood samples of the men from the Jewel House show traces of Scopolamine and Thiopental Sodium, both well, known anesthetics. The guards were taken out harmlessly, except for the one Warder who tried to stop the woman. He'll have a sore neck and testicles for awhile. They made every effort to prevent injuries. The grenades and bullets were made of soft clay cleverly put together. The cannisters of tear gas contained an extract of onion juice combined with a minute amount of Benzyl Bromide, the toxic carrier in normal tear gas, and some other substances we're still checking out. This is a new gas to us, just as effective as standard CS tear gas, but nontoxic."

Kingsly shifted uncomfortably, and went on. "We've had some sighting reports of helicopters going South and we have a team around Oxted and East Grinstead checking further." Kingsly was a meticulous man and he paused as if to catalogue all the information in its proper order.

"What about the woman?" asked the Prime Minister trying to hide her nervousness.

"Her personnel file is empty; all the papers missing. No reason for anyone to check on her during the last three months, so we can't tell when or by whom they were taken. No one working at the Tower visited her apartment or is sure of the address, although we're certain she lived within walking distance of the Tower. We're conducting

ASSAULT ON THE CROWN

a house-to-house search with an artist's sketch of her face," and he handed the Prime Minister a copy of the artist's drawing.

"Rather ordinary looking, not very attractive, middle aged, interesting mouth, though," she observed as she studied the drawing.

"This afternoon we're interviewing the personnel man who hired her," continued Kingsly. "The tugboat company called to tell us that the captain who hauled the barges is at sea and not due back until tomorrow. I have a man flying out to talk to him. We just received the papers used to hire the barges.

"Our laboratory people will be tracing the origin of the cannisters, the grenades, and the ammunition. The Army has identified the helicopters from the video tape as French, Aerospatiale-Westland Gazelle, a type they've used for a number of years in a utility role. It's small, reasonably fast, and highly maneuverable. Our research department is enlarging the video tape to its maximum resolution to see if we can identify the pilots. Until we find the helicopters or any of the thieves, we don't have a lot to go on."

"But do you think you can find the jewels?" asked an anxious Prime Minister. She was settling down now, her sharp mind getting organized. The shock was subsiding and she started bearing down.

"I honestly don't know. We have no real leads at the moment. So far the Jewel House is clean, no fingerprints, no loose hair or clothing, and nothing left behind, except one titanium loop used to secure the entry door on the west side. The helicopters have disappeared and so have the criminals. I would say our chances are not good for a quick recovery." Kingsly felt as if the heat in the room had suddenly been turned up. He was on the defensive.

"You do realize sir, that this is the worst national emergency since World War II." The Prime Minister was getting angry now. "It overshadows the Falklands episode. We may lose a strategic segment of the United Kingdom or lose our most treasured of treasures. I have put on extra people just to answer calls of assistance from all over the world and here at home. The Queen and the Royal family are extremely upset, and so is my Cabinet and the members of Parliament. I'm upset! And I have to talk to that man at 1:30 p.m. today, and I don't have any answers."

The Director-General of MI5, who had been reading the letter while listening to Kingsly's report, interrupted. "Madam Prime Minister, if stealing the jewels is a plot to gain the independence of Northern Ireland, then it's a colonial affair, and our E Branch has a significant amount of current information that may help in the recovery operation."

"That's right," she said, "it seems to me you were here a few months ago requesting more help for that group and we agreed. Let's see, Director Yates is in charge of that unit, correct?"

"Richard Yates, a very talented man. He's been following the activities of the Independence Party for some time. His last report included references to fund raising and certain clandestine activities that he was unable to penetrate. I am sure he can provide you with full background information."

"Please get him over here as soon as possible."

The Director-General left the room, and the Prime Minister turned to Kingsly and asked, "How would you classify the Tower raid, violent or non-violent?"

Kingsly reflected for a moment: "Well, it was designed to create mass confusion, and it worked. There was no communication system, no power, and the place was a smokey, exploding dense cloud in which no one could move about or get their bearings without fear of at least temporarily losing their sight. None of the grenades or ammunition were designed to hurt anyone; on the contrary, they were designed *not* to hurt anyone, a real risk on the part of the raiders. I would have to classify it as something to give the appearance of extreme violence when none occurred. That's hedging a bit, but that's the best definition I can give."

The Prime Minister sat silently evaluating Kingsly. He was good at his job. But he was constantly hedging. *That won't do.*

The Director-General returned, and within a few minutes a breathless Richard Yates entered the room. He began with a brief review of the professor's background: "Born in Belfast fifty-seven years ago; father Protestant; mother Catholic; raised Catholic; sent to Queens and graduated in economics; joined the IRA but quit when it turned PIRA; renounced Catholicism, now Protestant; has three sons, two businessmen in Australia; the oldest, Kevin, received military training at Sandhurst, served in the British Army in Northern Ireland and with distinction in the Falklands, after which he resigned his commission to work with his father."

The Prime Minister prided herself on her judgment of character. It was the first time she had witnessed Yates in action, under pressure, and she liked what she saw. Aside from the brief shortness of breath, he was succinct, but thorough, and he displayed a quiet calm. She knew him to be a bulldog, never quitting until he had his prey. She suddenly realized that Kingsly must step aside.

"The professor enjoys a vigorous academic and political career," continued Yates. "He's a respected economist and head of the Economics Department at Queens University. He at first formed a small Freedom Party, then changed it to the Independence Party in 1979. Membership had been slow growing up until about a year ago. Three years ago he had about 4,000 members and two seats in the now-defunct Assembly. It's been growing rapidly, and today we're fairly certain the membership is over 150,000, split evenly Protestant and Catholic. Quite a feat, considering the history of tribalism in the North."

"You know about the elections he wants?" asked the Prime Minister.

"Yes, Madam, the Director-General briefed me on the phone."

"Then could he win them today?

Yates didn't hesitate. "He will win in England

and lose in the North. However, having the jewels could change things dramatically. We've found out he's having a large number of propaganda brochures printed and ready for distribution."

"I see. Please go on." Yes, she was sure Yates was her man.

Kingsly had been listening intently. Finding the jewels would be the biggest coup of anyone's career. Not finding them would mean abject failure and possible loss of a job. He could sense that Yates was going to head up the operation. He had the critical information. He suddenly breathed a sigh of relief, happy to play a secondary but no less important role.

Richard Yates wanted more help. "As you know, we've been handicapped by lack of manpower and have not been able to infiltrate their party. Professor Banks spends most of his time at group meetings, committees he calls them, and talking to new recruits. His son runs the administration office and coordinates the reports of the committees for their ten-man Board of Directors. We're limited in how often we can follow him. We've a phone tap at the professor's home and taps and bugs at the party office. Most of what we hear is routine. They never discuss money or membership, at least not where we can hear it. We estimate they have over one million pounds, but only three-hundred thousand is on deposit in the Bank of London, the rest is probably in a Swiss bank.

"If the professor's team did take the jewels, that clears up some clandestine movements during the last five months. It tells me how the missing money might have been spent." And Yates described to the group Fred Press's recent activities, beginning at the farmhouse. "It would take about four or five months and a considerable amount of money to obtain the equipment and manpower for a raid. The professor went on a fund-raising tour to the United States and may have picked up as much as five hundred thousand US dollars. We suspect he may have deposited it in Switzerland."

The Prime Minister mulled that one over. Dealing with the Swiss was difficult. You needed an indictment and evidence that would hold up in court before you could access a bank account. She decided to wait a while before going to the Swiss.

Yates continued, "Kevin Banks has been out of Northern Ireland for over two weeks now, supposedly on vacation in Scotland. The assistant office manager expects him back in the next day or two, but as of yesterday he had not returned. We don't know where he is. Yesterday evening the professor received a call from a woman and quickly took down a phone number; we had no one assigned to follow him last night. We assume he called it back a few moments later from another phone somewhere. We traced the number to a phone booth here in London, but our London man was too late getting there. That covers in brief what we've accumulated to date."

The Prime Minister let out an exasperated sigh. "Well, I suppose you have plenty of leads to work on now. I want you to take as many people as you need immediately from all branches of our intelligence and police communities and put them in Northern Ireland, in London, or on the continent immediately you need them."

She turned to Kingsly. "You still have much information to collate, but understand that I must now place the entire problem in the hands of E Branch and Director Yates. The Director-General will be nominally in charge, but all information and reports will go directly to Director Yates. He'll be in charge at any meetings with you people here. The Director-General and he will meet with me daily on an unscheduled basis whenever information is received that is meaningful. I will schedule a press conference for each day.

"I know this is an unfair question to ask you, Kingsly, but I must, for I will meet with the Queen and my cabinet soon and need something to tell them. Now that you have heard Director Yates, at what point will we have enough information collected to predict whether we have a chance of recovering the jewels by April fourth — one week from today?"

Kingsly squirmed a bit in his chair and the heat went up again. "There will be new information coming in all the time, and I am sure everyone will be working around the clock," he hedged again. "Most probably one could predict the answer by day after tomorrow."

"That is not good enough," and the Prime Minister turned to Director Yates with a frown of disapproval: "I should think you will be able to do better than that." She looked at the Director-General sitting next to Yates. "I will call you at ten a.m. to schedule tomorrow's meeting. I need not remind all present, the information on who has stolen the jewels will be withheld from the press as long as possible.

"Now then, as to the freeze on air and sea travel from the island, what have you to report?" asked the Prime Minister.

The Secretary of State for Transport cleared his throat, "We are working everyone overtime at the airports, including Army personnel who are helping with baggage and parcel inspection. Flights are now leaving in the order scheduled on the twenty-eighth. All international airports are operating slowly, together with several freight terminals, a total of about fourteen.

"Seaports are going slower, everything aboard has to be inspected. Every crate opened. We've unloaded and reloaded several ships that are now on their way out. The Navy has responded magnificently, as has the Army."

The Secretary of State for Defence added, "Not even the smallest skiff or sailboat has escaped our attention since 11:45 a.m. yesterday. Navy sea patrols overlap, and both the Navy and Army air patrols make it impossible for anyone to come in or go out of our waters without a hands-on inspection."

The Prime Minister had been contemplating lifting the freeze, but decided to wait. "Things seem to be going along about as well as can be expected. I want the Home Office to clear any hardship cases that need to leave the island in a hurry. We'll hold onto the freeze a little longer. Thank you for coming, that's all."

* * *

At 1:30 p.m. the Prime Minister nervously answered her phone. The long wait had tested her patience and she didn't like the way she felt; she didn't yet have full control of her emotions.

"Madam Prime Minister, this is William Banks. Did you receive my package and letter this morning?"

She was surprised at the richness of his voice. She hadn't remembered much about him from a brief meeting a few years ago. "Yes, I did. Thank you for returning the Sword." She resisted the urge to call him a bastard and a traitor.

"Have you considered my proposals?"

God, do I have control of myself? "My dear sir, you do realize what you ask is impossible. England will never concede to terrorist blackmail."

"You know full well we're not terrorists. No one's been hurt and there are no hostages. The people of Northern Ireland are your hostages. We've sequestered your sacred symbols of the Crown in return for our independence. Let us be free!"

She continued to grapple with her emotions. "You know you don't have the majority vote. Otherwise you wouldn't resort to stealing. You know you can ask for an election at any time. You have the British Guarantee when the majority votes in favor of separation."

"All you've done, Madam, is re-assert the Guarantee with the South in the Anglo/Irish Summits. That doesn't guarantee independence, only slavery to the South. No, Madam, you and I both know that when the people of Great Britain vote on the question of our independence, over seventy percent of them will vote to get rid of us."

"You have no majority vote for independence in Northern Ireland and I cannot consent to an election in Britain knowing that your vote will fail. If there are to be elections, then both elections must carry the question or there will be no independence." She was irritated by the man's gall. The whole idea was preposterous. "You must return the jewels. When you feel you have a majority for independence, all you have to do is request an election."

"Madam, the original 1949 Act of Ireland was not formulated by people but by politicians, and it gave us the original Guarantee of Cessation by a vote of the Parliament of Northern Ireland. You abolished Parliament and changed the Guarantee to a majority vote of the people based on unification with the South. You know that will never happen. A clever way to keep Northern Ireland as the Western perimeter base of your national security grid for NATO. Why else would you spend four billion pounds a year and countless troops trying to hold Northern Ireland? The South has never supported you in any war and it never will. For reasons of security you can't allow independence unless you are forced into it."

The professor had sensed the Prime Minister's extreme irritation by her rapid delivery, although her voice had remained calm. Good, he thought, she knows she's in a bind. He continued: "I can't return the jewels. They may wind up at the bottom of the sea unless we have those elections. It's not just the elections, Madam, we must have guaranteed economic support from you for several years until we can stand on our own two feet. As for national security, we want it too. Our Transition Plan guarantees English and US bases in Northern Ireland."

"You are wrong about security, wrong about independence, wrong," replied the Prime Minister. I mustn't lose control, she thought, and she willed herself to relax. "Our commitment has always been to protect the people of the North from harm. You deserve that protection. You are beneath the umbrella of protection of the United Kingdom, and so you shall remain."

She was feeling better now, but she realized she was getting nowhere at this point. She tried to picture what he looked like close up. The photos were not the clearest and it had been a long time since she had met him. His voice was strong and direct, without a trace of anxiety. He is a formidable adversary, she thought. Now I've got to put him off for more time. "Professor Banks, England seeded the North with Protestants many years ago and we have a commitment to support them as long as they believe they're English. Furthermore, we have a commitment to the South through the Anglo/Irish agreement to work towards breaking down the barriers to unification on issues of common interest."

"You mean you need a Western Front," said the professor. "Let's face it, the South really won't support you, and they don't want any part of the North if it's going to cost them. Five and a half million people in the South can't afford to pump four billion pounds a year into the North. The violence continues because the PIRA is uncertain about the future of the North, the loyalists are uncertain about the future of the North, and because the South is uncertain about the future of the North. Independence will answer all those questions for good.

"Madam Prime Minister, you've been searching for a solution to the 'Troubles' for years, but you've never established any long-range policy. You surely must realize that a solution to the 'Troubles' that includes either England or the South is unworkable.

"What we have now in the Independence Party is excitement and a new energy. It is a quiet, nonviolent revolution. May I remind you again that since the Norman invasion, England has raped, pillaged, and sucked Ireland, North and South, dry. The jewels are our symbolic conquest of England and for that we have earned our freedom!"

"Sir, you are insane. No matter how you say it, your request is pure blackmail, and a government founded on blackmail will not go very far."

"No, Madam, we now have over 195,000 members, half Catholic, half Protestant, middle-of-the-road people, and our recruiting effort is bringing more in every day. We do not fear the results of an election. If, after our victories in the elections, the Army is removed, the UDC and RUC disbanded, and the UN takes over, we'll have no violence."

The number of members surprised the Prime Minister. *Our estimates must be out of date.* She was irritated with the poor intelligence. The Prime Minister silently agreed with much of what the professor said. The situation had always been frustrating for her, dealing with the South, fighting the PIRA and pumping money into an economic black hole. Now she was sure she needed time to sort things out. "What is it you are planning to do next?"

"Issue a statement and the letter I sent you containing our six separate requests. I want to withhold the Transition Plan for a while until I have a positive response from you about the elections. I would prefer to issue my statement at the same time you issue yours. If you need time, I suggest we wait until tomorrow, or the day after." He was stalling until Kevin returned.

"Yes, that's fine. I need a little time to talk to the Queen and consult with my Cabinet." She needed more time to locate the jewels.

"I might make the point that if the Queen dissolves Parliament, you and your government will be off the hook. It will be the people who decide the issue. Also, how do you feel about amnesty?"

"I am opposed to it." But she knew if she decided to jail the professor and the others involved it might polarize his movement and world opinion against England. "I will have to think about it some more."

"Then may I call you again tomorrow, the thirtieth, at 11:30 a.m.?"

"Yes, you may; good-bye professor," and she hung up. He is definitely stalling, she thought. Why? He's confident enough, no reason to wait. Something nagged at her. It was his son: Kevin, she remembered. He seems to be missing. She picked up the phone, called the Director-General, and asked him to locate Kevin Banks. He gave her a brief update which yielded little new information. She asked him to be certain that security was tight on all flights and all shipping into Northern Ireland.

* * *

At three that same afternoon the Prime Minister met with her entire cabinet. It was not a pleasant meeting. When she revealed who had the jewels and briefed them on the investigation, the members were outraged beyond reason. A few excited members gave a number of suggestions on how to improve the search, including replacing Kingsly and Yates. It turned into a shouting match, and she guessed that at least half of them would gladly give up Northern Ireland. Some wanted to hang Professor Banks. One thing was certain, they all wanted the Regalia back as soon as possible. She did her

ASSAULT ON THE CROWN

best to assure them that with sound investigation and a little luck they would recover the jewels before it was time to dissolve parliament. "I expect complete silence from all of you until I'm forced to inform Parliament and the public of the professor's demands," she ordered. "I've scheduled a conference with the press at four p.m. and I fully expect to put them off." She adjourned the meeting.

* * *

The professor heard the Prime Minister's press conference and was relieved that she held her ground and only issued very sketchy information. He was still formulating his speech when the call came: "Professor Banks, if you don't stop your independence movement you'll never see Kevin again. Think about it; we'll call you again," and the man hung up abruptly.

The professor stood in shock. *Dear God, someone has Kevin. Who? They couldn't know about the jewels, but Kevin has the ring and maybe they found it. Perhaps if we start a search we can find him by tomorrow.*

He was about to call his Board when the doorbell rang. A breathless John Larkey of McIver's church stood facing him. Before he could speak the professor motioned silence, stepped outside, and closed the door behind him. When they were far enough from the house the professor said, "The house is bugged. It must be important, you took a big risk coming here. What is it?"

"The reverend has Kevin and I think I know where."

When Jason's call came through, Professor Banks got the number and called him back from another pay phone. "I've bad news, Perry, Reverend McIver has kidnapped Kevin and threatens to kill him if we don't stop the movement. I'm pretty certain he doesn't connect us with the Tower project, but he may have found the ring on Kevin. I know where they're keeping Kevin. I've got to get him out without someone getting hurt."

"Where is he?" asked Jason, just a little startled by this strange twist of fate.

"Kevin's in the basement of the reverend's church. The reverend doesn't suspect that I know."

"If he says he'll kill him, I know he'll do it. Look, Professor, none of your people have been trained in this sort of recovery operation, except perhaps Kevin. I believe I can get him out of there without hurting anyone. I have the kind of equipment to do that sort of thing and you don't. Let me do it."

"You've done more than enough already, I can't let you risk your neck any further."

"It's all right, Professor, I can handle it. I know the man and I know how he thinks, don't ask me how I know, but I do. I'll be in Belfast tonight as soon as I can catch a flight. Locate a small .22 automatic pistol with silencer and two live cartridges for me, please. I'll bring along some special cartridges of my own. Have someone ready to meet me with all the information on the church and its activities for the next few days; someone who can drive me around Belfast."

"This wasn't part of the agreement, I didn't pay you for this. I guess I can't really stop you. But you're right, we don't have anyone qualified for this."

"I'll call you from my hotel when I get in." When Jason hung up, his hands were clammy and he had a chill, even though he was dressed warmly enough for the cool night air. His ribs and nose hurt and his face stung. Damn brain anyway, he thought. Funny what it will do every time I think of home. Why couldn't I forget it? My big brother! My misdirected, mind-poisoned brother, sick and getting sicker. Not satisfied selling clothes. He had to make his own religion to feed his hatred. No doubt he'll kill in the name of God. No concept of peace, no concept of good will, just evil. Why anyone would follow him is beyond my ken.

After the professor's call, Maria drove Jason home. When they were settled in the library Jason told Maria and Craig that he was going to Belfast.

They protested. "You can't go, Jason," said Craig, "you'll jeopardize the whole operation if you get caught."

"Not possible; I'll be traveling as Robert Brian McIver. I still have my old identity papers. My brother will identify me if it ever comes to that. The professor and his people still know me as Perry Wallace." He sketched out a plan that required Craig's assistance.

Craig listened intently. "It's risky, Jason, security at the airports must be tight going over. Don't know how it is coming back. Could be bad. I'll make the arrangements and be waiting for your call. "

Jason packed his gear carefully, selecting just the right clothes for the trip, and Maria drove him to Heathrow. He kissed her good-by. "I'll miss you, Maria. You and Craig did a great job this morning with the delivery. I'll be back before you know it."

"Can't wait," said Maria as she kissed him softly, "and be careful."

10

March 30th
Riposte!

The Prime Minister sat staring into the fire, fighting exhaustion. She had been up most of the previous night pondering the problem, and today would be hectic. She had learned that Kevin Banks had been kidnapped. The call was monitored by E Branch and word passed quickly. She ordered his recovery and wanted him in London. Perhaps he could be used as another bargaining chip if he indeed participated in the raid. *I wonder how long I can hold out before telling the media who has the jewels?*

She reflected on her meeting with the Queen early this morning: the two of them sat in a quiet sitting room on the west side of the inner courtyard at Buckingham where the morning sun shone through the richly draped windows, casting a golden glow on an otherwise gloomy conversation. She had made it a point throughout her tenure in office to keep the Queen fully informed on government affairs, more so than any of her predecessors. The

Queen had responded with enthusiasm, and the two women formed a quiet friendship. Over a period of time the Queen became more open and direct in asserting her opinions, always informally given and received. She felt deeply for the people and was passionate in her efforts to push for certain reforms. The Prime Minister had been able to put a few of the Queen's suggestions into effect.

This morning the two of them felt more unsettled than ever before. She remarked to the Queen. "It's clear to me that the jewels are in safe hands. Whether it's blackmail, 'kidnap' for ransom, or 'sequestering' isn't too important at this point. We'll never see the jewels again until Professor Banks has his vote. The professor is calling again at 11:30 this morning and I expect he'll set a date for his announcement even though his son is being held, apparently by some extremist group. I'll try to stall him as long as possible to give us more time to find the jewels. The reports of yesterday and last night tell me the investigation is going slowly. I'm afraid, your Majesty, that I'll be soon asking you to dissolve Parliament on the fourth so we may hold an election on the fifth and vote the question. At least that will take all of our esteemed politicians off the hook."

"You seem to be caving in very soon." The Queen was direct, and the barb stung her.

"I lost a few hours sleep last night over the question of the 'Troubles'. Can you think of any other way we can end the 'Troubles' and avoid wholesale bloodshed except through independence?"

The Queen sighed. "No, not really. It seems the Irish problem is a stalemate that is eternal. Is there to be a civil war too?"

"Too many groups in the South and the North will welcome our withdrawal and the North's independence; a few skirmishes perhaps, but no civil war. The professor's movement is growing by leaps and bounds. If gerrymandering is eliminated, as their plan proposes, and the Catholics have a fair say in the government, the Catholics will stay in the North. I don't think any of them really want to move South, they like the North. The professor's Transition Plan separates church and state, and if we support them economically for a time, with the help of the United States and others, they'll make it on their own eventually."

"How do you know the voting will be in favor of independence?"

"We've had a number of polls here at home that tell us our people would just as soon be rid of Northern Ireland. As for the vote in Northern Ireland, the new movement appears to be getting the upper hand and will very likely gain a majority. Anyway, in twenty-five years the Catholics will have the majority through faster proliferation, and it's possible they would vote for a union with the South. I would rather see independence first."

The Queen rose and went to the window as if to gather strength from the fleeting sunbeams. She was thinking about the others. She always regarded the Scots as Scotland, the Welsh as Wales, and the

Irish as Northern Ireland as well as the South. "You know, Irish history is filled with bloodshed and tears brought on by my forefathers and their predecessors. But English history has been fraught with bloodshed and tears, triumphs, and defeats. We have risen to great heights as a world power and now we are slowly shrinking back to our origins. I am proud of the United Kingdom and proud of our people." She returned to her chair and looked directly into the eyes of the Prime Minister, who recoiled from the deep sadness in her eyes. "We have been free here at home of internal violence over religion for more than 170 years; we are economically sound; perhaps it is time we let the Irish find their own way."

The Prime Minister was surprised by the Queen's directness. She knew the Queen to be a strong woman not prone to give in easily. She answered the Queen: "Some have accused us of not programming the future, of sidestepping issues and dragging our feet. Perhaps we have; the North has been an exasperating, frustrating problem. We haven't solved very many problems there, but independence, correctly handled, might be the answer. It is not an easy matter letting go of a valuable possession. Perhaps it's time to consider the next hundred years and prepare ourselves for a better future here at home."

The Queen took a last sip of tea, then the two women stood and the Queen said with a deep sigh of sadness: "Thank you, Madam Prime Minister, for sharing your thoughts with me." And she left the room looking a little older and a little more tired than when she came in.

The Prime Minister suddenly felt very much alone in the room warmed by sunbeams that could not brighten her thoughts. It struck her that the Queen no longer cared about the jewels.

* * *

It took Jason forever to get to Belfast. Security was tight and flights were delayed. But he had no problems getting through. He was dressed in a dark blue, lightly striped business suit, white shirt, striped tie. Looking every bit the English gentleman, he carried a rather bulky, medium-sized suitcase. He wore heavy rimmed, thick glasses and a thick, bushy brown mustache. His hair was streaked with grey and his stuffed cheeks made him appear heavier. When he stepped on Northern Ireland soil at Aldergrove Airport for the first time in over twenty years, those submerged, unwanted feelings came back. He fought them off, muttering to himself that he had more important things to worry about. When he concentrated on the job ahead, the pains went away.

The taxi dropped him at the Forteham Hotel on Great Victoria Street, and after passing through the hotel's security check, he registered as Brian McIver, omitting the first name Robert, with an address in London. The clerk recognized the name and asked if he was related to the Reverend McIver.

"No," lied Jason, and left for his room.

The clerk, a paid informer for MI5, picked up the phone and reported the new traveler who had just checked in.

It was almost 11:00 p.m. when he reached his room. The professor recognized Jason's voice when he called, and quickly gave him a telephone number to call: "This person will help you," and he hung up.

Jason was surprised to hear a woman's voice answer his call. "I'm just in from London, and Professor Banks asked me to phone."

"You must be Mr. Wallace. I've been waiting for your call. This phone is not tapped and I am too far down in the organization to be followed. Where and when can I pick you up?" Her voice was young, soft and lilting, and her thick Irish brogue brought back memories of Patricia.

"How about at the northwest corner of Grosvenor and Durham at nine in the morning? I have heavy rimmed glasses, a thick mustache, and will be wearing a dark blue sweater with grey pants."

"Good, see you then. Pick you up in a gray Fiat."

Next morning, March thirtieth, Jason got in the small Fiat at exactly nine a.m. and sat next to a bright, cheerful girl in her early twenties. She was wearing jeans and a pink sweater. Her hair was black and her smiling eyes sparkling blue. She put out her hand, "Hi, I'm Chris Cook, and you must be Wallace. I'm your guide for the next few hours until John gets off work. Then we can have dinner at my house and you two can talk."

* * *

At precisely 11:30 a.m. the professor called the Prime Minister. "Good morning Madam. I trust you have given my proposals a considerable amount of thought. Are you prepared to agree to the terms?"

"No, I am afraid I cannot agree to your terms now. My government needs more time to study the alternatives."

"If I may interrupt, you have no alternatives."

"We can let you keep the Regalia, wherever it is, for starters, and we are pursuing other options."

The professor was not surprised at the stalling tactics and didn't mind because it suited his purpose. "I see. Perhaps you can tell me when you might be in a position to give me a positive answer."

"That will depend on when you plan to make your announcement claiming responsibility for the theft."

"Sequestering, Madam, sequestering. I can't wait beyond ten p.m. tomorrow night in order to set up a press conference for nine a.m. the morning of the first." He was hoping that Perry Wallace would have rescued Kevin by then.

"I think we might have something developed by then. Call me at six p.m. tomorrow," she replied. She knew that withholding the information from her people and the world press would create a great deal of criticism. Stalling until after April first was beyond a sensible time.

"Fair enough," answered the professor, and hung up.

* * *

The meeting room down the hall from Director Richard Yates's office looked like a war room. The rectangular room, with a long, polished meeting table and cushioned chairs, included one wall of windows that overlooked the surrounding buildings and provided a clear, magnificent view of Hyde Park. Now, most of the windows were covered with maps and photographs blocking out the pleasant view. The inside walls were covered with more maps. There were maps of Belfast, Northern Ireland, England, Scotland, London, and every major country in Europe. The photographs included huge blowups of the Crown, the Orb, the Sceptres, and the Coronation ring. The blackboard was covered with scribbled questions. A large TV screen and VCR stood in one corner. Off in another corner were five telephones linked to local and international lines, next to which sat a small computer. A large coffee pot next to the computer puffed a lazy plume of aromatic steam that seemed to soothe the tightened nerves of those present. Yates had established this room as his principal place of business for perhaps twenty hours out of every day for the next several days. He had a cot placed in his office in case he became too exhausted to go on.

Yates sat opposite the screen with his Deputy Director, David Browning, Kingsly of Scotland Yard, General Graham of Army Intelligence, Captain Mellon of Navy Intelligence, and Forsythe of MI6. He was certain that Kingsly was thankful at being relieved of the responsibility for the investigation. And who wouldn't be, for Yates knew it would be only the best of luck for anyone to locate the jewels by April fourth, the day before the proposed elections. It was noon, over fifty hours after the raid, and he had been without sleep since the meeting with the Prime Minister the morning before. At this moment he did not have enough information for his next meeting with the Prime Minister at five p.m. He was grateful the Director-General was able to talk her into an extra two hours. These women, he thought, they do get impatient. The information was coming in meager and slow. It was enough to make a man believe this was only a bad dream that would soon be over.

It would take all his years of experience and training to bring all the forces together into one cohesive effort. The group had just finished reviewing the German's video for the third time and were interrupted by a secretary bringing in the latest reports from each of the agencies. Yates ignored them and remarked to the group, "It was brilliant, the audacity of it all, the quickness; it includes all the elements of clear precise planning."

"Did you notice the precise flight paths that each of the units took?" asked the general. "They dropped their cannisters with great accuracy and timing. It was like a flying stunt group, every pattern was timed to the second. And they hovered far enough up and away so prop wash wouldn't affect gas distribution. They couldn't have trained together, someone would have noticed. It was all paper planning and the pilots were very good. They must surely have had a lot of flight time in a number of different types and sizes of helicopters."

"It may not be apparent to the casual observer," remarked Yates, "but this was a sophisticated venture costing a great deal of money for the three helicopters, tear gas, smoke bombs, percussion grenades, fake bullets, barges, car rentals, housing, and payoffs. There were three pilots, two co-pilots, three other men, and one woman. Where did they come from? Where did they stay? Where did they get their equipment? How did it get here? Where was it stored? Where did they all go after the raid and where are they all now? Where are the jewels?"

Kingsly got up and poured another cup of coffee: "As of yesterday morning two were still in London when they delivered the sword. The rest are probably still in England because of the travel freeze. No clear ID on either the driver or the delivery boy. Oh yes, the delivery boy was very young and wore thick, horned rimmed dark glasses but was a little effeminate. It's possible 'he' was the woman. The woman may be the key. You saw the sketch developed from the people who knew and remembered her. There's remarkable agreement on all the details of her features. We have not yet located her apartment, but when the sketch is published on TV and in the papers this evening, we should get a fix on it. The newspapers will have a field day making up lies about her.

"We've traced the titanium wire loop, the only evidence found in the Jewel House, to special packaging wire that can be bought at a number of specialty houses by the spool. It's impossible to trace an individual purchase. We know the drugs involved and are checking all possible sources. They're easily obtained, with forged documents, through chemical companies or hospital supply companies. It will take a long time to trace down a purchase that's not valid and could have been made at any time within the last five months. It's also possible that the purchase was made long before, as part of someone's regular stock."

Kingsly continued, "For hours we've grilled the personnel man who hired Mrs. Ashford, trying to piece together the forged documents that were stolen from the files, but the poor man is exhausted and doesn't remember much. It seems that she captivated him in some way. He was more interested in her voice and her mouth."

Richard Yates held up his hand to stop the Scotland Yard man and thought for a moment. "That's it!" He got up and fished out the sketch from among the mounting pile of files that covered the long table. The artist had done an outstanding job. The note that accompanied it said he interviewed ten men and ten women. The women were sharper, more critical, and thought Mrs. Ashford old fashioned and matronly to an extreme. She offset this with her persuasive manner, quick wit and good sales ability in the shops. The men couldn't pin much down except that she was nice, brought them cookies, had a nice voice, and they all could vividly describe her mouth and lips. Yates looked at the sketch of a middle aged woman, perhaps in her early fifties with a bumpy broad nose, arched, sharp eyebrows, grey streaked hair pulled back in a bun, brown eyes covered by large horned rimmed glasses, and an attractive mouth with pale red full lips.

"David, take this down to our artist and have him change the sketch to a young woman with regular features and a good hair style. Let's see what he can develop knowing the bone structure and approximate size of her features. Tell him to put her in her thirties, give her a good nose, no glasses, full head of hair, soften the eyes and eyebrows, and leave that mouth just like it is." His assistant took the sketch and left. "Let's talk about those helicopters."

Kingsly began again. "We all agree the video shows all three flew off in a southerly direction. This coincides with the reports of sightings we've been getting, except for the first few reports that came in from almost everywhere in England. There were numerous sightings southwest over Oxted, south over Tonbridge and Royal Tunbridge Wells, and southeast over Haywards Heath. They seem to end in the vicinity of Ashurst, Lamberhurst, and Oxley's Green, the farthest about thirty-five miles away." Kingsly went to a large sectional map of the London area for a hundred miles around and circled the Tower and all the sighting locations with a bright red pen. Then he connected them with a bright yellow pen, and clearly, three distinct flight paths jumped out at them, but ended abruptly in the middle of nowhere.

"General, is there any chance those helicopters can float on that personnel carrier between the skids?" asked Yates, more alert now. "Only one chopper carried men. They didn't use the other two, why put them on all three?"

"Not likely, old boy, too thin; let me run it through my technical group. I have a man on his way over with some blowups from the video that will give us a closer look," and the general went to a phone.

Kingsly continued, "We have a few square miles of empty land in each of those areas, with thick wooded sections that make it possible to ditch the choppers or scuttle them in shrouded places where they wouldn't be discovered for days."

Yates, unhappy with that prospect, went to the sectional map and with a blue pen circled five reservoirs at Saint Hill, Ardingly, Bewl Bridge, Hollingrove, and east of Rusher's Cross. He was interrupted by an Army lieutenant who entered the room carrying huge blowups of various shots of the helicopters and placed them on a stand. Two more men followed with eight or ten more blowups. Yates asked the lieutenant to explain them.

The lieutenant stood almost at attention, in his most military manner, and began to describe the work they had done. "The first batch of blowups cover the equipment, the last batch concentrates on the pilot and copilot's features. The sun was popping in and out that day, and from time to time bright reflections interfered, but what we have is not bad. When one of the choppers banked, we could see the cockpits were stripped bare, except for a large clock that's not standard equipment. The markings are standard British Army. The faces of the men," and he flashed several blowups of the pilot or copilot, each dressed in fatigues, wearing a beret and dark glasses, "were not very clear to begin with, but we did some computer enhancement work to remove their glasses and the features sharpened up a bit. They all look strangely alike and bear a faint resemblance to a young Winston Churchill."

Yates thought the blowups excellent. The features were very sharp considering the resolution of the video and the distance from camera. "These are excellent. Even if we can't tell the men apart, that single fact tells me more about the planner or one of the planners of this operation. Thank you very much." And the Army men left.

Yates turned back to the map. "Do you suppose, General, that one of our security satellites picked up the three helicopters?"

"We've already checked and the heat sources in London and the surrounding area make them difficult to distinguish through infra-red analysis," answered the general. "Visual and computer analysis of satellite pictures usually takes weeks." The phone rang and the general picked it up, listened for a moment, hung up, and returned to his seat before adding, "If the choppers were stripped down, carrying two men of average weight and little else, they would float on that thin pontoon."

Yates turned to Captain Mellon. "Could you start a team of divers and sonar men searching these five reservoirs for the remains of the helicopters as soon as possible? I believe that'll keep you busy for the for the next day or so. Please report on progress every four hours or sooner if you find something."

"Yes, sir," responded the captain, and he left the room.

David Browning returned carrying two sketches and, with a wry smile of triumph, put them up on an easel for everyone to see. "She's beautiful," he said. "The artist felt there was something Mediterranean about her, so he made a blue-eyed blond and a brown-eyed dark-haired woman. Both strikingly beautiful."

"It's the mouth," said Yates, "look how it fits perfectly with the rest of her features. Fascinating! That's what made her face so, so incongruous, the mouth and those lips." Yates started issuing orders. "David, get this off to every intelligence group in Europe, and Kingsly, how about every police station in England and Interpol. I want to keep this under wraps. Don't want to alert her if we are fortunate enough to turn up her ID."

The four men continued their review of the bits and pieces of information trickling in. They had been at it steadily since early morning and it was getting on to four p.m. The Director-General would be by to pick up Yates at 4:45. "Let's try to sum up the rest of the loose ends," said Yates. "Forsythe's group is making a list of free-agent mercenary pilots throughout the world known to take on any kind of dangerous operation. General, I understand your group is compiling a similar list. There must be hundreds. All those men have got to still be in England. We closed off outgoing travel quick enough to keep them here. But where?"

"Unfortunately, there are hundreds of possibilities," replied the general.

"We've started a search to pin down the whereabouts of each man on our list during the last two or three weeks," added Forsythe. "It's a process of elimination that may take too much time, but we've pulled out all the stops."

"Do you suppose," Yates asked Kingsly, "you could cross check each name on the list with customs for entering the country?" But Yates knew it was a long shot; they could have flown the helicopters here undetected. "How about the barges and tug?"

"First," responded Kingsly, "yes, we can cross check with customs at every entry point in the UK, but you can be sure they used forged paper work. We can only work from the passenger lists of flights and ships, a long and tedious job. It's a very slim chance that these fellows made a mistake. Second, the tug people know next to nothing. The names on the forged documents, which are very official British Army looking, mean next to nothing. We are trying to identify the manufacturer of the barges. The barges' nameplates and numbers were stripped. Shipping companies in the UK have accounted for all their barges, so we are still looking."

Yates frowned, "All right, we still have a few minutes, let's go over all the ordnance they used."

Kingsly continued, "The cannisters were aluminum, no markings, production-run pipe, could have been made anywhere, and bought anywhere; tips equipped with battery-operated nozzles that sprayed the smoke or tear gas in a large circle for excellent coverage. Some, those that were to be delayed, had a simple digital timer that was activated when a ball held by a spring hit a switch on impact. The lab analyzed the tear gas as three times more effective and a hundred times less toxic than standard CS gas, something very new to us."

"All high tech and shrewd chemistry," responded a disappointed Yates. "It bothers me that these people were not concerned about being traced with what they left behind. Who manufactures specialty ordnance materials such as cannisters of smoke and gas, clay ammunition, and grenades that scare the hell out of you, but don't do any more than shake you up? More questions for you, Forsythe."

"We're already working on it with all the available information given us by Kingsly's lab people."

Yates left the meeting and returned to his office to finish off his notes. The years at Eton, in the Army, Scotland Yard, and these last in MI5 seemed so far away now. He had left his mark wherever he served. He was a tenacious bulldog, thorough, and he rarely failed. Now it all came down to this one case. The past meant nothing. Now it was imperative he solve one of the most daring political crimes of the century.

He got up and looked out his window at Hyde Park. The streets were busy now with commuter traffic, but the park was peacefully green. The sight had always relaxed him before, but not now. He felt uneasy. He didn't like to think of failure; in fact he never thought of failure, and he wondered why the idea had suddenly struck him. It sent a cold chill down his spine. Nothing like early retirement, he thought. Well, can't worry about that now. He walked back to his desk, picked up his papers, stuffed them into a battered briefcase, and left for his meeting with the Prime minister.

* * *

Chis headed the Fiat out of central Belfast. Jason turned to her and asked, "Do you know what this is all about?"

"Yes, the professor told me you're to get Kevin out. I hope you can. John is John Larkey, my fiance´, and a member of McIver's church; our agent in place, so to speak. Funny, I guess you can say I converted him to our movement. After I met him, I convinced him the reverend was up to no good, and he became interested in the idea of independence. It wasn't long before he joined us. John's the one that found out they kidnapped Kevin and where they're keeping him. The professor told me to tell you that you have to get him out no later than tomorrow night."

"That sounds fine," said Jason. "If all goes well, we should have him out of there on time. It will depend on the activities going on at the church tomorrow night and where the reverend will be at the time. I wonder if you can drive me to the church so I can get familiar with the place."

Chris circled around the pedestrian section of downtown over to the Old Park Road in Cliftonville where the church was located. It was a small church constructed of stone and mortar, with a single spire pointing to the grey sky. The wall completely surrounding it was overgrown with thick ivy. Jason thought the place looked dreary and unkempt.

As they circled the block a second time, Jason looked beyond the iron gate guarding the cobblestone courtyard with space for several cars. The small house in back was, presumably, his brother's manse. They discovered a narrow one-way street behind the churchyard rear wall and drove through it on their last turn around the church. Then Jason directed her on an exploration of the surrounding streets and back alleys before they left the area. "I'll come back tomorrow for another look," he told her.

Jason asked to go to Milltown Cemetery, and Chris drove him along Old Park Road though the dangerous Shankhill Protestant area and then to the intersection of Falls Road and Divis. Jason was sick at the sight of the "War Zone" as Chris drove carefully through the Falls Road Catholic ghetto towards the cemetery.

Chris frowned and looked over at Jason. "This is the worst of the areas, although Turf Lodge up Glen Road, with all its bricked-up shops, and the huge Catholic housing estate of Andersontown, are just as bad. The Army squaddies are forever marching up and down, one always walking backwards to cover their ass, getting support from helicopters buzzing the roof tops."

Jason could not believe the drastic changes of

over twenty years. He was still shaking his head in disbelief when then arrived at the cemetery.

She stopped the car and Jason walked to Patricia's grave, where he stood in silence, allowing the turbulent memories and pain engulf his very soul.

Patricia had been a leader. She earned her entrance to Queens with excellent grades and her ability to lead other students. She was active in both school and community service. At Queens, when the Peoples Democracy, an informal civil rights group, was formed, she immediately joined. They were a fiery, intelligent group bent on correcting social injustice and discrimination and getting full civil rights for all the people of Northern Ireland. They stood for one man, one vote; fair electoral boundaries; freedom of speech and assembly; repeal of the Special Powers Act; and more and fairer allocation of housing and jobs. It was right for her temperament. She believed deeply in freedom and saw too much tyranny in the government. She felt she had a cause. The Peoples Democracy was misunderstood by the loyalists and Unionists, who assumed they were a front organization for Catholics. Robert Brian kept out of it. He was too busy with his studies and working for his father. Politics was not his thing.

When Patricia told him about the planned march from Belfast to Derry on New Years Day, 1969, he asked her not to go. "I've heard there is bad feeling from some quarters about 'that group of young radical students wanting to serve the Catholics'." Indeed, he had heard his father rant on about them.

His brothers were strangely silent on the issue. Loyalists had broken up several meetings and caused trouble at one of their marches in Derry in October.

"I have to go." She was adamant. "It's only seventy-five miles," she exclaimed, "and the police promised to protect us. You know Tony McGee, our secretary. Tony promised to stay close to me. Besides, no one has really threatened us, only the loyalists are rumoring trouble."

They argued for days. He forbade her to go. She was stubborn and in the end he shrugged his shoulders in hopeless defeat.

The "Long March," as it became known, to Derry, served to rekindle the "Troubles" and start today's war in Northern Ireland. The march began in Belfast with twenty-five dedicated people which by the third day had grown to an estimated six-hundred. The number of press and television people following the event had also increased. There had been some anxious moments along the way, but nothing serious.

Through it all Patricia showed her strength of character, determination, and most of all her composure. She was a tower of strength, urging people on through the confrontations. The tiredness she felt was a good tiredness and she seemed to gather more strength as each day passed. Robert Brian was worried and unhappy. True, no one had been hurt after three days, but he didn't trust the loyalists. He didn't trust his brothers.

The fourth and final day of the Long March began with the ominous news of an unruly mob torching a police car in Derry the previous night. Tired but determined, the marchers plodded on through the last ten miles to Derry without incident.

Tension mounted during the last mile before the Burntollet Bridge on the outskirts of Derry. The marchers linked arms while the police put on helmets and riot shields. Patricia walked between Tony and another man she did not know. Keeping a steady pace, they kept their heads down expecting a stone to fall at any time. None did, and they were relieved — until they reached the bridge. They moved forward peacefully, and some of the police moved out of the way.

Suddenly from side lanes and streets a wild mob began throwing bricks, boulders, and bottles, and charged the marchers. Patricia started to run with Tony, but was hit in the head during the first salvo and fell to the ground. She got up slowly, dazed, not knowing which way to go; Tony was not in sight. The mob was running fast, carrying an assortment of weapons: wooden planks, crowbars, iron bars, sticks, nail-studded cudgels, and rocks. They kicked and beat and stomped anyone in their path.

Patricia was still dazed when the first wave caught up with her. A man with an iron bar hit her viciously across the back of the neck. She tripped and started to stumble. Another hit her in the hip with a nail-studded board. The long nails penetrated her soft white flesh and scraped her hip bone. She cried out, but no one heard her; the now-hysterical, blood-thirsty crowd screamed obscenities. When she fell, it was all she could do to cover her head with her arms. Someone kicked her in the stomach, and someone else did it again. Then someone hit her with an iron bar and broke her arm and she passed out. And the mob, with Sean and George McIver among them, passed by. About half the mob were off-duty B Specials, some with known sadistic tendencies, and the other half were loyalist extremists.

Only a few of the policemen tried to stop the carnage. She lay there in a pool of blood, bleeding from the head, when she started to hemorrhage internally. Two men tried to put her in a police truck, but a demented policeman pushed her out. Two other policemen, more sympathetic, got her into the truck and took her with a half dozen others to a hospital. Fortunately she was among the first to arrive, and she received immediate attention.

Eighty-seven people were hospitalized. Besides her battered head, broken arm, and severe hip wound, Patricia had miscarried and hemorrhaged so severely she required eight pints of blood. They operated and removed a ruptured spleen. She nearly died, but somehow hung on.

Robert Brian heard the news of the attack on the radio and went into a panic. He phoned his close friend Donald McVay and borrowed his car. Traffic was heavy, filled with sightseers. It went agonizingly slowly. He kept telling himself that she was all right and that he would never forgive himself if anything had happened to her.

By the time he reached Derry the marchers had arrived at the city center, given their speeches, and disappeared into the various hotels to spend the night; many had started their journey home. Patricia was nowhere to be found until Robert Brian spotted Tony standing outside the City Hotel.

"I'm sorry, Robert. I was linked arm-in-arm with her when the whole thing started. She started to run with the rest of us. Then I turned around just as she got hit in the head with a brick. She started to fall. I tried to get back to her, but the crowd was in a panic and I was pushed backwards, away from her. Missiles were flying in all directions. I turned around again and saw this big wild eyed guy with an iron bar closing in on her. I was knocked down then and clobbered good. I saw Sean and George among them.

"When things quieted down, I began checking the hospitals until I found her at Altnegelvin. They wouldn't tell me anything or let me see her. I tried to call you, but you must have left. God, it was terrible! They beat the women as bad as the men. I'm sorry, Robert. I hope she's all right."

"Oh my God, I hope she is too. Thanks, Tony, for letting me know." And he got back in the car trying to quell the fear, trying to keep the tears back, praying all the way. He located her in the recovery room, under post-operative care. The doctors had just finished the operation. He told the nurse that Patricia was carrying his child. The nurse saw the panic in his eyes and, sympathetically, told him she had lost the baby and lost her spleen.

"She's on the edge," she said sadly to Robert Brian.

He turned away and wept. He remained at the hospital all night, and when she seemed out of danger, they moved her to a room near the nurses' station. He stayed with her through the next afternoon until she finally woke. He kissed her softly and murmured, "You're going to be all right. You'll be out of here in no time, just as good as new."

"I've lost the baby, haven't I?" She started to cry. "I can feel it. I'm different, I know it. Tell me."

"They say you did."

"Oh, Robert, it's all my fault. I've lost our baby. I won't have another one, I know it. I feel different. Oh, God, I'm sorry. I want to die."

"It's not your fault. You're going to be just fine. We'll get married. We'll have another baby. I've a place picked out where we can live until I find a job in London."

"No, no, no, I know it won't work. You won't love me if I can't have any children. Oh dear God, let me die."

He tried to console her, but it was no use. He finally got the nurse to give her a sedative to quiet her. Then her family arrived and came to the room; her mother, father, and two sisters. He explained to them, awkwardly, not knowing what to expect, who he was and what had happened. They were shocked by the extent of damage to her body. They just stood there and looked at him, not saying anything. He left them to cope with their fears and anxiety.

Robert Brian stayed at the hospital for three more nights. A kindly nurse took pity on him and each night located an empty bed where he could sleep for a little while. Patricia would wake for a while, talk a little, and then start to cry again. The nurse would bring a mild sedative. Her family came every day, usually one by one. He would try to talk to them, tell them about the future; but they treated him as an intruder into their silent grief. They were polite but aloof.

As the days passed Robert Brian became more concerned. Patricia was not responding to treatment. The doctor couldn't explain it. All the vital signs were improving, but she didn't seem to be coming out of it. "Be patient, tonight or tomorrow she'll be back with us," the doctor told him.

On the afternoon of the third day, she became hysterical. He tried everything to help her out of it, but failed. He talked to her softly, then harshly. Nothing worked.

"Why can't I die," she cried, "I'm no good to you or anyone. Why can't they let me die?" He called the nurse and got another sedative.

That night while Robert Brian was sleeping and shortly after her bed check, Patricia awoke with a terrible cramp in her stomach. She began hemorrhaging again. She didn't call the nurse. She smiled and prayed to God for forgiveness. Her life had been good. She remembered the tenderness of Robert and the wonderful times, but she had made her decision. She lay there and let the life spill out of her. She was holding her rosary when she died.

They woke him and told him what he had been half dreading, half expecting. The doctor explained that it was most likely post-miscarriage depression aggravated by the pain and shock of her other injuries. The doctor also told him that her injuries had been too severe to allow another pregnancy. He went into the room and kissed her and held her hand for as long as they would allow. He could not cry any more. He would never cry again. Then they took her away.

He left the hospital and ran. He ran until he fell. Then he would get up again and run until he dropped again. Then he would get up and do it again. He was seeking punishment for letting her go, for seeing her die. Finally he fell exhausted in the middle of the night alongside a small road outside Derry, and slept.

Jason didn't know how long he had been standing there. He said a short prayer, then took the small gold wedding ring from his key ring, dug a little hole in the ancient earth next to Patricia's marker, and buried it. He fought back the tears and told her that he was sorry; that perhaps in some way what he was doing would make amends and stop the unholy bloodshed. "I will always love you, Patricia," he said aloud, "but I can never come back to you again. Good-bye." He turned and walked back to the car.

Chris drove him north on the west side of the city nestled beneath the green, steep mountains that slope and curl gently around the city, guarding it from some unknown, giant marauder. The city, once no more than a fort at the River Farset ford, grew into a major industrial community fostered by the plantation of Protestant immigrants from Scotland and Wales during the 17th century.

Chris turned back towards city center at Greencastle, mixing in with the fast moving traffic on M1 along Belfast Lough, the city's proud twelve mile waterway leading to the North Channel of the Irish Sea. Back in the center of the city she turned east around the ferry terminal, and Jason caught a glimpse of the great shipyards, now struggling for survival, where such magnificent ships as the Titanic were once built. She turned east along Sydenham bypass and parked at Belfast Harbour Airport while Jason went into the administration building and checked the directory of aircraft charter companies.

Jason returned to the car and looked at his watch saying, "We have a little more time, I wonder if you could drive by Queens and the Gardens and then out on the road to Crumlin."

The University hadn't changed, but now Jason appreciated much more the Tudor-style design of Charles Lanyon. He wondered if graduating from Queens would have brought him the same success he enjoyed today. She drove along the Crumlin Road out towards Aldergrove Airport where the familiar scenery brought back a flood of pleasant memories. About half way to Crumlin Jason suddenly asked her to stop, park alongside the road, and wait for him. He walked over a small rise and disappeared from view.

Chris, who had been quiet during the drive around the city, watched him until he was out of sight. Throughout the trip the man appeared to be concentrating and the silence was not uncomfortable. He seemed to her to be sensitive and gracious, something that was rare and enjoyable. It occurred to her that he knew the city well and someone here was close to him. He didn't talk as though he was from Belfast, but the thought crossed her mind. In fact, the more she thought about it the more she became convinced he was Irish.

Jason walked almost a mile before he found the remains of the old feed barn that long ago had succumbed to the ravages of time and weather. He remembered the first time he made love to Patricia, and the many times after. The pleasant memories of their young love gave him a good feeling. He stood for a few moments beneath the tree where they first picnicked, gave the rough bark of the tree trunk a little pat of affection and said another goodbye.

When he returned to the car Chris noticed his steps were a little lighter and the sadness that gripped him earlier had disappeared. He smiled at her and said, "Thanks, Chris, I guess you can take me to your place now and we'll wait for John."

* * *

Fred Press sat in his office thinking about his delightful predicament. Richard Yates had offered him anything in the world he wanted in the way of equipment and manpower from any of the services. His problem was what to do with them all. He had ordered three surveillance vans fully equipped with men, recorders, cameras, and high tech listening gear. He stationed one at the professors house, one at the Independence Party office and the third at the Reverend McIver's church. The van assigned to McIver arrived and parked across the street from the church an hour after Chris and Jason drove away from the area.

I just don't know what that maniac minister is going to do, Press thought. I suspect he's the one who's holding Kevin Banks. He seems to be stepping up his activities against Professor Banks. Up until now Press had not had the manpower to infiltrate; now he was frantically searching for someone who fit in and could make a connection. His efforts to wire tap and bug the church had so far failed; lately the church appeared to have a twenty-four hour guard. It was a little curious, but the man did have a paramilitary unit and was known for his paranoia.

He picked up the dossier on McIver and browsed through it again, hoping to get an idea: "Never married, a womanizer, and running with an extreme Unionist bunch. He didn't think the church he belonged to, one of the largest in the North, was hard enough on the Catholics, so he split and started his own church about five or six years ago. Calls it the New Protestant Convention Church. The man is a raving, maniacal, lunatic preacher that typifies the fearful Protestant. He denounces Catholicism and Rome. He pedals fear to his parishioners. He feeds them fear of becoming a Catholic majority, fear of being sold out by the British, and fear of losing their liberty to the Catholic laws of the South.

He keeps his people in line; a cruel disciplinarian demanding unquestioning obedience. Has established an illegal paramilitary force, believes in answering murder with murder, and would never give in to the PIRA. His group has been suspected of inciting the PIRA to violence. So far none of his people have been caught."

Press put the dossier down. *The surveillance van would be our first step to finding the right time for installing the bugs; and while we're watching we may pick up something new.*

When Press read the report from the clerk at the Forum Hotel, he checked the reverend's file again and found that his missing brother's name was Robert Brian McIver. Could be coincidence, he thought, but we had better check him out over the next few days. He assigned a young man named Brady from MI6, who was new to the service, to follow the man registered at the Forteham Hotel as Brian McIver.

He then called Yates and told him about the new arrival, McIver, then asked him to run a check on the London address. "Time is critical," said Yates, "we are shooting for the third as the last day we have to recover the jewels."

"I could use four more technicians to install bugs in the houses of the Party's ten-member Board. The Board are all so damned straightforward about everything but membership and money. They probably don't know about the jewel connection yet. I don't expect much, but it's worth a try. I've had a twenty-four hour watch on the professor since yesterday, and everything is normal. We're checking out a telephone number the professor gave someone in a rather cryptic phone call late last night."

"We'll send over the technicians today," replied Yates. "Keep up the good work."

Press hung up the phone feeling more anxious than ever. It'll be an uneasy wait until we get some sort of break, he thought.

* * *

At five p.m. the Director-General entered the Prime Minister's office followed by Director Yates. Yates went over the entire events of the investigation and gave her the new sketch of the woman. He pulled out the original sketch of Mrs. Ashford and put them side by side.

"Marvelous," said the Prime Minister, "congratulate the artist for a job well done. If we find her, we find the jewels. It's the first time there's been anything good to talk about since the day of the Tower. Nice work, Director, I do appreciate your efforts. Some of my colleagues are screaming for your neck. This will quiet the barking dogs." A look of triumph crossed her face.

"Thank you for the support, Madam," replied Yates. "I believe we'll find out who the woman is once the European agencies have a look. She's a professional and well trained; she must be known to someone on the Continent. I want to wait for a day or two before releasing her picture to the public. If she believes she's safe, she may make a mistake. Once we know her identity we can trace her movements during the last few months. We might link her with others on the team and track them down. I realize you want to know when we might locate the jewels. I believe we can fit all the pieces together by the day after tomorrow, that would be April first. It'll give us at best three days to find the jewels."

"I suppose that's the best you can do; I wish we had a guarantee. The professor plans to hold his press conference on the first. I intend to issue a statement shortly afterwards. Let's meet again at this same time tomorrow." After the two men left, the Prime Minister felt encouraged, almost happy with the news. She scribbled a few notes for her press conference at six p.m., wishing the day were over.

* * *

When John Larkey came through the door of Chris's apartment Jason recognized him as the young man in the gray suit who five months ago had followed him from his farmhouse meeting with the Professor to Dublin Airport. John did not suspect this Perry Wallace was the old man who had given him the slip.

Disturbed and wary of the young double agent, Jason spent the better part of two hours questioning him about his past, his philosophy, and the origin of his alliance with Reverend McIver. It had been John's father who started his prejudice by constantly preaching against the Catholics. Jason was reminded of his brothers Sean and George, who were sucked into the morass of religious bigotry by the same kind of preaching from his father.

Once, while Chris was out of the room, John confessed to Jason that he had taken part in the killing of a man at the reverend's orders, and that he had been in a state of remorse ever since. A chill ran down his spine as he told Jason that Reverend McIver, vengeful over the PIRA murder of a parishioner, a barrister who defended a Protestant killer and won the case, ordered the killing of a PIRA man: "An eye for an eye my Bible says, and by damn, we'll do it," the reverend told them, "now go and find him." John, Jack Brinker, and George Dermont had tracked down a PIRA man in a barn in Derry and killed him. They had been excited, egging each other on, mesmerized by the reverend.

John had squeezed the trigger. Squeezed again. The softness of the silencer did not leave a vivid impression, just a quiet grunt. The man fell over. Didn't move. Dead. John turned back through the door, went outside, and vomited. No matter what, he thought, never again. It was his first and last murder.

Later he met Chris, quite by accident, in a pub. She and two friends came recruiting for the Independence Party. It was courageous of them. They were all three Catholics in a Protestant pub in a Protestant neighborhood. They let on they were strangers in town. One word led to another and John and Chris agreed to meet again. They fell in love. Three months later he joined the Independence Party.

He had deliberated a long time, listening to the rantings of the reverend, listening to Chris preach the value of independence and the sorry state of civil rights. He confessed to her his connection with the reverend. Chris brought him to Professor Banks and when it was over he had agreed to become a spy

It shook him up, he told Jason, and this was his way of making amends; besides, he was deeply in love with Chris. Jason, using all the intuitive ability and judgment skills at his command, finally decided the young man was telling the truth.

After a lovely meal prepared by Chris, Jason chided John, "You won't remain slender very long once you marry Chris."

Over an after-dinner brandy he began firing questions at John: "Where will the reverend be tomorrow night? What is scheduled at the church? How many people will be milling about? How many men will be on guard, and where? What kind of car does he drive? Where are the keys to the room where Kevin is kept? How big is the office? Where is the door to the room?"

John answered them all without hesitation: "The bible class starts at 7:30 p.m. and the reverend almost always remains in his office until about 8:15 p.m., when he comes up to the meeting with his message for the week. At that time everyone is upstairs in the church except one or two fellows who cover the courtyard. Sometimes it's one man and sometimes it's two. You just never know."

"Does the reverend carry his keys to his car?" asked Jason.

"As far as I know, always."

"John, I want you to obtain an ambulance and have it parked at this spot at 7:45 p.m. tomorrow night," and Jason drew him a map. "Then I want you to arrange for a doctor from City Hospital to fill out official transfer papers for Reverend McIver from City Hospital to Oxford University Hospital. Finally I need a chartered flight ready at eight p.m. to fly to Oxford. Think you can do it?"

John whistled softly. "I'll need help from some of the Board members, but I believe it can be done. I guess I should get started now. By the way when do you want the .22 pistol?"

"Chris can bring it when she picks me up at eleven in the morning." He looked over at Chris: "I hope you don't mind. I'll be wearing a dark grey suit. Meet me at the same place. I'll have to spend some of my free time here with you until it's time to go tomorrow night."

"That's fine with me," she answered. "I'll make you and John a good dinner."

When Jason returned to the hotel he noticed the young MI6 man sitting in the lobby looking bored. Out of the corner of his eye he saw the clerk nod to the young man as he picked up the key to his room. Jason went up to his room, made a close inspection, found nothing disturbed, returned to the lobby, and went out for a walk. He walked down Great Victoria Street to Chichester and strolled past

Donegal Square. He spotted the young man following him when he turned the corner. He walked slowly past his brother's shop, disappointed that nothing much had changed since he left, then made a complete circle around the town center and returned to the hotel. Well, he thought, there have been some changes and a few remodelings, but much was the same as before. The young man continued to follow him directly into the hotel, and Jason smiled to himself.

11

March 31st
Mission: Rescue !

During breakfast, Jason paid little attention to the young man who sat a few tables away reading a newspaper. Jason settled his hotel bill and told the clerk he would be leaving at noon. Once in his room Jason removed his suit from the closet and carefully turned it inside out, revealing a dark grey wool suit typically worn by Protestant ministers. From his suitcase he extracted a small, battered valise, and emptied its contents on the bed. He took the empty suitcase down a back stairway and dumped it in a large trash bin behind the hotel.

At 10:55 a.m. an aging minister dressed in a grey suit with an ecclesiastical white collar, white mustache and goatee, greying hair at the temples, and a battered grey felt hat walked through the lobby and out the door. The clerk saw him leave, but thought no more about it. The young MI6 man, Brady, watched the old minister leave the hotel and went back to pretending he was reading the paper. A few moments later another agent entered the lobby and told Brady, "It took a while, but they finally talked to the apartment house supervisor in the SOHO district in London and discovered that this guy you're tailing never lived there. Press wants to bring him in for questioning." At 11:10 a.m. the two men entered Jason's room and found it empty.

Jason opened Chris's car door and said: "It's O.K. Chris, it's me."

"You gave me a fright, I wondered if some old minister was about to attack me." She drove him to within three blocks of the church and he got out.

"Wait here for me, Chris, I won't be too long." He took the narrow lane behind the church, approaching from the south along Old Park Street. About mid-way along the rear wall he found the small wooden door locked. He took his time walking around to the front wall along Old Park Street that included a pedestrian gate next to the vehicle gate. John had told him the small door was always open, but the vehicle gate was closed late at night. The church was a poor imitation Tudor design. The heavy stone and mortar walls overwhelmed the small, plain arched windows; its slate roof showed signs of repair, but more work was needed. Some stones were crumbling, some were repaired. A haphazard job, he thought, and guessed the church was poorly managed and not very wealthy.

Jason walked past both gates to the corner, but the man on duty in the courtyard did not see him. He turned around and retraced his steps along the walk, as if inspecting the wall, and carefully checked the surveillance van parked opposite the vehicle gate. He noted that the periscope was cleverly mounted on top of the van inside what appeared to be an air vent. He entered the large courtyard paved with cobblestones. A tall, heavyset man, with a scrubby beard, dark eyes, a flabby face, wearing a heavy woolen sweater, baggy pants, and cloddy shoes left his post at the top of the stairway leading to McIver's office and confronted Jason.

"Can I help you, Reverend?" the man asked in a rough, curt voice.

"Why yes, young man. I'm on holiday and checking out old churches. It's a passion of mine. I collect history and design. Is the reverend about?"

"No. He's gone for a few hours. But I'm sure he'll show you around if you come back later."

"Do you know anything of its history?"

"No, I'm sorry, all I know is that it's old, maybe a hundred years or so."

"Is that his office back there?"

"No, that's his house. His office is down those stairs."

"I see. Well, maybe I can come back tonight."

"He'll be busy with prayer meeting and Bible study tonight, maybe tomorrow would be better."

"Yes, well, maybe so. Thank you," and Jason, satisfied with his plan, returned to the car. He was looking forward to another good meal with Chris and John.

Late in the afternoon, while Chris went shopping, Jason took a stroll trying to forget his younger days, and yet failing somehow to do so. The surrounding territory kept jogging his memory. He remembered Patricia. Then the dark memories of his brother crept in and the unwanted feelings returned. He fought them off, yet wondered if he would see Sean tonight. And then it all suddenly came back, unstoppable —— It was the day after Patricia died when Robert Brian reached home, dinner time, and his two brothers and father were eating. "Where in the hell have you been?" asked his father.

"To Derry, a friend of mine was hurt."

"Damned ignorant kids. Shouldn't get involved. The Papist pigs got what they deserved."

"Damn you, you don't know what you're talking about. Protestants marched too. Marching for civil rights, social reform. You know, it's called freedom. The right for any person to be treated like any other person. Instead you get a bunch of Protestant Nazi thugs who don't have any sense, beating the hell out of everyone. No one understands. It's not a Catholic movement ... "

His father got up out of his chair: "You can't talk to me that way, Robert! Get the the hell out of here, now."

"Not until I tell you, the three of you, that you are bigots, rotten fucking bigots who can't see beyond your orange noses. Your false fears, hate, and prejudice will lead to your destruction; the destruction of this country. You wait. You've started a goddamned war and the killing won't stop."

His father was sputtering. None of his sons had talked to him like that before. It was blasphemy. Sean was getting more and more angry. "Listen, you little bastard," he said, "your thinking has never been right. If a war was started, then I'm damned glad I was there to help it along. You should have seen the buggers run. It felt good taking out a few."

Robert Brian's rage was suddenly and irrevocably uncontrollable. He dove across the dinner table, spilling, scattering, breaking everything in sight, grabbed Sean by the throat with both hands, and squeezed as hard as he could. As tired and exhausted as he was, his grip was like a vise. Whatever guilt he carried was all in his hands; whatever pain he felt was all in his hands; whatever frustrations he had were all in his hands; whatever hate possessed his soul was all in his hands. His brother tried to break his grip, but couldn't.

Sean felt the breath, the life, going out of him. His face turned red and his eyes began to bulge. Robert Brian was yelling into his ear. "You fucking murderer, fucking murderer, fucking murderer." Before Sean would die, before his last breath would be taken, his father and brother George managed to get each of Robert Brian's arms and break his grip. They picked him up, struggling to get free, and pinned him to a chair.

Sean McIver was holding his throat, gasping for air, breathing heavily; he had been near death, and it scared hell out of him. Then he saw his brother in the chair and a cruel, maniacal rage gripped him. He got up, steadied himself, and hit his brother as hard as he could. The first blow broke Robert Brian's nose. The second loosened four of his front teeth and split both lips. The next broke a rib and the last broke another rib.

"Enough," and his father stepped between them. Robert Brian had passed out with the blow to the mouth. His father took his drooping head and slapped at it unmercifully. "Wake up, you little bastard. I want to talk to you." They paid no attention to the heavy bleeding from his nose and mouth. They carried him upstairs to his room and dumped him on his bed.

Sometime later, when Robert Brian regained consciousness, it took him an eternity to figure out where he was. He lay face down, and that had saved him from choking to death on his own blood. He tried to move, but the pain in his side wouldn't let him. He fought exhaustion. He couldn't breath through his nose. He struggled to get up and finally, with excruciating pain, managed to raise himself off the bed. He got to the bathroom and washed his battered face. Sensing they had left, probably to the pub, he worked his way down the stairs to the phone, and called Donald McVay.

Donald drove him to Altnegelvin in Derry where Patricia had died. He had become friends with the doctors and nurses and they would know what to do. A horrified nurse took him to emergency. The doctor strapped his ribs, sewed up his lips, and straightened his nose. Years later, when he could afford it, he would have plastic surgery to remove the bump on his nose and the scars on his lips. The hidden scars of love, hate, and terror would remain in the dark recesses of his brain forever.

Robert Brian had missed Patricia's funeral. Four days later Donald picked him up at the hospital and drove him to the cemetery, where he laid a wreath. They drove home, where he stayed with Donald and his family for two weeks until he could move without pain.

One day he waited until his father and brothers were out of the house, went in, and packed his things. He cashed in his bank account and took his stock certificates with him. He thanked Donald and his family for their help and caught a plane to London. Robert Brian McIver died that day.

* * *

The MI5 surveillance agent was in his twelfth hour of boring duty and his relief hadn't arrived yet. He put the film in the processor and waited for it to come through. He examined it carefully and found the results perfect. He tracked the minister on camera from the moment he came into view, following as he went to the corner, turned around, and walked back to the courtyard. For once he was lucky, because the man on duty in the courtyard stopped the minister in his line of sight, the center of the gateway, and he was able to record all of their conversation. He would get it all to headquarters as soon as his relief showed up.

* * *

It had been a busy day for Fred Press. The extra

agents were submitting a constant stream of reports. Most were meaningless, except for the report on the arrival of Brian McIver. The man puzzled him. His address was false and he gave no indication that he was aware of his surveillance. Then he pulled a neat move on young Brady and simply disappeared. It was nearing five p.m. when he found time to review the film from the three vans. He selected the two films covering the professor's activities first, read the transcriptions, and found nothing of interest except that he had met young John Larkey at the University in the morning. No conversation had been recorded. That's odd, he thought, Larkey is one of Reverend McIver's men. He told his secretary to assign the next available man to Larkey.

It was nearing six o'clock when he began the review of Reverend McIver's church activities. The report told him there had been virtually no unusual activity except for a visiting minister. McIver had left at 10:30 a.m. for a tour of parishioners and had not returned at shift change by 1:30 p.m. The visitor had arrived about 11:30 a.m. and stayed for just a few moments. He read the transcript of the conversation between the man in the courtyard and the minister and switched on the projector.

The minister walked back and forth and then entered the courtyard. As Press studied the film he suddenly realized it was the walk of the man he had followed in Calais five months ago! He sat there stunned, trying to fit the pieces together. Why was a man left in the courtyard all day long with nothing to do? It had been a practice for just a week now. Maybe the reverend suspects we're watching, he concluded. But what's this minister doing at this church five months after meeting young Kevin? Press's intuition nagged at him about Kevin. *McIver has him somewhere; he must!* He listened to the tape of the conversation at the church and compared it with his tape from Calais. He had caught very little of the conversation in Calais, but enough to tell him the voice of the priest and the voice of today's minister were identical. When Press reached Brady the young man told him that he did see a minister leave the hotel shortly before eleven that morning. A priest, a minister, and Brian McIver; were they the same man? Press grabbed his coat and left for the church.

It was a little before seven o'clock when the MI5 Chief parked his car just four car lengths behind the van across from Reverend McIver's church. Two of his agents were in place as night "strollers" on the streets surrounding the church. Their small walkie-talkies were working perfectly and all four of them began a running conversation. The man in the van brought him up to date. Nothing unusual, except the reverend and two of his men spent two hours in his office during the late afternoon.

At seven a few early arrivals for the church meeting parked in the courtyard until it was full. Late arrivals parked on the streets nearby. The constant dialogue with the "strollers" indicated the large crowd was ordinary and subdued. The man in

ASSAULT ON THE CROWN

the van explained to Press that he had a limited view of the courtyard and could see only part of the reverend's manse, but had a clear view of the entry stairwell to his office. He reported that McIver had gone down to his office at 6:55 p.m. The man on duty in the courtyard chatted with some of the people before they went inside the church; all small talk.

Fred Press sat listening to the chatter and became more unsettled as the minutes ticked by. *Something is going on. I know it. I can feel it.* His years of experience had given him a sixth sense in situations like this. He continued to sit and watch people straggle into the churchyard and then to the church. No one seemed to use the small pedestrian gate.

* * *

Chris drove Jason to within two blocks of the church and left him there alone. He was thankful that John had arranged everything so quickly. He didn't want to put off this mission. Everything had fallen into place; the equipment and the documents were all prepared. It was left to Jason to do the rest. He had called Craig from a pay phone during the day and made certain that arrangements were complete on his end. It will be another stomach twister tonight, he thought.

At 7:35 p.m. he began his walk to the church. He was wearing the new leather jacket that Chris had bought for him, a beret, grey pants, heavy rimmed glasses, and a thick brown mustache. He passed the

MI5 "stroller" and his instincts told him the man was most likely an agent. When he rounded the corner the van was parked in the same spot. He did not see Fred Press slouched low in the car parked a short distance behind the van until he neared the courtyard entrance. He suddenly slowed and almost turned to give it up. *The surveillance is heavy. Why are these fellows here? Are the ambulance and charter ready after all? Has John turned us in? He can't know about the jewels yet.* He weighed his chances. It was overcast, hiding the moon. Without the light over the stairwell the courtyard would be dark.

Jason, more tense than he had been in a long time, made his decision, walked through the vehicle gate into the courtyard, then turned towards the parked cars where he would be out of sight of the van. The tall, heavyset man with the scrubby beard and cloddy shoes, did not recognize Jason: "If you're here for the meeting you have to go to the front entrance."

"Sorry," said Jason, "I don't go to the meetings. I'm here looking for my car. My wife says she goes to these meetings, but I don't trust her. I didn't see it along the street. I thought she may have parked it in here. I think she's fooling around with a friend of mine."

The big man looked at him with a grin. "One of those, huh?"

Jason maneuvered his way in between two cars drawing the big man into the darkness next to the east wall of the courtyard. "Maybe so and maybe not, this looks like it here. Got to get a better look."

He was out of sight of the van and the cars behind it, the big man close behind him; Jason whirled and caught him in the nose with spray from a small can he held in his hand. The man grunted in surprise and fell in between the parked cars. Jason quickly taped his mouth, tied his hands behind him, and bound his feet. He waited a moment, heard no sounds, then casually walked across the courtyard to the top of the stairs and went down. He didn't switch off the stairwell light.

The man in the van saw him and reported it to Fred Press: "It looked like the man who just came up the street; leather jacket, beret. Don't see the other fellow yet, he's taller."

"Let me know the moment you see him," ordered Press.

Jason used a small penlight to examine the lock, selected a pic from a small case, and went to work. In a few seconds the lock clicked and he quietly opened the door, listened for sounds, then stepped inside, closing the door softly behind him. In the dim light he could see one wall of the office and little else. He heard nothing but muffled murmurs from people above. Then he thought he heard the rustling of paper, but couldn't be sure. He felt for his gun, as if to reassure himself, took a deep breath, and moved silently, quickly, into the room. The dim light cast dark shadows on the face of the man at the desk until he looked up at Jason: "I thought I told you to stay upst ——"

Jason moved close to the desk nearer the light.

"What's a murderer like you doing masquerading as a reverend, Sean?"

"Who in the hell are you?"

The flashback in Jason's mind was unstoppable. He fought it off; didn't want to lose control, interfere with what he was doing.

"Remember me?" and Jason removed his beret, the mustache and glasses.

Sean McIver looked astonished: "Robert, Robert Brian, my little lost brother, my scared brother. Older and a little heavier. What the hell are you doing here?"

Jason stared at him. "What kind of man are you? What kind of reverend are you? Who would follow you anyway with your sick ideas?"

"Ah, little brother, I'm a good reverend. People pay and I preach the truth, as I see it. They love it and they love me. I know who my people are and how to tell them what they want to hear. Are you friend, or enemy come back for revenge?"

"You'll have to decide that. Why aren't you up with your flock?"

"My boys take care of the first hour and get them all whipped up, then I go up and put the capper on. What happened to my man in the courtyard? How did you get in here? Why are you here?"

"Your man is sleeping on the job now. You'll have to do something about him. Perhaps you didn't teach him well enough. How's George?"

"Running the store and paying homage to me. He's married, got two kids. That's not why you're here; what is it you want? I'm due upstairs in a few minutes. Why not join us so I can convert you."

"Not on your life, dear brother. You haven't changed those warped, insane ideas of yours in twenty years. In fact, it sounds like you've gotten worse. Northern Ireland doesn't need you to murder Catholics to force them out; they won't go. I've come for Kevin. Where is he?"

The reverend gripped the desk, knuckles white, trying to control his anger. "I don't know what you're talking about. You're still raving for those Pope-loving bastards who want to take us over. Well, it won't happen. We will always be British and I'll die first before I let it change." His eyes were getting that wild look and his face reddened as he stood up facing Jason, looking down at him.

Jason remained calm. "Always the bully, always the bigot, always the racist, always your way, peddling your own private hatreds. You and the idiots that follow you will let this country run down into economic and social ruin and kill it. You keep it up and there'll be no more Ulster."

"Here, now, little brother, you're getting excited. I've got followers of the same mind. We believe in our Protestant rights. The Papist dogs need not live." His voice was rising, his lips were moist as if he were frothing and his face became bright red. "We'll not stop; we'll keep on until we drive them out, the IRA and the Catholics; we'll win! And now, little brother, get the hell out of here and go back to wherever you've been cringing for the last twenty years. No! Instead, why don't you go straight to hell!"

"Where is Kevin?"

"I don't know. If you don't get out I'll take you out myself, just like I did the last time." He was excited and his big frame shuddered a little as he stood there scowling at Jason, who noticed that the deep lines of hate and misery in his face made him look much older. Jason guessed Sean weighed close to sixteen stone, overweight and out of shape, but he did not underestimate his cruel strength.

"You'll not jump across at me again, dear brother," said Sean, and as he moved around the corner of the desk towards him, Jason drew the small gun quickly and fired once. The bullet hit his brother in the cheek, disintegrating in a powdery cloud of smoke spattering his cheek with a red dye. The bullet's impact stung Sean, the surprise shook him and stopped him in his tracks. He reached up and felt his cheek, withdrew his hand, and stared at what appeared to be a bloody mess. "Jesus, oh Jesus Christ what have you done?"

"I almost killed you once, and now it would be easy. You're as good as dead, big brother, if you decide to move again. The next one is real, now sit down."

Sean sat down fingering his cheek, the sting still smarting. No one had ever pointed a weapon at him, let alone fired one. He was always telling someone else where to point them, when to fire them. No one would dare shoot him, he was invincible. He was right, wasn't he? He had always been right before. He stared at his brother and for the first time recognized the look of determination on his face, the fire in his eyes.

Jason was fighting back those unwanted pains with his every fibre, the memories still burning in him. He went to the door that led to the inside stairway upstairs and locked it. He came back to the desk and looked down at his brother. "You murdered a long time ago and God only knows how many times you've murdered since. I really don't think you're fit to live. Now for the last time; where is Kevin?"

"I don't know . . . "

Jason squeezed the trigger and shot him in the other cheek.

His brother recoiled in horror. He was stunned and sat there in disbelief. For the first time in his life his body began to shake with fear. "You're a madman, you son of a bitch."

"I don't have any more of those funny bullets. The next one is the real one, so where ——"

There was a knock on the inside door and a muffled voice said, "Reverend, are you in there? We're ready for you upstairs."

Jason imitated his brother's deep brogue and answered, "I'll be up in ten minutes, keep them busy."

"All right," the voice answered, and Jason heard muffled footsteps go up the stairs. He turned to his brother again. "For the last time, where is he?"

"I don't know . . . " and Jason shot him again, but this time the pop of the silencer was a little louder from the heavier charge of the live bullet as it ripped through the shoulder of his brother's jacket, tearing a little flesh, bringing a little blood, a spike of pain, and burying itself with a soft thud in the back of his wooden chair. His brother slid back in his chair in horror and capitulated. "All right, all right, you crazy bastard, no more. He's in the storeroom, there."

"Keys, please."

"There on that hook next to the door."

"Now, brother, get on the floor face down, hands behind your back, and stay there." Jason, gun leveled at his brother, put on his mustache, glasses, and beret, eased back to the door, reached the keys, and unlocked the door. "You can come out now, Kevin, it's Perry."

Kevin recognized Jason's voice and slowly walked out of the room holding his left side.

In the dim light Jason could see that his left eye was almost swollen shut and there was an ugly, open cut on his left cheek that could probably use two or three stitches. His lips were swollen and puffy. "What happened to you?" asked a disgusted Jason.

"I made too much noise this afternoon and they decided to shut me up. I heard you just now, but couldn't make out who it was, so I shut up."

"Nice gentle men of God. Can you travel?"

"I think so. My ribs hurt like hell, I think they're cracked."

Jason kneeled down and pulled a ring of keys from his brother's pocket, then said, "Get up, you slimy bastard. We're going for a walk to your car. If you try anything, anything at all, I'll kill you.

When you get to the top of the stairs, Kevin, reach around and turn off the light above the stairwell, keep low and go straight across the courtyard to the row of parked cars. Once there we can work our way between the cars and the east wall. We want the reverend's car, the blue BMW at the far end of the courtyard next to his house. Stay out of the line of the surveillance van across the street, it's probably MI5." Jason reached around and slapped tape on his brother's mouth, jabbed him very hard in the back, and said, "All right, get up, and move quickly now."

* * *

Fred Press was sitting in his car nervously waiting for something to happen. Everything appeared normal enough; people going to a weekday church meeting; nevertheless, he felt uneasy. The last straggler talked to the tall man guarding the courtyard and they walked out of sight towards the parked cars next to the east wall.

The agent in the van was bored when he adjusted the camera for night filming and switched his little periscope to the infra-red range. He was tired of listening to the chit-chat on the radio and his thoughts turned to the fishing trip he was about to take next day. He saw the two men, then lost them.

Still daydreaming, a few moments later he saw the straggler go down the stairs to the office and duly reported it.

"Keep watching," Press replied.

As the minutes ticked by, the agent's neck stiffened and one eye became a little blurred. He was wondering what happened to the tall man when it suddenly went dark in the courtyard. He called to Press, "Did you see that? The light above the stairwell just went out and it's darker than hell over there. I think I see movement. I'm adjusting the infra-red unit now. Yes, I see one, no, two, no, three men just ran towards the cars next to the east wall. Now they're gone, out of my line, can't see or hear anything."

Fred Press sat upright. "Look again; see anything?"

"Nothing. I swear there were three men."

Fred Press switched on his engine and called his "strollers": "Get your asses to the church gate on the double. I'm going in there and take a look." He stepped hard on the accelerator and spun the car out from behind the van. As he began his skidding turn into the gateway two ultra-bright lights, appearing enormous in the darkness, suddenly thundered towards him. The bright glare caught him by surprise, momentarily blinding him, forcing his survival instincts to take over; he swerved to the right and stopped inches from the ivy covered wall. The blue BMW missed him by a fraction of an inch as it sped by, turned a sharp right, and headed towards the corner.

Jason, behind the wheel of the BMW, turned a sharp right again and hit the accelerator. One of the "strollers", who had been running hard, stopped suddenly, did a double-take, and turned in time to see the BMW reach Cliftonville Road and turn right.

Jason saw no one in the rear view mirror, but didn't ease up. His hands were sweaty, his heart beating fast, but he was in control. He cranked up the speed for another four blocks, turned right again, and doubled back towards the Old Park Road following a route he had mapped out during his scouting trip with Chris. Jason turned into a side street, slowed, pulled up behind a parked ambulance, switched off the engine, switched off the lights and waited.

Sean was lying on the floor of the back seat, Kevin holding the gun against his head. "Keep him still for a few moments," said Jason. Then he got out of the car and ran to the ambulance. "John, Kevin and I will get McIver into the ambulance. Once inside, move it!" Jason pushed his reluctant brother into the ambulance and onto the stretcher, where Kevin helped him strap Sean down.

John Larkey gunned the ambulance and, once clear of the area, turned up the speed, siren blasting, all the way to Belfast Harbour Airport. Jason injected Sean with a small dose of Thiopental Sodium to shut him up. He removed the tape from his mouth and wiped the dye from his cheeks.

Before the drug took effect Sean McIver, angry and vicious, spat at his brother. "You can't hide me or keep me anywhere. I'll get out and I'll find you, bastard brother. And when I do I'll kill you with my bare hands," and with that last burst of enraged energy Sean McIver passed out.

Sean's remark did not go unnoticed by Kevin: "Is he really your brother? Are you a McIver?"

"It's a long story, not worth repeating," said Jason.

And Kevin dropped the subject, remembering that his friend had called him Jason when they left the Tower on the chopper.

The ambulance roared through the airport gate, stopping just long enough for security clearance. Fortunately, all the attention was on flights arriving from Britain. Security was lax on flights to the great island. Jason showed the guard the papers signed by the doctor at City Hospital transferring the patient, Sean McIver, to University Hospital in Oxford. The guard looked at the patient, shook his head in sympathy, and waved them through.

John pulled the ambulance up to the ramp of the chartered flight and helped Jason carry the stretcher, with his brother on it, on board. Jason thanked John for his help and wished both men good luck. The jet took off for Oxford Airport, a short flight of forty-five minutes. John drove Kevin to Chris's place where Kevin could stay out of sight and call his father.

* * *

Fred Press' moment of fear cost him the chase. *Damn! I should have let the bastard hit me head on, at least I would have had him.* He called the van as he swung his car backwards, straightened it out, and took off after Jason. "Christ! How many in the car?"

"One driver, that's all I could see. It's McIver's car, a blue BMW sedan, turned right next corner."

The "stroller," still puffing, reported as Press turned the corner, accelerator to the floor: "He went as far as Cliftonville Road and turned right." By the time Press reached Cliftonville he could see no sign of the BMW, but continued on for a mile or so before doubling back to the church. When he arrived in the courtyard, his two "strollers" were removing the tape and binding from the tall man with the scrubby beard. "Found him lying between two cars. A little groggy, but seems to be OK," said one.

"Police, what's your name and tell me what happened?" Press prodded the tall man.

"William Spinner; I was just minding my own business when this fellow came along looking for his wife's car. Next thing I know he sprays this stuff at me and I go out."

"What were you doing out here all day?"

"I just help out the reverend, see that nobody bothers the place."

"Did you see anyone leave a few minutes ago?"

The man hesitated. "No."

Press was sure he was lying. Two men from the church entered the courtyard and walked towards the stairwell. Press intercepted them: "I'm with the police, where are you two going?"

"To get the reverend," said one, "he doesn't answer our call and he's overdue for the meeting."

"Please wait here until I check his office." Press

went down the stairs to the dimly lit office. The desk was piled high with papers, books and magazines, but the room showed no signs of a struggle. He noticed the red splatter stains on some of the papers on top and the small hole in the back of the chair behind the desk. He took a small pen knife from his pocket and jabbed it in the hole, satisfied the bullet was still there.

The storeroom door was ajar, and the overhead light cast an ominous glow over the small room. As he entered, the stench of urine and excrement made him choke and forced him back. In the dim light he saw bloodstains on the floor and re-entered, holding his breath. Bloodstains were on the floor and on the cot. In one corner sat a bucket full of urine and excrement. In another corner, on the wall, scratched into the surface of one stone was the letter K.

Back in the courtyard, still trying to clear his nostrils, he said to the two churchmen, "McIver has left and probably will not be back tonight. I want to seal off his office for our laboratory people. Please continue your meeting. I'll be in to ask a few questions of your parishioners before they will be allowed to leave."

He turned to Spinner and waited until the two men were gone before saying, "You know that in Northern Ireland I can put you in jail with little reason and hold you there until you rot. I'll be dead before they let you go. If indeed they do. Now a lot is going on here that you don't understand and I'm not going to tell you. If you don't give me straight answers it's into prison for you. Tell me, did you see anyone leave here within the last few minutes?"

"Uh, yes."

"Who?"

"Reverend McIver."

"Who else? We know of two more."

"A stranger, the man who knocked me out."

"And the other man, who was he?"

"I dunno."

"You're lying," and Press turned to one of his men. "Take him down and put him away."

The tall man with the scrubby beard had been in Long Kesh prison once and knew that if he was put away again it might be forever. "All right, all right, the other fellow was Kevin Banks."

"What was he doing here?"

"Visiting."

"You're lying again. Was he locked up in that little room?"

"Look, I just help the reverend do his church work. I don't know what Kevin Banks was doing here. He was here for the last two days. That's all I know."

Press looked at the man with disgust, turned to one of his men, and said, "Take him to prison, get his urine and blood tested, then put him away for a day or two until we straighten this mess out." To his other man he said, "You stay here and wait for the lab men. I want those red spots on the papers on his desk checked out, the blood spots in that little room analyzed, and the entire office checked for fingerprints, and oh yes, the bullet in the back of the chair behind the desk."

Back at his office he relayed the events to George Yates. They both suspected the stranger and Kevin were connected with the Tower raid. They decided to arrest Kevin if they could find him. Press called for a complete check of all ports of entry, including the airports, and put every available man he could spare to work on it. Just under an hour had elapsed since the BMW came roaring out of the churchyard at him. The chartered jet carrying Jason and his brother was just making its approach to Oxford Airport.

* * *

Craig met Jason at the airport with an ambulance he had negotiated from Shady Glen. It was a very old second-hand machine recently repainted white. Neatly painted on each side was the word *Ambulance* with no other identification. The security guard at Oxford airport passed them through without question.

An hour later Jason sat across the desk from the director of the Shady Glen Sanitarium located on the River Dom not far from Ledwell in a remote, heavily wooded section on the edge of the Cotswolds. He had just handed him five thousand pounds for the first month's care of his brother.

Jason thought the director looked like Dracula. He was soft spoken, slender, with thin, long hands. His nose was much longer than average, narrow and bony, accentuating his sunken eyes and cheeks. He wore a white coat over his suit highlighted by a bright red tie, the color of blood.

The director fingered the money with genuine pleasure. "Ah, yes, thank you. We'll take good care of the gentleman."

"He's a violent man, clever and wild. He may need sedation. I'm sure you know what to do," said Jason.

"Ah, yes, yes indeed. His stay here will be pleasant enough, old chap. We'll see to that. Our rooms are plush and he will have all the comforts of home. The TV and news from the outside will be withheld as you request. He'll be supplied with gentle music and plenty of books to read. Sometimes we get the patients to start their autobiography. Good therapy, you know. He'll be put in the inner sanctum. If he should get violent and actually overpower someone, not likely you understand, not likely at all, we can stop him. Our attendants are specially selected, you see, so they are larger than most patients, and much stronger. Ah, yes, once in his room he would have to get through two security checks to escape. The second level is especially well guarded. He's in good hands; just leave him to us. You say he claims to be a reverend?"

"Yes, his name is John Sanders, but he claims to be Sean McIver. Keep him here and quiet. That's all I ask. I'll see you get another month's payment if it's necessary and a bonus if you keep him here and keep him quiet. Thank you."

Jason left the director's office and walked down a long carpeted corridor lined on either side with doors, each with a wire-screened porthole, all apparently locked. The attendant's station, with only one man on duty, contained over twenty-five TV scanners. At the main entrance a security guard removed Jason's visitor's badge and buzzed an automatic lock that opened the door. Jason took a few steps through it and stopped until the guard pressed a second buzzer opening the door to the outside.

"That man gives me the creeps, in fact the entire place gives me the creeps. It's a jail within a jail. How did you ever find it?" Jason asked Craig as he drove away.

"Never met the man before I arranged things. Just heard about it from a friend of mine a few years ago. Seems he had a cousin who was raising hell with the family after a grandfather died and left everyone a pile of money except this fellow. He was a lazy good for nothing and he was granted one pound. He went wild and threatened everyone in the family. When they found out he'd bought a gun, they hired two men to bring him here. The family all chipped in and kept him in the sanitarium for three months. When the poor man was released he was so afraid of going back that he left London for good and no one has seen or heard from him since. Seems the place is classified as a private resting home and the health authorities don't check on it."

"Any new developments, Craig? asked Jason, relieved and exhausted.

"I don't know. That ambulance had no radio, so I didn't catch the PM's eight-thirty press conference." Craig turned on the radio in Jason's Jaguar as he drove to M40 and pushed the car to top speed. They would be home by ten o'clock. Jason began twisting the dial on the radio to find out what the PM had said.

12

March 31st
Belfast Nexus.

It was almost five p.m. when Richard Yates left his "war room" wishing he had more time before his third meeting with the Prime Minister. The pieces would fit together better if he just had a little more time. Reports were coming in fast from everywhere with hardly enough time to digest them. He briefed the Director-General on the way to the meeting.

"Christ! Richard, we look like a pack of amateurs. We haven't found Kevin Banks yet. He has to be somewhere," remarked an exasperated and worried Director-General.

"Fred Press thinks McIver has him and he's set up surveillance on him and his church. He's going to move in on him soon," responded Yates. "I could've used more time for this meeting putting the pieces together. He was thankful they had reached 10 Downing quickly, although he expected the Prime Minister to be just as harsh as the Director-General.

The fire in the fireplace of the Prime Minister's

office was the only thing warming the chill in the room. The Prime Minister opened the meeting with a shocker. "Gentlemen, we've run out of time. A very good friend of mine in the media tells me that someone in my Cabinet has leaked the news. I'm afraid I'll never know who it was for certain. The media, by this evening's press conference, will want to know about the Northern Ireland connection. I fear I cannot delay any longer letting them know that Professor Banks is responsible for the theft of the jewels. It will have a great impact on our people. A huge media crowd from all over the world has descended upon us. I've moved the conference to Victoria and Albert Hall in order to handle the crowd. I've put off the professor's call until seven p.m. Perhaps you can give me something to quiet the press. Please proceed with your report."

Yates wheeled in a television set, plugged in a VCR, and reeled the tape made by the German. "We think all of the devices used in the raid, except for those small knockout spray cans, were made by one man, name of Speltz, in Amsterdam. The Dutch Intelligence Service has been trying for a long time to put Speltz in jail, but they've never been able to get hard evidence. He makes excellent firearms and small munitions and is very clever at hiding his little factory. They've never been able to find out where he makes the stuff he sells. He operates a small tobacco shop in Amsterdam." Then Yates explained how the Dutch had set up elaborate traps to get evidence, but had failed.

"If the Dutch Intelligence people believe he's guilty of illegal arms trade, why don't they bring him in for questioning?" asked an exasperated Prime Minister.

"They have from time to time, but to no avail. Now they can't. About two weeks ago Speltz closed his shop, sold his house, and moved to Spain. Apparently he has decided to retire. Without solid evidence to back up charges, the Dutch authorities can't extradite him. The Spanish authorities questioned the man. He was very pleasant and cooperative, but they learned nothing."

"That's the most ridiculous story I've ever heard," replied an angry Prime Minister. "The Dutch should have arrested the man a long time ago. To let someone work right under their noses making guns for people certainly is not good form at all."

The Director of E Branch flipped a page of his notebook and changed the subject, trying to find something that would calm the Prime Minister, but he knew this next bit would irritate the hell out of her. "The three barges were made in Italy and leased from an Italian shipping company in Genoa. Forsythe of MI6 is certain that an official of the company was paid a great deal of money to push the lease through at a very high premium. MI6 obtained copies of the papers filled with false information. They were leased to a fake French company and signed with a false name. Forsythe was unable to get any identification of the man who leased them." Yates paused as the Prime Minister fidgeted with a pencil, a grim look on her face. He then went on to explain how the Italian tugboat captain who, for a price, had told them the full story: how he took the barges to England, then floated them up the English Channel at night and crossed over to the Isle of Wight, changing his colors and the identification of his boat along the way. He brought them round the coast, close to shore, into the mouth of the Thames and anchored them, as instructed, in a cove off Canvey Island. He left for home on the same night, the twenty-sixth of March.

"We spend billions on national security and let an Italian tugboat captain make fools of us!" The Prime Minister did not hesitate to show her irritation. "Incredible! I'll get together with my defence minister on that one. Go on."

Yates turned to yet another subject guaranteed to upset her even more. "We located all three French helicopters, scuttled in three separate water reservoirs about thirty to thirty-five miles south of London. The navy divers are bringing them up now. We don't expect to find much, they're stripped bare of most instruments. Forsythe has been working with the French authorities to determine who bought them. They traced them to a French arms dealer who, though reluctant to talk, said the man who bought them was British."

"British! The man was British? Not Irish?" asked an agitated Prime Minister.

"The report says definitely British, not Irish. But of course we have people in Northern Ireland who take great pride in their British accents. He would not or could not give a description.

"The helicopters were flown to a small farm in France about twenty miles from the Spanish border and left there. The farmer said he rented space for a few francs to a man and an acrobat. A few days later the two men showed up and the acrobat flew each of the three through all sorts of maneuvers. Put on quite a show for the farmer and his neighbors, then suddenly flew off in one of them to the south, towards Spain. The next day he came back, flew the second one out, and a day later repeated the operation. We have the pilot's height, weight, and hair color, but his face was covered with a mustache and very large dark glasses."

Yates continued on, feeling the heat, and wishing the meeting were over. "The pilot did not speak to the farmer. The man who drove him there each day spoke fluent French; he was about six feet tall, medium build, older, with grey hair, a mustache, and goatee. We theorize the pilot flew each helicopter into Spain and stashed it somewhere for the next two months while the pontoons and tubes were installed. Two nights before the raid they were flown to England onto the barges off Canvey Island. It was a neat bit of flying, because the Channel weather was a little stormy and rough that night. A few Canvey fishermen were curious about the barges that appeared one day empty and the next full and covered with tarps, but no one reported it to any authorities.

"French Customs are combing their records to locate visa records that might connect with the pilots. Forsythe is cross-checking the descriptions of all the free-lance mercenary pilots for a match with the farmer's description of the acrobat. The Spanish authorities are not cooperating very well with MI6, and it would be helpful if you could call their prime minister and give him a boot."

"I'll see what I can do," responded a bitter Prime Minister, "but we've had problems communicating lately."

"The people who raided the Tower took only minutes to reach the reservoirs, then left in vans. We're tracing all the car rental and sales agreements made in England and Scotland within the last few weeks, but with well over two thousand, it will take time."

"What about the professor's son? Any word?" she asked.

"Nothing yet, but we expect something to break soon," replied Yates.

"Still no closer to the jewels Director Yates?"

Yates could sense the Prime Minister's anxiety and frustration and had been waiting for the question. He had saved the best for last. "One or two things have improved our chances, but we may suffer a wait before we get results. First the woman, Mrs. Ashford. We now know who she is. The Italian and French police recognized her from our artist's sketch. She is Maria Donna Costell, thirty-two years old; she is Italian, but is now a French citizen and lives in an expensive condominium in Nice with her housekeeper." Yates went on to describe Maria's background.

"Why do you suppose she would participate in a

criminal act?" asked the Prime Minister appearing just a little impressed with the woman's record.

"Remember, this is more a political statement than a criminal act," Yates responded. "Perhaps it's love, or politics, or maybe the cause of freedom or humanity. Or perhaps it is a challenge to cure boredom. She's wealthy enough. Money is not the motive. We just don't know her reasons at the moment. The housekeeper is mum, but she did say her mistress has been gone for almost six months.

"So far we've confined the release of the sketch to authorities here and abroad. It may be tipping our hand, but now we need the help of the public; therefore, I request we be allowed to release the sketch and her identity to the press and the world."

"Perhaps you're right, Director Yates, I will do that at my press conference this evening," said the Prime Minister, a little more relaxed now. "In only three days you've identified one prime suspect. I didn't think it possible. Now it seems all we have to do is locate her and we'll have the jewels back. Do you have any idea whether we can get to them by April third or fourth before the election?"

"Madam, I would like to say yes, but I cannot. We need a great deal of luck to locate her by the fourth, and the chances are remote. The men and the woman can hide almost anywhere in England with the jewels until after the elections and we would have a devil of a time locating them." Yates squirmed to get more comfortable in his chair. He could not tell from her expression if the PM truly understood the nature of the problem.

"That's not what I wanted to hear, but I concede you are no doubt correct." She seemed to relax a bit as she sighed. "So in the end it may be luck and the public who come to our aid. When the professor calls, I'm sure he will understand why I must release the news before he does. And if he doesn't, well, that's just too bad. He can set up his own press conference tomorrow. I'll release the woman's name and picture. Better have several hundred printed up and sent over to me. Is there anything else I should know?"

"Yes," Yates replied, "the Swiss bank account. It seems the Swiss will do nothing until we file formal criminal charges against Professor Banks. The monies transferred to the Swiss account exceed the legal limit of transfer without notification to our government. Therefore, we have two different charges to file against the professor, the jewels, and the funds to steal them. Do you want to file charges now?"

"I'm willing to take our chances and wait."

Yates finished up with, "I don't believe any of the men or the woman have left English soil."

"It's almost time for the professor's call; thank you, gentlemen, we'll meet again tomorrow."

* * *

The call from the professor was brief. She explained about the leak. He was not unhappy; with luck Kevin would be out of the church tonight and he would have the ring. He was ready to meet the press, regardless.

"I cannot accept your terms," the Prime Minister gambled, "we must evaluate the impact on the United Kingdom before I can concede to blackmail. It's never a good idea to concede to blackmail; I find it an appalling thought."

"Madam Prime Minister," he said, with a touch of exasperation in his voice, "you are now talking about two governments, yours and mine. And mine has sequestered the jewels, by my authority, in return for the lands of Northern Ireland. It's an even trade as I see it, nothing more. We simply are using the jewels to focus world attention on our right to govern ourselves. If you prevent these elections for whatever reason, your reputation in the free world as a champion of freedom will come crashing down. I have no fear that both elections will be in our favor. If you do not agree to the elections, then of course it may be a millennium before you ever see the jewels again."

"I must remain firm on this. I will not agree to your terms!" And the Prime Minister hung up sharply.

* * *

The Prime Minister called the closed, emergency meeting of Parliament and her Cabinet in the House of Lords at Westminster for 7:30 p.m. The meeting was hushed as she explained the professor's demands and her attempts to locate the jewels while stalling a public announcement.

"Unfortunately, there has been a breach of security," she said with just a touch of bitterness, "and now I must proceed to let the world know what is happening. I do not recommend acceding to their blackmail demands at this point. I fear once the news is out our people will want the elections, and world opinion will bring great pressure to bear for us to conduct them. It's my fervent hope that our intelligence people will recover the jewels before we are forced to hold elections. My press conference has been set for an hour from now. I would appreciate it if you would keep silent on this matter until after that conference."

The members of Parliament sat in stunned silence until the Prime Minister finished her briefing, then broke out in noisy outrage. The thirteen member representatives present from Northern Ireland sat shocked beyond belief as the rest of Parliament made noisy suggestions from all quarters, including a hanging for the professor, long jail terms for the top members of his organization for conspiracy, and an outright immediate severance of Northern Ireland from the United Kingdom with no economic assistance whatsoever. As the pandemonium and yelling subsided and reason took hold, it was this last option that began to gain momentum. Before it could develop more strongly, the Prime Minister adjourned the meeting and headed for her press conference.

The Members of Parliament from Northern Ireland, who remained mute throughout this display of anger and bitterness, decided to hold a caucus and prepare a joint statement to the press. However, they were completely surprised and confused by the events. They knew the professor's party had been gaining strength, but had no idea it was strong enough for him to risk a ploy as bold as this. If independence was now a distinct possibility, then it dramatically changed their political horizons. Violent argument among themselves over a course of action prevented them from making a joint statement.

* * *

Security was tight at Victoria and Albert Hall, where the Prime Minister's press conference was due to begin shortly. Visiting members of the press, radio, and television were required to pass through two checkpoints: The first was a rather slow and deliberate review of passports, company ID, and the special pass issued for tonight only; the second a delicate metal check that detected the presence of a single coin. Over twelve hundred people were awarded the special pass to attend the largest press conference ever held by the Prime Minister. It was a far cry from her press conference the day before when only a dozen media representatives were allowed to attend.

The media people seemed impatient and restless, the atmosphere tense. Those fortunate enough to be present suspected something special was about to take place. They had been warned that no telephone in the vicinity of Victoria and Albert Hall would be made available. Some were fortunate enough to have car phones and fax machines handy.

The Prime Minister, alone on the stage, looking a little tired, began her address to the assemblage amid the popping of flash bulbs and the silent recording of the television cameras.

"Thank you for coming ladies and gentlemen. I know you are deeply concerned about our investigation into the disappearance of the Crown Regalia. Please hold all your questions until the end of my statement, after which there will be a short question period. I do not guarantee I will answer all your questions. We know who has taken the jewels and why."

The giant hall became deathly quiet as she launched into the complete story of Professor Banks and his demands. She explained that her Cabinet would be deliberating alternatives. Then she released copies of the professor's letter and the sketch of the woman Costell.

Barbara Mitchell of Associated Press couldn't believe her ears. She's been stonewalling us for two days, she decided. Why? It must be hectic at 10 Downing. I'd love to get an earful of the PM and Queen together. Heads will roll for sure for allowing it all to happen.

When the Prime Minister finished her prepared remarks, the hall broke into noisy confusion and everyone seemed to be screaming questions at once. A number of "yellow journalists" broke for the exits to file their stories, typical tactics, before they possessed all the information. Mitchell saw them go, and the thought of all the half-truths and lies that were about to assail the public disgusted her.

A microphone in the center aisle and one on each side aisle were available for questions. After much jostling and shoving, members of the press formed queues and began firing questions at the Prime Minister. The crowd quieted as she answered each in turn.

"Yes, we waited until now to release the news because we were reviewing our alternatives. And no, I will not discuss those alternatives."

"No, we do not intend to arrest Professor Banks, at least not at this time. It would serve no useful purpose."

"Yes, he did return the State Sword in perfect shape, and it has been microscopically scrutinized and confirmed as the original. It's back at the Tower."

"No, we have no idea when the Tower will be reopened to the public. We are developing a new security program."

"Yes, to repeat again, we are asking the public here and abroad to help us locate the woman, Maria Donna Costell. We have no idea where she may be hiding, but we are certain she has the Crown Jewels in her possession or she knows where they are."

In a rare impulsive moment, the Prime Minister decided she could do something to encourage more help from the public. She had discussed the idea briefly with her Cabinet, but collectively they had dismissed it in favor of the confidence they placed in the investigative effort. Now, reflecting upon the final words of Director Yates in their earlier meeting, she realized that success meant luck as well as skill. And to recover the jewels before a forced election probably meant more luck than skill.

She realized the idea would cause a great deal of controversy in her government. She held up her hands to her audience for silence and as the crowd quieted she began: "I have answered all the questions for now, but I have one last comment to make. The United Kingdom will pay one million pounds to anyone who provides information leading to the recovery of the jewels. Thank you for your attention. Good night," and as she left the stage, pandemonium broke out.

* * *

When Jason and Craig arrived home after leaving his brother at the sanitarium, an excited and worried Maria threw her arms around Jason. "You're a welcome sight, both of you. Did you hear the news? They found out about me. The sketch is a perfect likeness. Now it's a million pound reward."

"We heard the news on the way home. It was quite a shock. I hadn't counted on them coming up with a likeness of you," replied Jason frowning, thinking. "It must be very good. The artist made some pretty good guesses and they must've traced you through the French or Italian police. This means you must stay here until the professor gets his independence and we get amnesty. You can't call Anne now, your phone is surely tapped."

"Jason, it could be months."

"No, I don't think so. Once the public gets to thinking things over they will bring great pressure to get on with the elections."

They fell silent as Jason got up and poured them each a brandy. "That one million pounds will cover a great deal of the cost of 'The Project'. Well, now," Jason joked, "perhaps that's a way to get the professor's investment back. All we have to do is turn them in."

Craig and Maria ignored the remark. "Jason, she sounds so firm in her resolve. Do you think we'll ever have a chance at amnesty?" asked Maria. "I would hate to think of becoming fugitives for the rest of our lives."

"Maria, I can never remember a time when the Prime Minister didn't sound firm in her resolve to do something. But many times she has backed off from a so-called firm stand. No, I believe she will have to yield to pressures from home and abroad and hold both elections. From that point I believe the professor will win. He has promised to hold out for amnesty. We just have to be patient."

"Tell me honestly, Jason, what makes you so sure he will win?" Craig asked.

"There's no doubt in my mind the British people will favor independence. Give the Irish back their island, they've been saying. If the professor and Kevin are accurate, then the election in the North will pass. It's a strange phenomenon going on there. Tribalism has taken a back seat. If two hundred thousand people, half and half, feel that excited and determined about it, then big changes will occur in the North."

Jason fell silent for a moment thinking about the big changes in his life. To his utter surprise and delight now, each time he thought of the North or Belfast, or his past, he did not get those old haunting pains. Visiting Patricia's grave and confronting his pathetic, deranged brother seemed to have cleansed his mind. Perhaps it was a hidden desire for revenge, or maybe the idea that at long last there would be an end to the "Troubles." Whatever the reason, he felt happy about it. He thought about asking Maria to marry him, but said nothing. After this was over he was certain his business life would change. Now was a good time to think about selling his brokerage; to think about his final moves in London.

The brandy was getting to him. The events of the last two days had made him bone tired. When he finished telling Maria what had happened, she led an exhausted Jason to bed and pouted a little when he fell instantly asleep.

* * *

It was late when a weary Prime Minister lifted the phone and listened to Yates report bad news and good news. "First, we didn't get Kevin Banks. Earlier tonight at a Protestant church in Belfast, a man rescued him from a Reverend Sean McIver who we believe held him captive for the last three days. The man who rescued Kevin used a knockout spray similar to that used in the Tower raid by the woman Costell. We think he took part in the raid, came to Belfast, registered at the Forteham Hotel as a Brian McIver, and got Kevin out. Coincidentally, the reverend has a missing brother whose name is Robert Brian McIver."

Now, the Prime Minister was really upset but she said nothing. She knew they had placed men on watch at a church in Belfast. And they let him get away.

"We are certain we now have one more Belfast connection besides Professor and Kevin Banks: One of the men who took part in the Tower raid was Robert Brian McIver! According to a third brother, George McIver, who runs the family clothing store in downtown Belfast, Robert Brian McIver left Belfast over twenty years ago after a family fight.

"We have not located Kevin Banks or Reverend McIver. Kevin is somewhere in Belfast. He called his father to let him know that he was all right. The reverend has apparently been brought to England. We found a chartered flight to Oxford that fits; a security guard remembered the destination of the 'patient' as the University Hospital in Oxford, but they never heard of the man. The flight was arranged in the name of Kevin Banks. An ambulance picked the reverend and another man up at Oxford airport and we've started the laborious task of checking on the whereabouts of every ambulance in England yesterday and tonight."

"What sort of man is this reverend?" asked the

Prime Minister, still trying to quell her anger.

"He was born in Belfast forty-eight years ago," answered Yates, and he recounted the strange history of Sean McIver and his fanatical background. "He is a staunch Orangeman," Yates concluded, "and radical loyalist, with a cruel streak that he tries to keep under control. His small, illegal, paramilitary unit is suspected of causing a number of PIRA deaths. He has never married, but has a number of women parishioners who favor him."

"What a terrible man, what sort of people would follow him?"

"People touched by PIRA violence; people who have been brought up to fear and hate the Catholics; people who are paranoid and violent; who knows? He does a good job, it is said, of provoking the hatreds. His group grew to about six hundred and then stabilized during the last couple of years."

"What about the missing brother?" asked the Prime Minister.

"More interesting," responded Yates, "we believe he's the same man who masqueraded as a priest in Calais; who visited the munitions maker in Amsterdam; the same man who bought the helicopters; who rented the barges; and who visited Professor Banks at a farm house in the Republic five months ago. We think he's an international free-agent like the woman Costell, and we think they have worked together in the past.

"The pilots and copilots were hired mercenaries, difficult to trace. That leaves only three men and the woman as the core group; the planners. If we are correct, they are Kevin Banks, Robert Brian McIver, the woman Costell and one unidentified man. He has left a trail of clues that fit together but are meaningless without his true identity. We have made up his profile and sent it to our European friends. He is Caucasian, approximately six feet tall, medium weight, westernized accent, intelligent, clever, good at disguises. Our own file comes up empty; identity unknown, except that he may be the man named Robert Brian McIver. We have a photograph, taken when he was sixteen years old. It's not a very clear photograph and he has no doubt changed by now. However, we're distributing it to the media at this moment."

The Prime Minister's anger subsided at the news of another connection to the jewels.

"Madam Prime Minister," Yates said, "I now believe Robert McIver is the man that planned this entire operation and that a man of his intelligence would not deliberately leave so many obvious clues unless he wanted to send us a message."

"What might that be, Director Yates?" asked a curious, now wide awake Prime Minister.

"The jewels are in safe hands and still in England. Whether he will destroy them if the professor asks him to do so remains to be seen. At least one thing is certain; our fugitives can't go very far; they are in effect being held captive by the jewels they're guarding."

13

April 1st
What Fools We Are!

Belfast was in an uproar. A constant stream of media types and the curious arrived by charter and scheduled flights at both airports all night long, completely filling all the available accommodations within several miles of Belfast. The professor's public relations committee, now numbering over one hundred members, finally resolved the questions on security and a hall in which to hold the press conference. They rented the Grand Opera House and set up strict security checks at its entrance. They feared not from the PIRA, but from some extremist loyalist group. One had already been neutralized, perhaps the most violent — Reverend McIver's.

Since the professor's demands included a temporary end to the Royal Ulster Constabulary and the Ulster Defence Regiment, the police were noticeably absent, allowing traffic to pile up and get out of hand, resulting in gridlock for blocks around the approaches to the theater. The line for admission formed at six a.m. and grew increasingly longer as time for the press conference drew near.

Shortly before nine a.m. Professor Banks sat on the stage with his ten member executive Board; he wished Kevin were with him. John Larkey had turned into a real asset. He had raced Kevin to City Hospital where the Doctor who had signed the transfer papers for Reverend McIver worked on Kevin's wounds. The x-rays revealed three cracked ribs; fortunately none were broken. Kevin's nose was bruised but not broken, and the deep cut on his cheek required five stitches. John drove Kevin to Chris's apartment where he could stay until his wounds healed a little. Then John delivered the small package given to him by Kevin to the professor. Neither realized that MI5 had launched an intensive search for Kevin.

The professor reached into his pocket and the feel of the ring gave him a measure of reassurance. He was surprised at how quickly the Prime Minister's people had turned up the identities of Robert Brian McIver and Maria Donna Costell. He was uncertain about McIver. That news had been broadcast early that morning, together with a picture of him at age sixteen or so. If it were true, it would explain the Magician's desire to help get the jewels and to risk exposure rescuing Kevin.

As he waited to begin his statement, he felt a little uncomfortable wearing the light application of makeup that his public relations committee insisted he use. They had even slipped a small block of wood in front of the podium to give his already tall figure a larger-than-life appearance. Now I have to be a television cutie, he thought.

Finally, at a signal from one of the public relations committee members, he walked to the podium and began his speech. The room became absolutely still.

"Ladies and gentlemen, thank you all for coming. We're not equipped with microphones for questions. If you have a question, please write it down and hand it to one of the three men standing in the center aisle, and I will do what I can to answer it. Incidentally, copies of this statement will be made available to you afterwards at the exits." His deep voice resonated throughout the hall, where it quickly became apparent to the experienced journalists that this man, with his poise and quiet self confidence, possessed strong leadership qualities and that special charisma.

Barbara Mitchell was one of them. She had raced from the PM's press conference, phoned Logan for a charter flight, reserved a small bed and breakfast outside Belfast, and called in her story, all from her car as she drove to Gatwick. Now she was sitting in the front row amazed at the events and at the man standing at the podium. Her office had dug up his background and called it to her. She knew he had been Original IRA, once a Catholic, now a Protestant, and a shrewd economist. She didn't know until now that the man possessed a presence that few leaders had.

The professor paused and his glance caught the inquisitive stare of Barbara Mitchell. "Many of you in this hall may not recall the troubled history of Northern Ireland. If you will allow me a moment to digress, I would like to give you my views on some of the events leading to today's situation. The current 'Troubles,' our war in Northern Ireland, began over twenty years ago when the People's Democracy marched for civil rights from Belfast to Derry. It's hard to believe that even in those modern times a march was necessary for such simple civil rights as one man, one vote; an end to gerrymandering; freedom of speech and assembly; repeal of the Special Powers Act that gave police unlimited power of arrest and detention; and more jobs and more housing. It was not a religious march but a march for the underprivileged, for the unemployed, and for freedom. This misunderstood march created fear among the loyalists, fostering hatred and violence. And thus began the uncivil war we have today.

"Since then almost three thousand people have been killed, most of them innocent bystanders. Where in this world do soldiers march in fear of their lives to keep the peace, except in war-torn countries? Where in this world are men kept in jail for little or no reason, except in states of anarchy? Where in this world are men kept from self governing and deprived of full civil rights, except in states of dictatorship? Northern Ireland is one place in this world where all these things happen. And they happen every day. But the war is misunderstood as religious, tribe against tribe. It is the gangs who use religious differences to further their own ends.

Economics, plain old bread-on-the-table economic deprivation, lies at the heart of our struggle in the North. The efforts to balance government programs and the private sector have failed. And we want to change that!

"And what about civil rights? If you cannot walk around your own town without fear of confrontation with soldier, terrorist paramilitary, gang, or murderer, you have somehow lost a civil right. If there is blinding bigotry, a judicial system twisted by politics, no jobs, and inadequate housing, someone has lost a civil right... And we want to change that!"

The professor paused and looked over the hushed audience. He knew this was his only chance. He thought he had their complete attention. The theft of the jewels would soon be forgotten if he could convince them independence was the only solution.

He purposely changed the tempo and deepened the tone of his voice, "To bring peace and prosperity to the North, three things must happen: The British must withdraw; the South must eliminate Articles 2 and 3 from its constitution that claim the North as their own; and the North must vote for independence. There is no question that a settlement to the 'Troubles' cannot involve either the British or the South, but only the North, alone. The two powers must recognize this. Great Britain has deprived us of our right to govern while continuing to foster the insanity of war through the Anglo/Irish Accord, a smoke screen of political debauchery that fantasizes unity with the South, a country that can hardly afford to care for its own. Great Britain on the other hand supports mediocrity, encourages the dole, and deprives us of our economic independence in favor of their own.

"Ladies and gentlemen, go to any soccer match or to the continent and meet someone from the North, then ask them if they are British. They will tell you they are Irish! Be they Catholic or Protestant, Republican or Unionist. And you can tell they're Irish. We are Irish! We are a special brand of Irish, Irish of the North, and proud of it. I started the Freedom Party a number of years ago to encourage independent thinking and action. As our party grew, our member's thinking has matured, shifting our focus to independence.

"Yes, the North still has its tribes of Catholics and its tribes of Protestants, and yes, its lunatic fringes; but overshadowing that mistrust, independence promises a successful peace, freedom, and economic stability. Today we have over two hundred thousand members, half Catholic and half Protestant, middle-of-the-road, sensible people. They have studied and worked hard, without the help of politicians, to develop the structure of a new government. They have pledged to recruit another two hundred thousand. They will do it; I guarantee it.

"We now ask the Republican, the Unionist, the Socialist, and the Independent to join us in this great adventure. The people of my party are not politicians and bureaucrats; they are people from all walks of life, some unemployed, seeking a better way."

Kevin, watching television at Chris's, could tell that his father was excited, but the audience did not see this. His presence was commanding, his voice deep and strong, his elocution so perfect that the group of hard-bitten journalists were being subtly but unavoidably moved by the passionate speech.

"Ladies and gentlemen, ours is not a unilateral declaration of independence; it depends on a vote of both the British people and the people of Northern Ireland. We propose a step-wise road to independence involving the participation of the British until we can stand on our own. Our Transition Plan outlines the direction we must take to achieve our goals."

Barbara Mitchell knew he was winning. This guy is good, she thought, as she sat scribbling her own impressions of an event that she felt was certain to be historic.

"You heard the Prime Minister say that we have stolen the jewels and that it's blackmail, and she will not yield to our demands. The fact of the matter is, and I have told her this, we did not steal the crown jewels. We 'sequestered' them by my authority. And when we get our elections and our land, the jewels will be returned. We do not want Parliament and the do-nothing politicians to vote the question, we want the British people to vote the question. No more apathy. We want to focus on our problems.

"I alone am responsible for 'sequestering' the jewels; those who actually obtained them for me deserve amnesty. If the elections fail I alone will go to jail and the jewels will be returned. If the elections succeed and the Transition Plan is signed by a new Prime Minister of the North and Britain's Prime Minister, the jewels will be returned. As a symbol of good faith I have already returned the Sovereign's Sword. As proof that we have the jewels, here is the Coronation ring," and he held up his hand for a TV camera closeup. There was no mistaking the shimmering brilliance of the large sapphire and cross of rubies, surrounded by flashing diamonds, as anything but the real article. It was real. Jason had made certain of that.

"The Crown Regalia is the very symbol of the strength and endurance of the United Kingdom, revered by the Royal family, the government and the people. It would be a shame to lose them forever, but I guarantee the jewels will find a watery grave if these simple requests are not granted."

Barbara Mitchell by now realized the man meant what he said. He will get his way, she thought, but what will really happen in the elections? He seems so sure of himself. Well, we'll see. Wonder if the British can locate the jewels before then? They're homing in pretty fast.

The professor read the six-point demand letter of March twenty-ninth without emphasis. "The Transition plan is now being reviewed by the Prime Minister and will not be released until she has completed her review."

William Banks decided to send the South a message. "Ladies and gentlemen, the Transition Plan does include a provision for the United Nations and Great Britain to insist that the South withdraw Article 2 and 3 from their constitution. It also includes a request of the United Nations to declare Northern Ireland a free and independent country. The South should be aware of this because they must allow us the opportunity to be free, as they have been free for these past fifty years, and give us time to work together to solve our mutual problems and strengthen the island's economy.

"The South must recognize the PIRA's violent activities as a scam to propagate terrorism in the name of a false dream. Before the Normans came, our island was united only briefly when the Gaelic Kings drove out the Vikings. True Gaelic unification is a myth.

"The people of my party are saying, 'I'm Protestant and I don't care if you're Catholic, or I'm Catholic and I don't care if you're Protestant.' Let the hurt, the hate, the tragedy, and the tribalism die. Bury them! Let us move forward! What really matters is freedom and a brighter economic future for each and every one of us.

"In conclusion, let me say to the people of the United Kingdom, their government and the Queen, that if you truly believe in freedom, give us ours! Ladies and gentlemen, thank you for coming; I will answer your questions now."

The hall was perfectly silent. Then suddenly the travel weary, tough-minded journalists broke into tremendous and enthusiastic applause. Professor Banks was stunned and his Board members astonished.

* * *

The Prime Minister picked up the remote, switched off the television set, and sat staring at her Cabinet in silence. The speech was not special. It was a delivery of facts without much rhetoric. But it was the way the man delivered the words, with a certain emphasis here and there or a cadence introduced at the right moment, allowing time for the audience to savor their meaning. She hated to admit the man had charisma, but she knew it was true.

"Professor Banks has a definite presence; you couldn't miss the applause at the end," she said. "His warm reception is a sure sign his popularity will grow. I received a very soft, polite, and half-hearted applause last night and that was all. Of course, I wasn't delivering a speech for independence, but nevertheless I see the momentum shifting in his favor. I'm open to any suggestions. You all know what has happened up to now."

The Minister of Agriculture spoke up. "We should jail the bastard now for committing a low and despicable crime against the Crown."

"Hold your temper, Jonathan, you know it's too late for that. Perhaps I should have done it that first day, but the risk of losing the jewels forever was too great. Besides, we don't need a martyr now. It's bad enough we have to deal with a man who appears to be a born leader."

"The professor has guessed, accurately enough,

ASSAULT ON THE CROWN

that our government does not have to grant independence even if there is a majority vote in the North," commented the Secretary of State for Foreign and Commonwealth Affairs. "You and I both know the intent of the guarantee applies only to unification of the North and the South. We're not obligated to grant independence, just as we're not obligated to re-establish a Parliament of Northern Ireland. What we give we can take away and that is as it should be; they are British subjects. There's no reason why we can't maintain control of Northern Ireland if we find the jewels."

"Easier said than done," replied the Prime Minister, irritated by the naivete of the man. "We're running out of time for that. If we are to hold elections on the fifth, then we must start the machinery for candidate ballots no later than tomorrow, the second, or else we will not be ready. Based on what we saw a little while ago and polls taken here, I believe that the elections, both of them, will favor independence."

The Cabinet broke into grumbling and small talk as the inevitability of the situation began to sink in. They had been waiting for the Lord Chancellor to speak. The noted historian and orator, who often set a firm course on an issue for the Prime Minister, was respected by his peers for his brilliance

As was his custom, the portly man rose from his chair before he spoke. He was a short man and it put him above the heads of his seated companions, giving more psychological weight to his words. "Like it or not, we have been placed in a most embarrassing and awkward position. Madam, gentlemen, we have been dallying with Northern Ireland's 'Troubles' for over twenty years. We have not formulated a long-range plan because there is no solution as long as the South will not change their attitude. For centuries we tried to keep the island for ourselves, however, through the ineptness of our ancestors who, for countless years, paid scant attention to Irish problems in favor of problems here at home, we failed miserably.

"We need Northern Ireland to protect our western shores. The South has been almost like an enemy during our recent conflicts: They failed us in World War II and turned their backs on us during the Falklands crisis. We need a defence buffer. The South knows it, our allies want it, we want it, and the professor realizes all of these things. And he is willing to concede any defences we want. What better time than now; what better excuse to establish a heavier concentration of defences, paid for by our allies, in Northern Ireland. We gain monetarily on both counts, defence and the gradual reduction of an unwanted drain on our economy. I agree with the Prime Minister after reading Yates' intelligence reports and listening to Professor Banks; independence will pass."

The Prime Minister, anticipating what the Lord Chancellor was about to say, attempted to cut him off. "I abhor blackmail, and that's what we're dealing with!"

The Lord Chancellor ignored her remark, remained standing, and continued. "True, it's a crime, an assault on the Crown. But it's water under the bridge. The important thing now is how we negotiate with a new government. We must see to it that our future economy is protected. In ten years, if all goes well and they develop a sound economy of their own, we'll be sending no monetary support to the North . We'll have a strong ally at our side in time of need if we are fair about it today.

"Perhaps many will call it blackmail, but the prospective advantages to us outweigh shallow name calling. I therefore recommend that we agree to the professor's requests and establish a task force to begin working on the problem." He looked around slowly, carefully, with his most serious expression, and sat down.

The Prime Minister was frustrated; she did not want to give in. "It's too early to capitulate. Next thing we know it'll be Scotland and Wales on our backs. We have yet to hear from the Secretary of State for Northern Ireland. "Can you shed some light on our problem?"

The Secretary was a very tall man. Seated, he towered over the rest of them. He remained seated as he answered the Prime Minister. "Madam, you know as well as I that the economy in Northern Ireland is in a sorry state. We can continue to cope with the PIRA and the extremist loyalists, and people will continue to be shot or blown up or God knows what. For as long as I've been there I have worked to bring the two tribes together; but for the deep political distrust, I might have succeeded. We are going to sell them out to the South, they say. I'm sorry, but in all my time spent there I have failed to create a stronger North working at the political level. The professor, working at the people's level, has made astounding progress. Madam, you and I have tried to make the Anglo/Irish Summits into something practical, but they are not working. Nothing will work so long as we are involved. I am afraid I must agree with Lord Chancellor. The time has come to make the break."

"It will be an embarrassment to capitulate, to give in to blackmail. There must be another way," lamented the Prime Minister.

The Chancellor rose to his feet again. "Madam, this is not an act of terrorism or blackmail. It's more an act of symbolism than an act of rebellion. They meant to harm no one nor did they intend to keep the jewels. You could tell from the television broadcast that his appeal for sympathy from the public and the world is going to work. I doubt seriously if you will be faulted for acceding to his demands. Furthermore, it may not be necessary to ask the Queen to dissolve Parliament and call for the elections. She may be of a mind to do it herself."

The Prime Minister remembered her last meeting with the Queen; the sadness that seemed to engulf her; and her final remarks. "Perhaps she may," said the Prime Minister, "the thought had never crossed my mind. It would be the first time in modern history. Gentlemen, you all know the situation now and have heard some interesting comments. I cannot guarantee the recovery of the jewels within the next three days without a great deal of luck.

Therefore, I now ask that you give me an advisory vote, by secret ballot, on the question of accepting the demands of Professor Banks."

Not since the Falklands had so serious a problem confronted the Cabinet. The United Kingdom spent millions protecting two small islands thousands of miles away and spends billions each year protecting the people of Northern Ireland. Which one is worth more to protect and save? Including the Prime Minister's there were twenty-two votes cast. The Prime Minister, without opening any of the ballots, adjourned the meeting by saying, "Thank you, gentlemen, I shall carefully consider your vote and your suggestions."

* * *

The Taoiseach, Prime Minister of the Republic of Ireland, the South, had been astonished by the announcement of the British Prime Minister the evening before. He was awed by the performance of the professor at his morning press conference. He had heard of the man, but did not realize the strength of his personality. Word of his party had been trickling in for the past several months, but he had felt no threat. Now he realized he had made a horrible miscalculation. Soon he would be besieged by the media, probing, questioning, placing him under global scrutiny, and pressing him for a response to Professor Banks.

He sat alone in his office gathering his thoughts,

trying out ideas, reviewing words and phrases he might use to describe his feelings. He scribbled notes to himself in a nervous hand. The more he pondered, the more he realized he needed more information. It had been a while since he had talked to the Prime Minister; he hoped she would not ignore him. He put in a call to her, but was told he would have to wait until she finished her Cabinet meeting. Damn, he thought, I don't have much time. I've got to meet with my own Cabinet and the President before the press is all over me.

As he waited anxiously for the Prime Minister's call he reflected upon his country's turbulent history, marked by long periods of desperate economic struggle for survival. The land was poor and unyielding, the strength of his people indomitable. For centuries their struggle for freedom survived the plague, famine, war, civil war, rebellion, rape, plunder, pillaging, scorched earth, terrorists, executions, reprisals, and captivity by the Vikings, Normans, and British. Now, he thought, a weakening economy with a huge annual deficit and high unemployment seems to be leading us towards more adversity. He was hoping his latest efforts at cost reduction in the government would turn things around, but it was too early to tell. He needed stronger economic ties with Britain and the North. It was he who helped modify the original hard-line approach of his party, improved relations with the United Kingdom, and paved the way for the Anglo/Irish Accord that could resolve some practical issues affecting the North and South. The idea that the Accord would become a firm step towards unification with the South had struck fear in the hearts of many Northern loyalists and created a cry of outrage that all but scuttled it.

Now relations had become strained with Britain again over the refusal of his courts to extradite to Britain a certain terrorist priest from the Republic and Britain's failure to prosecute certain Royal Ulster Constabulary members for originating a "Shoot to Kill" policy against anyone suspected as PIRA. Relations were anything but cordial.

The Taoiseach spent an agonizing hour waiting and wondering what in the hell was going on. Finally the call came through. "Madam Prime Minister it's good of you to return my call. I saw your conference of last night and Professor Banks's this morning. It's quite a shock. Can you tell me what you plan to do?"

"You know very well that our Accord established at the outset that any time the majority in Northern Ireland dictates a change, we both agree to honor it. My question to you is, are you prepared to remove Articles 2 and 3 from your constitution?" She was trying her best to sound as polite as possible.

"Can you tell me how you assess the outcome of the elections, or will you allow them at all?" he asked, sidestepping her question.

Damn! He's being slippery again. "What the professor said is true enough," she replied. "According to all the intelligence sources we can put to the task. The election in the North is a certain victory for them. He already has two hundred thousand votes and he will get the additional votes he needs from Unionists, Socialists and Independents who favor independence. It may go as low as fifty-two percent or as high as sixty percent in favor of independence. The handwriting is on the wall. What do you propose to do about it?" Her voice was icy, all the politeness gone.

"Madam, we've discussed this before, we have not the resources to handle the North. We have a few renegades who think so, but it is just plain impossible. Even so, getting the majority of the Dail to agree to striking the Articles will be difficult."

"Sir, you continue to coddle the criminals, the terrorists, the Provisionals who attack us. They are based in your country and you look the other way. You protect known terrorists from prosecution and will not put in jail even those who have been convicted. It's about time you changed. Once the North gains independence, we will introduce a resolution in the United Nations supporting their right to become an independent country. Your claim will be invalidated. As a peace-loving nation that has gained its own independence, you will be expected to allow the Northerners freedom. World opinion will force you to withdraw the Articles. And when you do, you face the consequences of an uprising in you own back yard."

"Madam, those are harsh words." He felt angry and frustrated, but he knew them to be true. "You are aware that as Taoiseach I have given much thought to the cancellation of the Articles, but have withheld a serious crusade to do so. It could lead to violence and bloodshed here."

The Prime Minister's voice became more piercing, the words forming a slashing knife travelling across the Irish Sea. "Sir, the professor was correct. Your Island, since its inception, has never been united. Unity is an illusory dream. It is time to face reality. You will soon have to deal with an independent North, and we will have little to say about their affairs. Perhaps in time, a long time, you can approach the North and discuss unity with some assurance of success. But not now. You can prevent bloodshed in your country with stern measures. Your people will not put up with violence. It's up to you to sell the idea to withdraw the two Articles, and I strongly urge you to do so quickly."

"Your words bite deep, Madam; you're convinced the movement will succeed despite the fact that it is based on blackmail? Independence in the North is a bitter pill to take."

"No more bitter for you than it is for us! Will you remove the two Articles?"

The Taoiseach's mind was racing over history and recent events, the status of his economy and the future well being of the Republic. He needed time to sort things out, analyze the situation, and turn events into a favorable situation for his party and administration. "I don't know," he answered, "it's all very sudden. I will need time to meet with my Cabinet and discuss the alternatives. I assume our Accord will be invalid after the elections. I take it you do not intend to prevent the elections?"

"Sir, it has been four whole days since the theft of the jewels and only three since we have known who was responsible. If we comply, we must put the machinery in motion by tomorrow afternoon for ballots to be ready for elections on the fifth. It will be confusion at best. Please call me tomorrow after you have reviewed the situation."

"I will be happy to do so, Madam," and the Taoiseach hung up, palms a little sweaty. He rose from his chair, walked to the large window, looked down at the busy street below, and pondered the task before him. He recalled the terrible Anglo/Irish war of 1919 and the equally terrifying civil war of 1922, all to achieve a degree of freedom that ultimately led to independence. During the ensuing years, the people had vacillated between two political parties; the Fianna Fail, a splinter group from the Original Sinn Fein whose motto, "One Island, one Ireland," can best describe their political posture; and Fine Gael, who from time to time had contemplated removal of Articles 2 and 3 from the constitution to erase their claim to the North. Now he worried about the impact of Northern Independence on the Progressive Democratic Party, who advocated constitutional reform and peaceful unification with the North. They now had become a prominent factor in the South's political framework.

For us, independence has been a long tortuous journey. Now the North, may achieve its independence, very shortly. He wondered if bloodshed might occur. Violence would be senseless, but then it always was. *The two of us, the North and the South, are as diverse in our attitudes and social customs as the Aborigines and the Australians. Their Catholics are not like our Catholics any more than the few Protestants here are like the Protestants in the North. What price unity? Bickering, headaches, unsolicited violence, and above all, economic hardship for everyone.* He gave a deep sigh of resignation and called a special meeting of his Cabinet.

14

April 2nd
Backtrack.

It was the morning of April second and Richard Yates was exhausted. At age sixty his reserve energy dwindled faster. After some ninety hours straight with no more than a few occasional naps, his frayed nerves created an edginess totally unfamiliar to him. He looked at his Deputy, David Browning, tired and pale, sitting across from him, and wondered if he looked that tired. He wanted to thank David for his dedication and hard work, but that would come later; then he would give him some time off to spend with his family and recuperate.

The "war room" had changed. All of the maps were put away except for one of London and the surrounding area. Two large blowups of Robert Brian McIver and Maria Donna Costell graced one wall, but the windows overlooking Hyde Park were once again clear, revealing the broad expanse of the park and the city. The blowups of the jewels had disappeared, but a blowup of the helicopter remained.

The two of them were listening to Fred Press on the speaker phone from Belfast: "Kevin Banks is still missing. We found out later that he was treated at City Hospital shortly after they skipped from the church. He was pretty well cut up and hurting. Kevin is holed up somewhere licking his wounds. I believe he somehow passed the Coronation Ring to his father, but of course there is no way to prove it. That was the only way we could link him to the Tower. We traced the ambulance to City Hospital, but no one knows how it got away from them. We traced the telephone number the professor gave to Brian McIver, at least we think it was him after we put all the pieces together, to a girl, Chris Cook, who works in the professor's office. We're checking her out now."

"Is there any sign of violence in the city?" asked Yates.

"Not yet," replied Press, "but Belfast is heating up since the professor's press conference yesterday. The Orange Order is planning a big show of strength with parades and meetings all over Northern Ireland. The Independence Party is planning similar parades. The Royal Ulster Constabulary is planning a sick-out holiday of protest supported by the Ulster Defence Regiment. There will be virtually no police in service tomorrow and the fourth, only the British military. Sinn Fein and the PIRA are silent, but our sources expect no trouble from them.

"A good many of the Unionists are swinging over

to independence. The real problem is the extreme loyalists and the worst of them, the Reverend McIver, is gone. Professor Banks has virtually no protection from assassination. He will not allow any of his people to have arms. This may sound silly, but do you want us to move in and protect him?"

The question startled Yates, and he looked inquiringly at Browning before saying, "Damn it, Fred, I can't believe we've come to that point. Here we are trying to find the evidence to put the man and his friends away for a long time, and instead we wind up protecting him? Northern Ireland is an enigma, to be sure, but this is ludicrous."

Press changed the subject. "Do you still want us to pick up Kevin Banks if we can find him?"

"No. He won't tell us any more than we already know, and it would cause a political scene. It wouldn't hurt to let someone in the professor's organization know that the British authorities are no longer interested in Kevin. Where's the professor now? At the university, or is he at home?"

"Two days ago he took a short leave of absence from his job, and he's everywhere. He must have a hundred meetings a day. He's traveling all over Ulster, almost like a political campaign. Usually he has no more than two or three people with him. He's an open target, but he moves quickly. A large group of media people are following him around."

"As distasteful as it is, I will ask the Prime Minister if she wants to protect him. Anything else I should know?"

"We've interviewed a man named Donald McVay who was a close friend of Robert Brian McIver over twenty years ago. He told me that the young McIver left Northern Ireland after his two brothers and father almost beat him to death shortly after his fiance died.

"Did he ever hear from him again?"

"Once, shortly after he left. He called McVay and told him that he was all right and that he would, in time, contact him again."

"Did he ever do it?"

"No, that was the last that he heard from him."

"Where did he say he was calling from?"

"London."

"I wonder what happened to him after that? Well, maybe someday we'll find out. Do you have anything else?" asked Yates

"No. How is your check of the kidnap ambulance coming? If we can find the reverend he might tell us about his brother."

"We've accounted for every ambulance in England for the hours in question. However, at least one hundred ambulances have been retired and sold off to individuals. We're trying to locate them through auto registration, but it's doubtful we'll have anything by day after tomorrow. I'll let you know what the Prime Minister says about protection."

Fred Press said good-bye and hung up.

Yates looked at David Browning, whose head was drooping, got up, and poured them both another cup of coffee. David shuddered when he put the cup in front of him and said, "I think I've consumed enough coffee to last me the rest of my life.

"Probably so," said Yates, "but it helps keep you awake. Now, David, I know this is difficult, but let's go through it all again. I meet with the Prime Minister in a little while."

David Browning wished he were somewhere else, anywhere else but here, trying to tie up the loose ends. He was tired. He knew they were close but couldn't imagine how the final bits would fit together. The Director was looking for something too, but couldn't put his finger on it. David began: "Well, the Tower, the helicopters, and the ordnance yielded nothing. We have narrowed the list of pilots to forty. Hell, they're all over the world. These pilots move around so much it's almost impossible to trace them. We have asked our friends on the continent to cross check the list against visitor visas and entry records during the last two weeks.

"The French have been very cooperative. They found the name of the man who purchased the helicopters. One James I. Donnally, British passport, stocky, about 5' 11", weight 13 stone, brown hair, mustache and thick rimmed glasses. Bingo! We have a connection, Donnally is the name of the man Press followed; that man was taller. The Spanish authorities tracked down a Donnally who stayed at a small hotel in Santander on the North coast of Spain and they're developing more information. In fact two men stayed in the same room but only one registered. They fit the description, one stocky, one tall; British passports, maybe brothers. A James I. Donnally died several years ago in Brighton and the file pictures show a very thin man with a long nose, bony face; rather ugly. Two passports were issued in different years to James I. and James P. Donnally. Both passports have the same ugly picture and, not surprisingly, the same address, the apartment in the SOHO. It seems they use the Donnally ID quite a bit for travelling."

Yates gathered from his assistant's tone that he had so far nothing to be enthusiastic about. *We've got to have something soon. We're treading water, almost drowning . . . .*

Browning looked up from his notes and went on, "The Italian tugboat captain, for more money, gave us a description of the man who leased the barges. It was the stocky Donnally. We located three vehicles rented by a James Donnally, presumably used to get away from the reservoirs after scuttling the helicopters. One was found at Hastings, one at Ashford and one at Heathrow. No one can remember a face, but he used a credit card! We thought we had him, but it turns out he has a special account at the bank; used the SOHO address again. Always has money deposited against the card and no statements are mailed to him. Never charges more than he has in the account. Comes to the bank so seldom to pick up his statements, once or twice a year, no one can describe him.

"Speaking of vehicles, we traced Kevin Banks

from Gatwick by charter, Logan Air, to Prestwick, where he checked out a car to Stranraer. The timing is a perfect fit with the Tower raid. He carried a small valise and looked strangely like our young Winston Churchill! He had to be involved in it! He was James Donnally on the plane, Kevin Banks disguised as young Winston when he checked out the car at Prestwick, and the genuine Kevin Banks when he turned it in at Stranraer. The ferry had been stopped and every boat in the Northern Irish Channel had been stopped. Unfortunately the patrol boats were so busy they didn't record the names of people on board. Only conducted thorough searches. Everything we have on Kevin is circumstantial."

"A neat little trail, all very clean, but why do you suppose they made it so easy?" The Director got up for more coffee.

"Not certain, probably wanted us to be sure to link the professor in some way to the raid."

"You're right, as usual. Go on," said the Director and he noticed Browning perk up a bit.

"The best for the last. The MO of Maria Costell's friend fits eight men who operate in Western Europe. We narrowed it to two, a Perry Wallace and Jonathan Sinclair. We found Jonathan Sinclair in Sicily working for a Greek entrepreneur. He is short and fat. Perry Wallace is our best lead. His reputation is impeccable. Seems to have been in business for about ten years and has worked a few times for police organizations in Europe."

"Not in England?"

"No."

"Isn't it strange we've never heard of him? Go on."

"He does 'recovery work' for private individuals, sometimes called the Magician for his amazing ability to disappear. He's noted for using darts, sprays, hypodermic needles, etc., to avoid violence. Sound familiar? He's a Black Belt and doesn't hesitate to use it if necessary. He has handled perhaps thirty cases for very high fees. Odd, but it's not a full-time occupation; he disappears for about six months each year. He has a class act, so to speak, is familiar with the arts and music, an intellectual of sorts."

"How does one obtain his services?" The Director was fully awake now adrenalin pumping up a bit.

"Very nicely. Write him a letter, tell him what you need and he will answer you." David Browning was smiling and trying to hide it from the Director.

"You're pulling my leg, aren't you?"

"Not really, but I thought you might do a double take. He has a secretary in Bern, Switzerland, a teacher, Juliana Keller, married to a Swiss banker. The inquiry goes to her address and she forwards it on to Wallace. MI6 has talked to her, but she will not give the forwarding address. We hand-carried a request for his services through our postal department and then through the Swiss postal department, where it was delivered to her in this morning's mail. We're going to intercept her forwarded mail, without her knowing of course. Hopefully she won't sit on it too long."

"Excellent. Where do you suppose she will forward it?"

"You are teasing me again. It's your turn," said Browning.

"All right. She'll send it somewhere in England, and I bet it'll be right here in London."

"Suppose he's not the right one?"

"Come now, who is teasing whom? The pieces fit too tight," said the Director.

"Glad you said that. The final piece in the puzzle is the flight record from London to Nice during the months of October and November last year. Mr. James P. Donnally visited Nice late in October, stayed two days, and returned to London. Our European friends verify that James P. Donnally is one of the aliases used by the Magician when he travels. No confirmation yet, but it's rumored he worked a job with Maria Costell."

"Good work, David." Yates was relieved that he had better news to report to the PM. He checked his watch and saw it was time to leave for her meeting. "Well, we don't have a positive ID on him yet, but it looks as if Wallace, Donnally, the Magician, and Brian McIver, or Robert Brian McIver are one and the same. I think the Prime Minister will be pleased with the news."

* * *

Juliana remembered what Jason had told her: "Never give out the address. If someone comes asking for it, be suspicious and very careful." The man who came asking for Jason's address was definitely British, his attitude a little condescending and manner a little coarse. It was her usual practice to forward his mail the same day she received it, but this last letter arrived just after the Englishman left. Her intuition told her something was wrong. Jason won't mind if I hold it, she decided. He already had plenty to do, judging from the mail she had forwarded lately. In fact, she wondered how he would manage both his occupations now that his reputation had spread.

She decided to wait one more day before forwarding this latest request. It was her usual practice to put the letter in another, larger envelope, and mail it from the corner postal box. But tomorrow evening she would take it to the Central Post Office and mail it from there. Posted on the third, Jason would probably get it on the fifth or sixth.

* * *

Yates finished with his report to the Prime Minister and was feeling better about the progress for the first time since the assault on the Tower.

"I like the progress you're making Director Yates," she told him. "Unfortunately, we're no closer to the jewels than when we started. I must make a move today. The pressure from home and abroad has been heavy. The phones have not stopped ringing during the last few days, and the mail is mountainous." Indeed, she had stayed until the early morning hours answering calls and mail. She desperately needed sleep. But, this was no different than other crises that she had weathered well. She made it a point to always look fresh in public. Makeup did wonders.

She went on. "The royal family is insisting that I request my government be dissolved and the elections held. The British Commonwealth of Nations have asked the elections be held. The President of the United States and the Premier of Russia have urged me to allow the elections to be held. The European Economic Community has followed suit, and members of Parliament are screaming for a meeting to settle the question. I'm holding off any decision until late this afternoon, hoping you will turn up something." She got out of her chair to stretch her body and relax her nerves. "I also want to find out what those rascals in the Republic of Ireland are up to. My press conference is scheduled for six p.m. Let me know if you turn up anything before then."

* * *

"Madam Prime Minister," the Taoiseach began in a low melodic voice reminiscent of an actor about to pronounce his lead lines; "I have met with my Cabinet and have reviewed the alternatives. You know that we, my party at least, have always advocated the peaceful unification of Ireland. We believe it is inevitable that one day Ireland will be one, not two countries. We believe in self determination; witness our long and often bloody struggle to be free. The *reality* of the present situation dictates that we support the independence of the Northern six counties. And we will issue a statement to that effect."

"Sir, you continue to talk out of both sides of your mouth," the Prime Minister replied, angry and irritated. "You have not answered my question. What are you going to do about Articles two and three of your constitution?"

"Nothing, at the moment." He was stalling. The Taoiseach's Cabinet had terrible arguments about removal of the Articles. It was he who stood firm on the retention of the Articles for the moment. However, one thread of argument caught his attention more than any other; the new Progressive Democratic Party could gain in strength and his party could lose members if the problem was not handled delicately.

The Cabinet had cautioned him that their own party membership was weakening on the issue. These are modern times, they said, and the younger generation, except for a few radicals, is inclined to treat the North as a separate and distant nuisance. Besides, our people are only interested in unification if it doesn't cost anything. It's time to consider another, more reasonable long-term approach to unification. Better we begin working together for economic coexistence and mutual support. The Protestants of the North have always done a better job at industrializing. It's true they've fallen on hard times, but their economic future could become quite bright with aid from England and the United States.

"No, Madam, we are doing nothing at the moment with the Articles," he repeated, "but that does not preclude a change of that policy."

"Do you realize that if you withdraw the Articles, the PIRA will have nowhere to turn? They will have to fight in the South as well as the North for unification. They are neither strong enough nor clever enough to do that. It would be futile for them. Sinn Fein will renounce the PIRA in order to promote their growth in the North and in the South."

The Prime Minister smiled inwardly and tossed in a strong barb: "But then you must deal with the unexpected growth of the Progressive Democrats. They seem to have a sensible outlook on the affairs of the Republic. Perhaps in time they will supersede you. If you do nothing about the Articles, I am prepared to introduce a resolution to the United Nations to force you to remove them. You will suffer the pain of world censure and humiliation." The Prime Minister wanted to be certain the South would never control the North. She was protecting her backside.

The Taoiseach knew that the Prime Minister was correct in her assessment of politics in the Republic. Northern independence drastically changed the dreams of unification, at least for the time being. It would require a severe overhaul of the Republic's policies toward the North. He would have to modify his own policies to meet the challenge of the growing popularity of the Progressive Democratic

Party.

"Madam, some day you and I will be able to sit down across from one another and smile without rancor, talk without painful memories of history, and negotiate constructive benefits for all three of us. I don't know when that will be, but perhaps sooner than we expect. We stand firm on the Articles but recognize the North's right to independence. What do you plan to do about the elections?"

"I believe you already know my answer. Listen in to my press conference at six p.m.," and the Prime Minister said a polite good-bye and hung up.

The Taoiseach, upset and angry since the first announcement, was now sad and weary from the constant stress of contemplating a major political decision that would affect the future of the Republic and his party. Now he knew for certain that Britain's Prime Minister saw independence as inevitable. Why else would she be so firm in pressing for repeal of the Articles? Of course! he suddenly realized. She wants to firm up her negotiating position. Without a threat from the South, she can negotiate a better program for the British economy and defence!

The Taoiseach knew that independence was a good road to take. But what of the Articles? He did not tell the Prime Minister that the arguments among his Cabinet were the most violent he had witnessed in all his years as head of the party. The word traitor was used more than once for anyone who suggested the repeal of the Articles. There were threats and accusations while old animosities, long since buried, surfaced among the members. For some it was life threatening. It was all he could do to hold the meeting in check. The split was almost fifty-fifty, and from that he drew the painful conclusion that he would suffer a disastrous defeat if the Articles were not repealed. He guessed that most of the Progressive Democrats, half of his party plus half of the other major party, would surely vote for repeal. That was a plurality he could never overcome in an election. He would do the only sensible thing to save his skin: put it to a vote of the people and bypass the government!

* * *

The crackle of the fire and occasional pop of a piece of wood overpressured by a small pocket of gas somewhere in its cellular structure was all that disturbed the silence of the room. The lights were out and the soft glow and dancing shadows made an effortless attempt to change the mood, to clear the air, to soften the stress, to relax the tension. The Prime Minister was, like so many others in the government, tired. The strain of the last few days was beginning to take its toll. This day was almost over. One last meeting with the Director-General and Director Yates of E Branch.

Her meeting with the Queen was almost anticlimactic. The Queen did not ask her about the jewels and she did not bring up the subject. Instead they discussed the many times in England's history that a Colony or Dominion had withdrawn from the Empire. At one time the British Empire had occupied one fifth of the world's surface and included a fourth of the world's population. Now it had eroded to the United Kingdom and Northern Ireland, a few remaining Dependencies, and the British Commonwealth of Nations.

During this meeting the two women concluded the best approach was to draw Northern Ireland into the British Commonwealth of Nations. The professor was not specific on the type of independence he desired, although it was plain enough he wanted complete separation, and certainly the ballot could be left unspecified. Northern Ireland would join the ranks of Canada, Australia, and New Zealand, all independent, but with the Queen as Head of State. While Britain held the purse strings, Northern Ireland would bear a common allegiance to the Crown. This would pacify the majority of Unionists.

The Queen had given the matter much painful thought and told the Prime Minister it was time to allow the North its due process. During her reign she wanted no violence and no barriers when it came to free determination of territorial status. If the elections were successful for Professor Banks, then it would be up to the Prime Minister to negotiate a settlement that included Commonwealth status with freedom to operate independently. They agreed to give notice to dissolve Parliament and the government on the sixth, election day, rather than the fifth, as requested by the professor, and reinstate the government on the seventh.

Following their meeting, the Prime Minister recalled the United Kingdom representative to the United Nations to prepare the necessary request to the United Nations Security Council for police and military support after the election, together with a formal request by Northern Ireland for admission to the United Nations General Assembly.

* * *

The Prime Minister's six p.m. press conference was stormy. Although the media speculated the British would be forced to hold the elections, no one expected this fearless and resolute woman to yield so soon. She fended off questions and told them the elections would be held on the sixth rather than the fifth as requested. Extra time was needed to allow all the candidates in Northern Ireland to submit their names and to allow the printing of the ballots.

She offered no new information on the jewels and told them she was reviewing the Transition Plan and the question of amnesty. If the vote for independence succeeded, UN assistance would be requested.

* * *

The Director-General and Director Yates sat opposite the Prime Minister waiting for her to begin the meeting. Only one small lamp in a distant corner of the room was lit; the glow of the fire and the flickering shadows still dominated the room.

The shadowy light cast weird and unflattering shades of orange and grey upon her face.

"Gentlemen, you heard my announcement. For all practical purposes I am temporarily out of a job. After tomorrow you can find me on the coast at Llandudno relaxing in the salt air. What of your report, Mr. Yates?"

"First is the election. Our figures now show the Independent Party reached the two hundred thousand mark, making it the largest political party in Northern Ireland. They need another 125,000 to carry the question if all 640,000 votes are cast. They should receive enough votes from all parties, except the hard line Unionists, to carry the election. A large contingent of Unionists favor independence.

"Each day the Independence Party signs up new members. The silent majority is suddenly moving fast. We finally have a couple of agents in the organization, and they report it is phenomenal. It's difficult to get a hard-headed Irishman to change his mind, clear away the prejudices; but it's happening. It's a difficult choice for most, but they view it as 'the end of the day'."

"What do you mean?" asked the Prime Minister.

"It is an old Irish expression meaning the end of the 'Troubles,' or to some it means the end of everything, it depends on who you're talking to.

"All the hundred or so committees are working on every imaginable phase of government, social, economic, and judicial operations. It's grass roots politics at its finest. The committee chairmen are scheduled to meet at the former Parliament House at Stormont the day after the elections to finalize their recommendations to the new Parliament. We hear the constitution and a bill of rights are already written and waiting for the new Parliament to approve. They have scheduled a Constitutional Convention during the week following the elections. The plans include contributing dialogue by constitutional law experts from the United States, Canada, and here at home. Incidentally, Stormont is to be renamed Independence."

Yates brought her up to date on tracing the Magician and the woman. "With the aliases used and lack of clear identification, it will be next to impossible to locate him. If the woman goes out in public she will probably be disguised. We are ninety-nine percent certain they're in London and one hundred percent certain they're in England. We hope to find his address when the woman in Bern forwards our letter. I don't know where this will lead us.

"The list of free-lance mercenary pilots has been narrowed, but we are several days away from anything concrete. We must know before you go whether or not you want to provide protection for Professor Banks."

"He is still a British subject and even after the election may well continue to be," replied the Prime Minister, "the answer is yes." Her voice was firm, the inflection emphatic, but Yates failed to catch her expression of disgust in the shadowy light of the room.

"It's time to start thinking about dropping your investigation and preparing to close the file," she continued. "The professor is the responsible one and he will either be the new prime minister of the North or he will be in jail. As for those who took part in the raid, it seems to me that unless you actually catch someone with the jewels, you have no solid evidence with which to convict: no fingerprints, no positive identification, nothing; it's all circumstantial. The pressure is now too great to prevent the elections. While we still hold the purse strings, I believe we must establish an aggressive posture at the negotiating table for favorable long-term results. Of course, I do not want to grant amnesty unless absolutely forced to do so."

Yates was upset; the dimness of the room hid the flash of anger as his face turned red. He was about to protest when the Director-General cut him off. "Madam, we have spent a great deal of time and money to get where we are today in our investigation. We have four days, including election day, to find the man and the woman. I believe we should cancel all our efforts to locate the others involved and concentrate on the man and the woman. There is no doubt they have the jewels. We'll send security people in to protect the professor and some of his people."

"Fair enough, you can continue to look. But if you find them, I want to know about it before any arrests are made, understood?"

After they left she called Professor Banks to establish the first negotiating meeting for the day after the elections, if successful. He agreed to return the jewels once a formal Transition Plan was signed by her and the new head of the government of Northern Ireland. He emphasized that amnesty was required before the jewels were returned. She remained non-committal

She then returned the call of the Taoiseach of the Republic to learn what he had done about the Articles.

***

The two men drove back to their office in silence. Yates settled into a chair across from the Director-General holding a glass of whisky the DG had poured from his private stock. The DG could see the exhaustion and frustration on the face of Yates. "Politics! Politics is pervasive in this job. Over the years I've tried to insulate you and the other Branch Directors from some of the more harsh, high-level decisions, and absorbed the blame for myself."

Yates could think of one or two times he had been irritated by decisions he thought came from the DG.

"The Prime Minister must think highly of you to include you in some of her intimate thoughts," continued the DG. "She's trying to think of ways to salvage this disaster and turn it into a positive opportunity for the Crown. A few days in Llandudno sorting things out and she'll come back like a tiger. You know, this may just be a primer for you. I plan to retire in two months and recommend you as the new Director-General."

"I didn't suspect," exclaimed a surprised Yates, "I thought you would be here forever. Good luck. Yes, I *am* upset with the Prime Minister. We have progressed further than I ever thought possible when I began, four, no five days ago. Plain hard police work, cooperation from our friends, and a little luck brought us close, so close, and now our hands are tied."

The Director-General smiled. "Some wag in this business once said it; 'don't let justice get in the way of what is good for your country'. What is more important, putting a man behind bars or helping the Prime Minister improve the future security of the country?"

Yates raised his glass in silent toast to the DG, rose to his fullest height, gulped down his drink, put the glass down carefully, and glared at the Director-General. "I can't agree to that! Good night," and Yates turned and left the room, tired and disgusted.

The Director-General smiled and raised his glass in silent toast to Yates, took a swallow, and in a soft, mellow voice said out loud. "Here's to you, old boy, may you have a good career as Director-General."

15

"The end of the day?"

Yates slept for ten hours. He was frustrated and restless when he climbed onto the cot in his office, and the long sleep did not change the way he felt. He was groggy and it wasn't until mid-morning of April third, after several cups of coffee, that he was thinking clearly again. He wasn't confused, he was angry when he told David to close down a major portion of the investigation. "It's not over, David. I will not give up yet. I want those people and I want those jewels. I want a little time today to rest and think about it. Keep on trying to find McIver and Costell." He went home that night, for the first time in six days, to his wife's delicious cooking. Back at the office the next morning he told his secretary to allow calls to come through again. There was an urgent message to call Fred Press. "Good morning, Fred, what's new?"

"We had a bomb attempt on the professor's house last night. Our surveillance van spotted three men; watched them plant it. We closed in and caught them trying to get away. The bomb was set to go off ten minutes later with enough explosives to blow up the entire block. We deactivated in time. The men were members of a small loyalist paramilitary group. The uproar it has created with this huge crowd of media people is astounding. We have hundreds of them looking around for any scrap of news they can get. It's a circus. As a result of the bomb attempt, all of the Unionists organizations, except two small extremist groups, have publicly stated they are willing to see the election through without violence. We are keeping close watch on the two groups, one of which planted the bomb. The Reverend McIver's flock has folded."

Press continued. "We put Professor Banks under house arrest against his wishes, but when we told him the Prime Minister ordered his protection, he agreed. We now have three men with him twenty-four hours a day, three more at his office, and have blockaded the entire area around his home. We are organizing security so he will be able to leave the area and go about his business.

"The professor has changed his strategy now. He is issuing the committee reports through the newspapers and television. The proposed constitution and bill of rights has been released; very good, by the way. He's trying to soften attitudes and prevent violence. Every organization is holding meetings and marches of some kind. It's wild but not unruly, a lot of excitement in the air. The police are ineffectual and the Army is doing its best to cope. So far a few fist fights, but nothing more. We have our work cut out for us for the next few days."

"Is young Kevin with his father?" asked Yates.

"Constantly. He took quite a beating. His eyes are blackened and he has a large bandage on his cheek. His ribs are still sore and he walks carefully."

"When you have your protection plan fully developed fax it over to my secretary." Yates wondered if they could save the professor's life.

An excited David Browning burst into his office. "We have it! The woman Juliana Keller waited until late last night to post the letter. The Swiss postal authorities agreed to cooperate and allowed us a look at all the letters in the box, about seventy-five in all. Only two to England the rest were local. One was a postal box here in London, the other a man in Oxford. It took all morning to locate the application card for the postal box and bingo, we have the same address McIver used in Belfast at the Forteham and on the passport applications, the apartment house in SOHO! The name used was Donnally!"

Yates knew there was something odd about that address. McIver was in some ways a creature of habit. If the address works, keep on using it; he used it a lot. Yates thought it could be some kind of connection. What was it? "David let's you and I go over to that SOHO apartment and ask a few more questions."

The apartment house manager, a large, dark skinned sloppily dressed fat man with food stains on his pants, was not the least bit interested in answering their questions. He didn't like police of any sort. He was certain one or two of his tenants were ditching the law and he didn't want any trouble. The apartment house was run-down, in need of major repairs and paint. During the last twenty years at least five managers had lived there and he was the sixth, or maybe the seventh, he said.

"How do you keep track of your renters?" asked Yates.

"In this book, a ledger for payments of rent."

Yates looked at the ledger. It covered the last four years and contained at least a hundred names.

"Do you have any ledgers that go back twenty-five years?"

"Don't know, only been here three years, got to start a new ledger one of these days."

"Where might they be if they were still around?"

"In the storeroom, or maybe up in the attic."

"Show us."

The man was visibly irritated by this intrusion into his usual afternoon of doing nothing. He rose laboriously from his chair. It seemed difficult for him to move around as he led them to a large storeroom beneath the main structure. The low ceiling forced them to duck down to clear the beams. Through the dim light they saw a chaotic tumble of wooden boxes, cardboard cases, old furniture, and plastic bags. After an aimless, unproductive search, the manager begrudgingly took them to the attic. The attic was smaller, but in the same junky and jumbled condition. When they finished their inspection, Yates turned to David and said, "Get several men over here as soon as possible and go through this place with a fine tooth comb. See if you can find those ledgers."

"Here now, you can't go through here without a warrant," said the fat man, breathing hard.

"We will have one," replied Yates with an expression of utter disgust.

* * *

By Monday the third, Jason had decided to sell out his brokerage business. He left Maria and Craig and spent the day at his office closeted with his company solicitor and his two senior assistants, both long-time friends, both vice presidents, both eager to buy him out. Together they worked out a buyout schedule and plan of reorganization allowing Jason to remain as Chairman of the Board for a year. The papers would be ready for signing on April fifth. Jason insisted that no public announcement be made until the following year.

The next morning, April fourth, he met with his personal solicitor and drew up papers to transfer the ownership of his house and car to Craig. Jason wanted to leave England and spend more time with Maria. He realized their common interests and intellectual curiosity fell along parallel paths. The more they talked and made love, the more solidified the bonding between them. For Jason it was total commitment, no turning back. He knew the timing was bad for a marriage proposal, but had to risk it. He wanted more than anything now to protect her.

Back home with Maria in the late afternoon, over a cocktail, Jason smiled and told her what he had done. "I want to live with you in Nice, and I want to marry you, will you have me?"

She was truly shocked. She was in love with him, yes, but he was not her first love, and at times she wondered if he would be her last. She never gave marriage much serious thought; pushed it out of her mind while enjoying the pleasures and excitement of their growing love.

Suddenly on top of all the chaos thrust upon her, the whole world knowing she took part in the raid, she faced the most serious question of her life. Now it was stress piled upon stress; was he that unfeeling?

"Oh, Jason, how could you at a time like this?" she cried.

"Because you're the first woman I've truly loved since Patricia. I want to spend the rest of my life with you. We can do so many things together. I know the timing is bad, but we can recover from this mess, with or without amnesty, much better if we are Mr. and Mrs. Jason Stark living in Nice."

"Jason, are you so sure? You'll be giving up all you've worked so hard for during the last twenty years."

"I'm not really giving it up. I'll be earning substantial money for a long time, until they finish buying me out. The harder they work, the sooner it will end. In the meantime, we can travel a bit and enjoy ourselves."

"Jason, there's so much I want to do with my life.

This is too sudden, I need some time to sort things out, O.K.?" And in the brief silence that followed she remembered how much he meant to her. "But I want you to come to Nice with me."

"All right, but remember I don't give up easily."

Craig came down to prepare dinner, and Jason gave him the news. Craig was overwhelmed. "I can't believe you're leaving and turning everything over to me. I am very grateful, but it isn't necessary."

"The house is a good house. I want to leave it with someone I know will take good care of it. We can visit you once in a while when we come to London. You can visit us often, any time you wish, in Nice. If we get married, then you must be my best man. If Maria decides against marriage I still want Nice to be my new base of operations."

Before dinner the three of them discussed Jason's art and antique collection. Jason decided to inventory all the items he wanted sent to him in Nice. Of the remainder, Maria could select anything she felt appropriate and Craig could keep the rest. They began listing items, and Maria noticed the small picture on a table in the library of two young men with a girl standing in between them. She turned it over and read, "Donald McVay, Patricia and me." Patricia's natural Irish beauty made Maria's heart ache that one so lovely could die so young. She remembered the story of Donald helping him after he was beaten. Jason told her that the Barbican apartment he leased was registered in Donald's name, a name he used on rare occasions to hide his identity. She put the picture down and continued her survey.

* * *

The SOHO apartment house basement and attic were a jumbled mass of junk. Some of the boxes were thirty years old. They had been moved and shuffled about so much the search revealed no rhyme or reason to their arrangement. It was dirty, dusty work, and the agents grumbled, but continued doggedly in pursuit of the ledgers that by now everyone believed had been thrown away. Working straight through without relief, the agents found the box mid-morning of April fifth; six ledgers covering the last twenty-five years.

"It was bad luck, damned near the last box buried under a hundred other boxes," David explained to Yates back at the office.

"What are we looking for?" asked David as they began reading through the ledgers.

"A name," Yates answered, "McIver, Donnally, Wallace, I'm not sure."

"You realize," said Browning, "we've already turned London upside down checking every McIver, Donnally, and Wallace we could find, and came up empty."

"Yes, but we haven't looked here, now keep looking."

By noon their search yielded nothing. Yates was clearly disappointed. "Damn it, I thought we would find a link, a connection, a nexus."

"A what?" asked David.

"A nexus, a connection; they mean the same thing." Yates couldn't leave it alone; he got up for another cup of coffee and paused at the window. The green stretch of Hyde Park in the distance never failed to delight him; the sky was patchy blue; people were walking about; traffic was normal; everything fell into place down there, why not here and now?

Suddenly he put the cup down, rushed to the phone, and called Fred Press. "Fred, what was the name of the fellow you interviewed who helped Brian McIver leave the country?"

"Just a moment," and Yates could hear Press rustling through some papers. "Here it is, Donald McVay. He said McIver left around March of 1969."

"Thank you, thank you very much."

It took David three minutes to locate the name. "God, here it is right in front of our eyes. A Donald McVay stayed at that cheap SOHO dump for six weeks beginning the first week of March, 1969. By God, there is your nexus!"

"David, we have 'til the morning of the seventh, the day after the election, about sixty hours from now, to find them. I'll be damned if I will give up. Now, where do we start to locate a Donald McVay in a London house, flat, or apartment? Christ! We have thousands!"

"It's a false name. It won't be on any public records anywhere."

"Perhaps, and perhaps not. We have to try. Let's

start with the postal service. Offer a sizable reward. One of the postmen may turn him up. Some of those fellows have phenomenal memories for names of people on their route. Sometimes hundreds of names."

"How about the phone company?" asked David. "He must have a phone."

"They are so screwed up they can't even bill properly. But it's worth a try."

David looked in the phone book and counted ten McVays. Two had a first initial D. "I'll start checking these and get someone on passports, licenses, permits, deeds, and utilities," and David rushed out to get help.

Yates sat in his chair feeling like a driven man. He had every right to give up the chase, but couldn't bring himself to do it. He had to know this man's identity. In all his years of service he had failed few times. Failure was not in his vocabulary. Losing was not his nature. "While we still have time, I will find him," he said aloud, and he reached for the latest batch of reports and began reading.

Jeffry Gaycraft walked into work feeling good. At least his feet had stopped hurting ever since he had bought a new pair of air-cushion shoes. It was election day, April sixth and he felt good about voting for Northern Ireland's independence. Maybe after they quit spending money on them, he thought, I'll get a raise. He'd been a postman for over thirty years and at times his age got the better of him. Now he could deliver the mail, which seemed to get heavier each day, with a small spring to his step.

Just like old times. He knew every person on his route, new and old. He hadn't met them all, but he knew them just the same. The mail they received gave their lives away. The magazines, letters from family members, maybe lovers, he imagined, legal notices, and bills gave all sorts of clues to their lives. Surprisingly many of those he met matched his imaginary image of their personality. He caught sight of his old friend Harry, who was quite excited about the new reward circular. "It's a big one this time, Jeffry, a thousand pounds."

"What's it for, Harry?"

"Looking for some bloke name of Donald McVay. Want his address."

"Jesus, Harry, that sounds familiar." He searched his memory as he walked to his locker. He passed the bulletin board and stopped to read the circular. One thousand pounds for the address of Donald McVay, and it gave a phone number to call. He didn't recognize the number.

As he was sorting his mail getting ready for his daily tour it suddenly came to him. He stopped sorting. *Yes that's it! The Barbican apartments; one box never gets any mail.* For a long time the mail box had no name card and he thought the apartment was empty. But that seemed odd, because as soon as anyone moved out of an apartment there it was immediately rented to someone else. It was a popular location.

One day he had bumped into the manager and asked him about it. He told Jeffry it was rented. The next day the manager put a little card in the slot with the name Donald McVay on it. Of all the long-term residents on his route, McVay was the one person he new nothing about: No mail, no history. He dropped everything, phoned the number, and was surprised to learn who was offering the reward.

* * *

It was election day and David Browning and Richard Yates were getting irritable. Neither had slept much the night before. "David I know we've got him. I can feel it. If we just have a bit of luck."

"All of the phone listings were clean; so far no luck with licenses, permit, passports, etc.," said David. "It took all afternoon yesterday to distribute the circular. We missed most of the postmen. Now it's nail-biting time." It was nearing lunch time. David ordered lunch, hoping to hear something soon.

Yates sat nibbling a sandwich, drumming his fingers on the table and reading a report that his eyes did not focus upon, when the phone rang. It was their fourth caller, Jeffry Gaycraft. He switched on the speaker so David could listen in.

"He's lived there about two years; never seen him; never gets mail; very strange," said Jeffry. "Apartment 302, the Barbican." Elated, they thanked the mailman and David put out an emergency search for the apartment superintendent's phone number.

They listened as the superintendent told them about Donald McVay. "The man pays by the year in cash, in person. See him maybe twice a year. He is about six feet, puffy cheeked, heavy brown mustache, large round and thick horned rimmed glasses, no discernable accent."

"That's our man!" and Yates looked at David. "Let's get the hell over there, now!" He told the superintendent to wait right there for them, they were just a few minutes away. Yates checked his watch; it was 12:32 p.m., April sixth; the elections were half over.

* * *

After one of Craig's most delicious dinners, the three friends sat over coffee discussing various options. "It would be a good idea," said Jason, "while we're marking things for the movers, to clear this place of all our technical materials and equipment."

They spent the rest of the evening planning the clean-up and Jason's move. The next day they stripped the lab and shop of everything except the ordinary tools and equipment found in any home shop. Craig carefully packed all the chemicals, instruments, and special gear for transport to a storage warehouse. Jason packed all his disguise paraphernalia and false papers into three large trunks for Craig to take to storage. Craig purchased a guitar case long enough for the two Sceptres and a small suitcase to carry the Crown, the Orb, and the Coronation Ring. Merlin's Nest became an empty room except for the two items. It was a long day for them.

Jason had one more chore: "Tomorrow, Maria and I will check out the Barbican apartment to make certain it's clean." He was getting an uneasy feeling about the place. He hadn't checked it since Kevin had left it on the morning of the raid.

On election day, April sixth, Jason drove Maria in his Jaguar to the apartment where the two of them spent the morning putting the place in order. When they left, the apartment was spotless. It was nearing 12:45 p.m. as Jason closed the door behind him and they walked to the end of the hallway to the two lifts. Jason kissed Maria on the cheek and said, "Mmmm, you smell good; you hungry?"

"Starving! Built up an appetite with all that work." She watched the dials above the lift doors. The lift on the left was on its way up, the one on the right, on its way down. It stopped and they got in, joined two other passengers, and faced the front of the car. The door to the lift on the left opened, just as theirs shut and Yates, followed by Browning and the apartment superintendent, got out.

Going down, the man standing next to Maria caught the fragrance of her perfume and tried to sneak a better look. The dark glasses and woolen cap prevented him from doing so, but the sensuous mouth told him she must be beautiful. He looked with envy at the puffy cheeked man with the heavy, brown mustache standing next to her.

* * *

David Browning had driven, as if possessed, half way across central London through the busy midday traffic at harrowing speeds. It was all Yates could do to keep from telling him to slow down. After all, he wanted them worse than David, or so he thought, but he wanted to live, too. The superintendent was waiting in the underground garage and led them to the lift. Once inside, he told them that about three weeks ago a tall, thin young man stayed in the apartment for about two weeks. He thought the man had a slight Irish brogue, but he only said "hello" once or twice and he couldn't be sure. "I've got better things to do than check up on everyone in the place," he told Yates.

When the lift arrived at the third floor and the door opened, Yates stepped out as the door to the lift next to them closed. He caught a whiff of a delightful fragrance that distracted him. Some beautiful lady, he thought. He directed the superintendent to stay by the lift until they needed him. He and David walked quietly to the door of the apartment and knocked. David had drawn his gun, knowing the man and the woman were both Black Belt and he would be no match for them. Yates carried no weapon, a long-standing policy of his. Yates knocked at the door again and got no answer. After a third try he summoned the superintendent, who gave him a pass key, and he opened the door. The apartment was empty! He took a quick look through the bedroom and kitchen and decided it was clean — very clean. He went into the bath, stopped, and yelled, "David, come here quick!"

"What is it?"

"Smell that?"

"Smells pretty good."

"They were just here. She got on that lift just as we got out of ours. I could smell her! David, quick, you're fast, stronger, take the stairs, get to the garage. Hurry!. Stop them! Don't kill them! I'll follow." And David took off as Yates locked the door behind him.

David burst through the door to the garage just in time to see the Jaguar going out the exit. It was silhouetted in the strong outside light and his eyes did not adjust fast enough to catch the license number. He ran. He saw the man and the woman. He wasn't going to make it! He stopped, drew his gun and aimed at the back of Jason's head. Too much background traffic, people, cars, damn them! He pointed the gun at the ceiling and fired a warning shot. The bullet flattened against the concrete ceiling and fell harmlessly to the floor.

Jason saw the man running, then stop and aim. He heard the warning shot and couldn't believe it. He stepped on the accelerator and spun the car out into the traffic almost colliding with a bus.

David ran to his car, spun out, burned rubber, turned again, burned more rubber, and leaped out into the traffic, only to discover the Jaguar was nowhere in sight. He slowed, wanting to shoot himself, then went around the block and picked up Yates.

"It was a Jaguar?" Yates asked incredulously.

"Yes. Black, dark blue, dark brown, dark, dark,

dark, damn it! It was silhouetted and I couldn't even make out the damned license number. I came this close to shooting him. Now I wish maybe I had."

"It's good you didn't. Let's get back to the office and start looking at all the Jaguars in England," said Yates.

David Browning, frustrated, upset at himself, and exhausted, angrily cried out. "Christ! You never give up! What the hell difference does it make? They'll get amnesty anyway. It's no good, Richard, we're not going to get them."

"You're wrong, absolutely wrong, David. Never give up. Keep on trying. It's still possible, but it takes patience, brutal, fingernail-biting patience; but sometime, somewhere the answer will come. Now let's get going; we don't have much time!"

* * *

A frustrated Director Yates sat in his office the morning of April ninth asking himself how they could have done better. He was putting the finishing touches on a report to the Prime Minister summarizing the entire affair. They had checked the registration of every Jaguar in the United Kingdom, and there were thousands, but found no connection to any of the names they had been working with.

He was positive the Barbican apartment belonged to the Magician; everything fit. It was clean, too clean. Not a fingerprint, not a hair could be turned

ASSAULT ON THE CROWN

up. No one cleans a place that well. *Damn it! We were just seconds too late.*

It was Sunday and he had not been home in three days. Ninety-seven percent of the voters turned out in each election. The British voted seventy-two percent for independence and the North voted sixty-six percent in favor of independence. The Independence Party had won ninety seats in the new 176-seat Parliament; the rest were split among the Unionists, Republicans, Socialists, and neutrals. The professor was elected the first Prime Minister of the Republic of Northern Ireland.

Today marked the official signing of the Transition Plan and maybe the return of the Jewels. The signing was to take place at nine a.m. He smiled at the turn of events. The first meeting between the two prime ministers had lasted a mere fifteen minutes. Professor Banks was furious. He had threatened to dump the jewels into the Irish Sea, but the Prime Minister stood like a rock. So long as she held the purse strings, Northern Ireland must join the British Commonwealth of Nations and the Queen would remain the official Head of State.

The professor called an emergency meeting of the new Parliament, where a ferocious debate ensued. They hadn't yet ratified a new constitution and were now debating Commonwealth status. In the end they had reached a compromise; five years of Commonwealth status, after which Northern Ireland could declare complete independence if it so desired. The Unionists and extreme loyalists were deliriously happy.

Today's signing of the Transition Plan set in motion the transfer of power and the agreement for interim economic aid. The United Nations forces, now beginning to arrive, would remain until the new government established a civil and military force of its own. Almost lost in the news coverage of the meeting was a small item reporting the declaration of amnesty for those involved in the raid on the Tower.

Yates went down to the meeting room and, with David, watched the television coverage of the signing with mixed emotions. Professor Banks assured the Prime Minister that the Crown Regalia would be returned before the day was out. Yates, hundreds of media people, and millions of others wondered how it would be done.

"Well, David, we were close," said a tired Yates, "maybe next time. You need some time off. How about two weeks?"

"Great! Thank you, sir," and David couldn't leave fast enough.

* * *

Jason was elated. The signing was his signal to return the jewels. The three of them had not missed the amnesty announcement and had already worked out a plan. He picked up the phone and dialed. After the fourth ring, Yates answered.

"Director Yates, E Branch, I believe you've been looking for me. I have something to deliver to you," said Jason.

"The Crown Regalia?" asked Yates.
"Yes."
"Where?"
"Please come alone to the church at Buckingham Gate Road and Castle Lane. At precisely 10:20 a.m. someone will pick you up in a four door, maroon Austin," and Jason abruptly hung up.

* * *

The maroon Austin pulled up beside Yates standing alone in front of the church. An old man in a battered hat, with grey hair sticking out from beneath it in tangled array, a white mustache and goatee, and wearing a well-worn raincoat, rolled down the window and said, "Please get in Director Yates."

"You look better than your pictures in the newspapers," Jason said as he drove slowly away.

"Thank you. You look very much like someone I have a few snapshots of in my files. You must be, let's see, Robert Brian McIver, Perry Wallace, James Donnally, the Magician and, oh yes, one Donald McVay."

"You are very good, Director. I believe I would want you on my side." Jason was interested in how he had traced Donald McVay to the Barbican apartment, but decided to work it out himself. "Your man almost shot me the other day. I suppose I should feel grateful he changed his mind. Perhaps with a little more time you might have tracked me down."

"No," the Director was candid, "as a matter of fact, we checked every Jaguar in England and couldn't find a connection. I received the last report this morning. You apparently have one more alias we can't trace."

Jason made no comment as he checked his rear view mirror and noticed the black Mercedes slip in front of Craig's car. Craig, with Maria sitting beside him, closed the gap and held his position. Jason turned down Victoria Street.

"Where are the jewels?" asked Yates.

"This is a rented car. The jewels are packed carefully in a suitcase and a guitar case in the boot of this car. They were treated with respect, handled with gloves, and not worn. The Coronation Ring is packed in the State Crown."

"I thought Professor Banks gave it to the Prime Minister this morning?"

"Well, not exactly. That one is an exact duplicate made by a friend of mine in Amsterdam. Just below the circle of diamonds in the main setting are two diamonds, one on each side of the ring band. Underneath one of them, in the base of its setting, is the date of the Queen's birthday. Very tiny."

"You went to great lengths to protect the Regalia, didn't you?"

Jason smiled at the Director: "I didn't want to break the law. In truth, I didn't want to see them in anyone else's hands. And I had a personal interest in the project."

"Yes, we reasoned it out. That is, if you are indeed Robert Brian McIver. Where is your brother, by the way?"

"He's resting comfortably. He'll be back in Belfast soon enough. I'm happy for the people of the North with their independence. In fact, I voted here in favor of it. They'll have a tough time for a while. It's going to take a long time to get the two tribes working together harmoniously, but the professor's organization has a good start."

"Speaking of fresh starts," said Yates, "you and your friends have been granted amnesty. I must say I admire your planning of the operation."

"Thank you. If you're ever in need of specialized service let me know. I believe you know how to get in touch with me."

"Yes. That reminds me, when you pick up your mail and find my request in it, please disregard it. We were hoping you would pick it up before the election."

"I almost did one day, but thought better of it."

Jason turned the corner and stopped in front of Victoria Station. The black Mercedes pulled up directly behind him and the two men got out and walked towards the Austin. Craig, wearing his young Winston mask, pulled up directly behind the Mercedes and got out with Maria, wearing her Mrs. Ashford disguise, close behind.

"Now, Director, it wasn't nice of you to bring those two fellows along," said Jason in mock surprise.

"Sorry about this," replied Yates, "you have one more identity; and it's hard for me to give up."

Jason got out of the car, but Yates remained in his

seat. Jason faced the two men walking towards him, their attention riveted on him as he raised his hands to fend them off. Craig and Maria walked up behind the two and gave each a quick chop on the back of the neck at almost the same instant. Both men went down in front of a surprised, busy crowd of travellers. Yates, still seated, caught somewhat by surprise, did not move when all three jumped into the car. Jason switched on the engine and stepped hard on the accelerator. He spun around one corner, then another, and stopped abruptly behind a taxi waiting for a fare in front of the Grosvenor Hotel. He looked at the Director. "Promise to be good now and get these damned jewels back to the Tower!"

"Sorry, old chap, but I just had to give it one more try."

"My friend's car behind your Mercedes is also rented," said Jason. "Have one of those fellows turn it in for us. Thank you, Director, and good-bye."

The taxi, with three rather odd-looking passengers, sped off along the busy, exhaust-choked streets of downtown London.

Never one to give up, Yates copied down the license number before the taxi was out of sight.

Epilogue

One week after the elections for independence, another election took place in the South. The people of the Republic of Ireland voted overwhelmingly to remove Articles 2 and 3 from their constitution. Northern Ireland would cost each of them too much money to support. This turn of events put the PIRA members in a state of confusion. Some of the less intelligent members of the organization took matters into their own hands and placed a bomb in the Dail. The explosion killed five legislators.

This violent act so infuriated the people of the South and members of the Dail that amidst the smoldering ruins, Parliament passed a law giving members of the PIRA twenty-four hours to leave the country or be tried and sentenced to life imprisonment without parole. Most of the membership fled. Some went underground. Four PIRA leaders protested, two were caught and immediately sentenced, and the other two made their way to the

North, only to be faced with a similar law passed by the new Parliament of Northern Ireland.

* * *

Three weeks after the election, the Reverend Sean McIver was returned to Belfast. Still recovering from his incarceration, he found his church in a state of disuse and most of his flock gone astray. When he heard the news that Northern Ireland was now independent, his mind snapped and he went into a state of mental shock that would take long months of care from which to recover. A middle-aged parishioner who had been close to him took him into her home where, it is said, his recovery is going better than expected.

* * *

Three months after the elections Richard Yates was appointed Director-General of the British Security Service, MI5. The London *Times*, in one of its more accurate articles, described his rather extraordinary and productive career. It included an intimate appraisal of his work on the Tower affair, portraying him as a determined and brilliant investigator who came within seconds of catching his prey. The article thrust him into public focus and gave him a big boost in popularity.

* * *

Maria and Jason moved his belongings to Nice and immediately departed on a three-month cruise around the world to consider marriage. When they returned to Nice they found a new house that suited their taste; large enough to hold their combined art collections. One afternoon, after they had settled in, Maria told Jason she wanted to marry him. That very same afternoon Maria received another request from the Italians. In the same mail Jason received a request for his services, transmitted through Juliana, from the new Director-General of MI5. They laughed uncontrollably for a time and then sat down, soberly, thinking of what to do next.

* * *

Craig Alexander was very lonely after the departure of Jason and Maria. It didn't last long however, for when he paid a short visit to Jason and Maria he met the most beautiful woman he had ever seen, a close friend of Maria. Her charming innocence captivated him and he soon fell hopelessly in love. He took her away with him to London where they will soon be married.

* * *

Two months after the elections, the Tower of London was reopened to the public. The crunch of visitors waiting to see the jewels was overwhelming. The center of attention was not just the Crown

Regalia, but the second and perfect duplicate of the "wedding ring of England," the Coronation Ring. During a private evening showing of the jewels for the Queen and the Prime Minister, the new Chief Warder explained the modernized secret security measures adopted at the Tower. The Prime Minister noticed more sentries on duty. Each was equipped with the standard loaded automatic rifle and each carried a gas mask pack.

The Prime Minister had enjoyed a tremendous surge in popularity at home after the negotiations with Professor Banks, and plunged forward with new economic programs riding the crest of her new-found popularity. While walking up the stairs from the vault of the Jewel House after marveling once again at their beauty, she remarked to the Queen, "It'll be a long time before we'll know if trading those jewels for a new nation was worth it."

The Queen looked at the Prime Minister with a twinkle in her eye. "When it is 'the end of the day' for the Northerners, the true end of their 'Troubles', then perhaps that will be the time to return the ring to Professor Banks." And the two women walked out into the cool London night air.

Remember!

Write now for additional copies of *Assault on the Crown* to Epsilon Books, 1026 Sheppard Road, Walnut Creek, CA 94598

Please send me _____ copies @ $6.95 each. I am enclosing $_____. (Please add $2.00 per order to cover shipping and handling.) Send check or money order—no cash or C.O.D.'s please.)

Name _____

Address _____

City _____ State _____

Zip _____

Prices and availability subject to change without notice. Please allow four to six weeks for delivery.

ASSAULT ON THE CROWN
IS A COLLECTORS LIMITED FIRST EDITION.

Each copy is autographed and numbered by the author.

EPSILON BOOKS
1026 Sheppard Road
Walnut Creek, CA 94598